GORSEMO

Marion Whybrow was bo
St Ives, Cornwall in 1980, with her husband,
Terry Whybrow, who is an artist. She began writing
for the local paper and these articles turned into
books on painters, potters and sculptors.
This is her second novel. It was shortlisted for the
Halsgrove/Western Morning News Peninsula Prize in
2003.

Fiction
Shadow Over Summer

Books by other publishers include:
St Ives 1883-1993 : Portrait of an Art Colony
The Leach Legacy : St Ives Pottery and its Influence
The Innocent Eye : Primitive & Naïve Painters in Cornwall
Bryan Pearce : A Private View
Virginia Woolf and Vanessa Bell : Remembering St Ives, *Marion
Dell & Marion Whybrow. Winner of a Holyer An Gof Gorseth
Kernow Award, 2003.*

Play
O.A.P. Rules OK

Smaller Books
Twenty Painters St Ives
Potters in Their Place
Forms & Faces : Sculptors in the South West
Twenty Two Painters who Happen to be Women
Studio : Artists in Their Workplace
Another View : Art in St Ives

ACKNOWLEDGEMENTS AND THANKS

My husband, Terry, for everything
My daughter, Kim, who designs my books
Cover illustration from a painting by John Piper
Ann K, Helen D, Karen H, Marion D, Susan S, Vanessa C,
who encouraged me
Ann, Judie and Liz from U3A
Porthminster and Porthgwidden Beach Cafes
Alison Symons book *Tremmeda Days*
St Ives Library Staff

JOHN PIPER
(cover artist)

The artist, John Piper, explores the landscape of Penwith -
its moors, cliffs, headlands, coastline, cottages and hedges.
It has been the constant inspiration and theme of his
paintings. Like the landscape itself, the paintings can be
stark, even forbidding, and have been described as
atmospheric or brooding, but the treatment of the subject is
unfailingly sympathetic.

GORSEMOOR COTTAGE

Marion Whybrow

BEACH BOOKS

First published by Beach Books
Fauna Cottage, St Ives, Cornwall in 2005

ISBN 0 9522461 5 5

Designed by Kim Lynch
Riverside, Lelant, Cornwall

Printed by T.J. International Ltd
Padstow, Cornwall

Front Cover – Painting by John Piper

GORSEMOOR COTTAGE

Marion Whybrow

CHARACTERS

Annie Shaw	b.1860	married Henry Care
Loveday Godolphin (nee Care)	b.1882	married Nicholas Godolphin married Ned Berryman
Karenza Pender (nee Godolphin)	b.1902	married Jack Pender
Mary Ward (nee Pender)	b.1920	married David Ward
Zillah Brook (nee Ward)	b.1966	married Carl Brook

1

She was so angry. At first the anger far outweighed her sorrow and carried her boldly into the funeral parlour, as though she would confront her mother and ask what business she had dying. Zillah had spent so much time, making plans, preparing the cottage in hopeful anticipation of her mother's visit to Cornwall. Now those dreams were worth nothing. Her carefully structured schemes, played out over the last few months, were shattered beyond redemption. Now she must face the reality that she and her mother would remain forever distant. A lifetime of resentment and anger could not be mended. The sorrow came later, after she had complained to the funeral director, in her final blaze of anger.

'I don't like the lipstick you've used on my mother's face.'

'But ...' he began, amazed that anyone should think to criticise.

Zillah wasn't prepared to listen.

'She never wore lipstick. She would not like it. I do not like it.'

'It's to make her look ...'

'Please remove it. She doesn't look like my mother.'

'People like to see their dear one looking well.'

'She's bloody dead,' Zillah shouted, and walked

quickly to the door and out to the noisy jolt of traffic, which hit her forcefully and shocked her into crying. Her mother wouldn't have liked to hear her swear, but it was an affront that some stranger should invade her mother's dignity, should smear her helpless face with lipstick, so abhorrent to her in her lifetime.

Why had her sisters not objected, she wondered? They, who had been so much closer to their mother. Zillah, the first born, had arrived as a disturbing, bawling nuisance, an inconvenience, an interruption to a life that was already coping with a new husband, a home, learning how to cook, and muddling through an onslaught of different experiences. It was too much of a responsibility for Mary Ward and she did not like mahogany-red-haired, blue-eyed babies resembling the colouring of her own mother. 'Go away. Go away!' she screamed. The new mother was angry and resentful of this new intrusion in her life. The trauma of the birth and its resultant tragedy had not made for an easy affiliation between mother and daughter, even allowing for time to heal post baby blues.

Two other girls, Amy and Ruth, were born in the next two years, dark haired and fine featured, like herself. Mary, knowing what was expected of her had coped so much better and learnt some skills for surviving day to day living. Zillah had always been her father's favourite, neither of her two sisters had measured up to his first born, and so the pattern of relationships had been created for life.

Zillah walked along the High Street, expecting to see her mother talking to a friend, instead one of the friends stopped her. 'You're one of the Ward children, aren't you? I'm sorry to hear about your mother.' She murmured her thanks, indicating that she was in a hurry and walked on.

She turned into the road where much of her childhood was played away with rounders and chasing games, and shared secrets with friends, and hot summer days when the children sat outside until it was dark and cool, and the day was over. And cold chilly winter days when they quickly built snowmen and waited for cars to drive along and knock them over. And rainy days when they sheltered in someone's doorway and still couldn't be enticed into going home, unless for something to eat, and then out again. They were street children in those days of not too many cars and very little danger from anyone. Today, there were no children in the street and the road was constantly the playground for cars.

As she reached the house the sad notes of her father playing the piano caught at her heart. *These Foolish Things* sounded particularly poignant at this time. He was playing her mother's favourite tunes; songs from a particular era. They never varied in their rendering. Her mother had odd obsessions about different aspects of her life. She liked routine, order, timetables, the habitual daily custom. The unexpected was anathema to her, but death had caught her unawares and unprepared. Amy, Ruth and Zillah hugged each other solemnly and sat glumly round the table, each engaged with her thoughts and memories, and occasionally making a remark.

3

'What will we do with that old Christmas paper, all smoothed out and piled up on top of the wardrobe?' Zillah said, still irritated and bad tempered, 'and the magazines of the Royal Society for the Protection of Birds, which were delivered every month and never opened or read. She wasn't the least interested in birds. And there's her collection of utterly useless bus time-tables, dating back to the first omnibus, I should think.'

'Why are you so cross, Zillah. There's no hurry. First we'll throw away the plastic bags and the chocolate boxes. Mum transferred her stuff into your room after you left. She got much more secretive about her collections. She kept the door locked. I hardly dare look in there for fear of what I might find, heaped up and saved for no good reason,' Amy said.

Ruth defended her mother's squirreling habits and oddities. 'We all have our peculiarities.' Then remembered how bored she had become with mother's manic insistence that she turn round three times if she caught a glimpse of the full moon through the window, and how she had to throw salt over her left shoulder if she spilt some. There was a pile of old sixpences to spit on for various other oddities. But she recalled an incident which made Amy and Ruth smile, and Zillah grimace.

'Just a little lipstick mum. You'll look lovely. It's only a very soft colour,' Ruth, her youngest daughter said, laughing and holding the lipstick ready should their mother agree. The two girls stood round expectantly.

Zillah slightly apart, looking on.

They had arrived early to dress her up, make a fuss, and style her hair. Mother had submitted to these attentions but occasionally she asserted herself.

'I've never worn lipstick in my life I'm not starting now.' It was one of their mother's definite dislikes.

Zillah listened impatiently. Her sisters laughed. They were much more relaxed with their mother, happy to tease and joke with her. 'Where are the pearls I bought you?' Amy demanded, 'They'll look lovely with your new twin-set.'

'I'm saving them both for best, when I go somewhere special,' their mother said. Zillah tutted impatiently. The girls laughed.

'Mum, you'll never wear them unless we make you. And you are going somewhere special. Zillah's bought tickets for The Sound of Music. That's special isn't it?'

Their mother shrugged.

'Might as well take the woman next door,' Ruth teased.

'Perhaps dad would like to go instead.' Amy suggested. 'Or, Zillah could cancel and get her money back, and we'll stay here and have a cup of tea and another piece of birthday cake.'

Their mother had the grace to look contrite. 'Oh well, as it's my birthday.' She took a sly look at Zillah to see how her slight insult had affected her. Zillah looked blank.

'Your father won't recognise me,' she went on, 'He'll think I look a bit tarty.'

'He'll think you look lovely,' Ruth said, and opened

the door shouting, 'Dad! Come and see mum before we go.'

The sound of the piano playing *I'm Confessing that I Love You* ceased. Their father appeared in the doorway. His wife turned towards him.

'David. Look what Amy and Ruth have done to me. Those girls and their glamour.'

'Well, Mary, you do look fine. Pretty as a picture.'

Above the heads of the three women, he winked at Zillah. Their mother accepted the compliment with an embarrassed smile.

'I'm wearing the clothes, but I'm not wearing the lipstick, or the make-up. Makes me look like a clown. Your dinner's in the oven.' She directed the attention away from herself.

Amy and Ruth bundled her into her coat and hat. Their father went back to his piano to play *I Can't Get Started* and their mother sang the words, 'I've flown around the world in a plane.' Her father sang, 'Still I'm broken hearted, 'cos I can't get started with you.' The girls escorted their mother through the front door. Neither Mary, nor David, had flown. Mary didn't like holidays and unfamiliar places and David would rather restrict his experiences to Mary's narrow views than be away from his wife and family. His life was governed by his wife's habits and peculiarities.

Zillah went to say goodbye and stood watching her father. He continued to play, but looked up at her, waiting expectantly.

'Dad, I'm thinking of moving to Cornwall.'

'Ah. I thought you might. Grandma Karenza always

wanted you to live there. I don't know what your mother will say.'

'She's got the others. She won't miss me. I'll tell her tomorrow.' She kissed her father, responding to the calls of her sisters to hurry up or they'd be late. Her father would miss her. It didn't need to be said.

For the first time since her mother's death Zillah began to cry. 'I wanted to make it up to her,' she sobbed. 'All those years that we spent not understanding one another. I always intended that she should come to Cornwall and stay. I've been decorating the cottage, making it nice; putting wallpaper in her room; planting flowers. I bought a garden seat - just for her - and now she's died.'

'Zillah, for goodness sake! It's hardly her fault. Don't get upset,' Ruth interrupted, angry at her sister's irrational petulance. 'Did you really think mum would travel to Cornwall on her own, without Dad?'

'I don't know. I hoped.'

Amy shook her head agreeing with Ruth's opinion. 'Be sensible, Zillah, have you ever known Mum to go back home? Wild horses wouldn't drag her there. I hardly think you could manage it.'

Her sisters' brutal attack on her idea of reconciliation with their mother humiliated her. Of course, Ruth and Amy knew mother so much better than she did, but why did they have to be so scornful of her hopes? Couldn't they see her disappointment in not being able to fulfil her earnest wish to be valued and loved, as they were?

Both her sisters were so calm and that angered Zillah even more. Why was she the only one crying and in a state of shock. Why weren't they complaining at their loss? She had unfinished business with their mother; how could they be so unconcerned? Naturally, the girls had to cope when their mother collapsed while picking daffodils in the garden. They were fortunate to have been with her. Maybe there was some consolation in having spent the last few hours in her company, drinking tea in the garden on a warm spring day.

Through the window Zillah could see the broken fence where the next door neighbour had been hauled over by Ruth to give artificial respiration, while Amy rang for an ambulance. Everything had been done to save their mother with efficiency and skill, but death was final.

Their father had arrived home to see the ambulance leaving the house and had followed in a neighbour's car. For the last few days he had sat at the piano all day and into the night, playing the tunes that Mary sang; the songs of their younger days. They hadn't adopted any others, and *Dancing in the Dark, Thanks for the Memory* and others of that era had remained to remind them of the early days of courtship. David Ward now played the repertory through and was tinkling and ranging over the keys in a trance-like fashion. Then the piano died away.

Ruth, mother's baby, sat with her own baby on her lap feeding her heaped spoonfuls of organic mush from a jar. Scattered around were the various articles of use designed to keep a baby clean, healthy and happy. Their father, walking forcefully into the room snatched at a couple of baby wipes and disappeared, without a word, through the front door.

'Dad didn't even say hello to you,' Amy remarked. 'He's been waiting for you to arrive, and then ...'

'He didn't see her. He didn't see any of us,' Ruth confirmed. 'He hasn't talked. He sits there playing the piano. Perhaps he'll go with you to Cornwall. I've come round every day but baby and me are more of a nuisance than a comfort. Poor dad.'

Ruth and her husband lived a few streets away. Ruth had been a daily companion to her mother since the birth of their baby. Mary had enjoyed a distant affection for her grand daughter, Lisa. She liked showing her off to the friends she met while shopping in the High Road. 'It was a brief but happy time,' Ruth said.

'Then why aren't you angry that it's over?'

Amy, who was unmarried and lived with a group of women who ran an art shop and gallery in Richmond, offered her own explanation. 'We have cried Zillah, but Ruth and I had a complete relationship with mum. There was nothing more to discover or learn about each other. We three were fulfilled, while you were always on the outside; except you had dad.'

Ruth emphasised these points. 'In a way, because everything was complete, we can get on with our lives and finally be independent. It sounds harsh to say it at this moment, but it's true. Amy and I have everything she gave us. She has left us secure, while you are still yearning and wanting something from her. Just reverse the situation with you and dad. You were always a pair, complete.'

With a shock Zillah took in the words of her two wise sisters, realising the truth. She remembered the mornings in her cottage in Zennor, the lovely fresh Cornish west wind blowing softly in from the Atlantic. Those early Spring mornings, offering hope after a wet winter and the interminable passage of men coming to rewire, fix the plumbing, install a kitchen, decorate and generally make the cottage habitable.

Zillah had done much of the painting and wallpapering herself. Her mother's room was a delicate shade of blue paint, with white woodwork, and curtains and matching bedspread of a small floral print. White rugs on broad planked sanded floors gave space and comfort. One upstairs room became a generous bathroom, serving two double bedrooms and there was a third room. Downstairs was a large kitchen extension, a dining room, and a good sized sitting room. Zillah was pleased with the simplicity of the overall design. The cottage was ready to receive visitors; the first would be her mother; when the telephone rang.

'Bad news I'm afraid Zillah,' Amy said, and then a long pause while she composed herself. 'Mum has died of a heart attack.'

'No. No, not Mum. No, not Mum.' Zillah had burst into angry tears.

She felt cheated. It should have been their father who had died. He had been in and out of hospital with breathing problems and chest infections. The expected death of their father had not run its course and their mother, who was never ill, was dead. It was not possible.

Zillah had dreamed of her mother in the kitchen preparing recipes that only she could do, telling her daughter to set the table, make a cup of tea, cut the bread, or put some flowers on the table, ready for their meals. She had imagined her mother sitting in the garden chatting; Mary telling tales of her childhood in the village, of the friends she grew up with, of the trips into St Ives to take butter and eggs to market. There would be no awkwardness, and that mysterious gulf that had existed between them would disappear. All it needed was for her mother to be in the place where she was born. But these dreams came from longings and regrets. They had no place in reality. The events had taken place in Zillah's head.

They had just finished lunch when their father returned. He looked directly at Zillah.

'I've done it,' he said. She knew immediately what he meant and smiled.

'Done what dad?' Amy and Ruth wanted to know.

'Wiped the lipstick off your mother's face. The cheek of it. The damned cheek.'

Zillah got up and kissed him. 'I'm glad dad. I'm so glad. I knew they wouldn't take any notice of me telling them.'

'I waited there while they ... while they put the lid on. They wouldn't dare defy me.' He shuddered and sat down. 'Cup of tea please loves.' The emotional trauma of it had exhausted him.

11

In church, the four of them occupied the front bench. The coffin was raised on the next level. They could hear shuffling and muted prayers from behind, but none dare look round for fear of being disrespectful. A boy server, in his white gown, entered from the side of the altar and lit candles, genuflecting as he passed. A pale sun shone through a stained glass window and lay its colours across the coffin. The dense silence nearly unnerved their father.

'I hate this. I hate all this.' He sat grimly in his seat next to Ruth, who held a restless baby. Ruth put her hand over his, soothing both him and the baby. 'Shush now. Shush. Don't be upset. We're here.' Zillah and Amy knelt with heads bent mumbling what prayers they could remember.

The congregation seated themselves as the notes of the organ announced the arrival of the vicar. The girls rose from their knees and snuggled up close to their father, surrounding him with a wall of sympathy and strength. The reverend, unnoticed by the family, began his ministrations and prayers. They listened in shock.

'Death, where is thy sting!' shouted the vicar in exultation.

The baby, suddenly aware of the voice, gave a high-pitched cry, which spiralled and echoed to the rafters, tinkled on the stained glass windows, and cascaded down on the congregation.

'She was a sinner ...' he intoned.

David broke away from his family's encircling arms.

'No. No. She wasn't a sinner. You can't make such judgements. I can tell you she wasn't a sinner. Don't use those terms for my wife, my dear wife. Don't ...'

He rose to his feet, shaking off the girls' restraining arms, and hurried down the aisle.

There was a stunned, momentary silence and stillness from the vicar, the mourners and the family of girls. The saints in their stained glass windows looked down in dismay at this unseemly interruption.

Amy and Ruth together, dragged Zillah to her feet. 'Go after him. Quick.'

Zillah stumbled from the bench and ran down the aisle, her feet clacking noisily on the tiled floor. She reached the church door at the same time as her father.

'Oh dad,' she said breathlessly. 'I've always wanted to do that. You are brave.' She kissed him fervently, took his arm, and steered him towards the High Street.

'Your mother would be shocked,' he said, and grinned. 'What'll we do now?'

'We'll get a taxi and be at the crematorium when Ruth and Amy arrive. We've only got the few relatives who've turned up coming back to the house.'

'I didn't want that either.'

'I know dad, but some of them have come some distance, and we couldn't let them travel home without something. Anyway, they'll want to remember mum, and I'm sure you'll find it'll help.'

'What'll they have to remember her for? Never saw her from one year to the next.'

There were only family flowers gathered in the courtyard of the crematorium. A collection was made in the church for various charities. No one mentioned David's outburst in the church, thinking it was due to extreme distress. The relatives milled around keeping a watchful distance, not knowing what to say, or how to say it. Zillah knew her father's outburst had been from anger, rather than sorrow. He had drilled into her his intentions for his own demise in the taxi.

'No church service. No expensive coffin; something easily disposable. No flowers. No words elevating me to the saints. No prayers. No people. No tears from you girls. A straight ending. Exit. Understand?'

'Yes, Dad, of course.' She agreed to everything he said.

'I'm not coming to Cornwall. I want to be here where your mother is. She hasn't left the house. Her spirit is still around and I don't want to leave her on her own.'

Her father's devotion to her mother was absolute. His Mary was as unchanging as a slab of Cornish granite, he would say, endorsing her peculiarities, even at the disadvantage of his family. There were severe restrictions on their lives because of her ingrained habits, like refusal to travel. Her, often irrational, rules governed the family.

Many of the relatives didn't return to the house. There was an embarrassment that they couldn't overcome. They had never experienced anything like the scene that had taken place in church. They needed to get over the shock.

David's two brothers, whom he hadn't seen for some years, slapped him on the shoulder. Their wives kissed the girls, nodding their unspoken sympathy, glad to be away and back to their normal lives, even if it meant travelling half the night to get home.

Zillah, sitting alone in the kitchen after Amy had gone home with Ruth, and her father was once again playing the piano and occupied with his own private thoughts, couldn't help but reflect on her past busy life. It was going to be a lonely existence in Cornwall compared to Highgate, with its continuous bustle of people and traffic, where she could look out over the rest of London, and yet lose herself in Kenwood, or among the trees on Hampstead Heath.

A few years previously, when Gorsemoor Cottage finally became hers, her life had started to change dramatically. It was the fault of the inheritance. When the letter from the solicitor came to release the documents, she had been having breakfast with her husband, Carl. 'It's addressed to Mrs Brook. Nothing to do with me.' He read the letter with distaste, knowing that she would go to Cornwall to see the property.

'I'm not going with you,' he said. 'I think you should sell the place and we could buy a house in Highgate or Hampstead with a garden, instead of living in a flat.'

'But perhaps we could have both,' she said placatingly.

'We can't afford both, especially if the place is as run-down as the solicitor says, and needs major repairs.'

'But it's been in the family for generations. I can't let it go.'

'Then why doesn't your mother want it?'

'It isn't hers to want and she doesn't like it anyway. It has been left to me. I practically spent my childhood there. It's my real home. It's not a farm now. It's only the cottage, a garden, a field, and the few outhouses. grandma Karenza sold most of the land to the neighbouring farm.'

Every morning and evening they discussed the property. Zillah spread out the photos she had taken on her brief visit, outlining her ideas, and vainly seeking his interest in the project. Carl resented the amount of attention Zillah was prepared to spend, planning possibilities for making the cottage habitable, and turning the units for holiday lets into a viable income. Carl wasn't prepared to sell their flat, with its great views over the treetops, for a run-down place overlooking bleak fields and a distant sea.

Zillah put the plans for Gorsemoor Cottage on hold. Meanwhile, it fell into further disrepair through wind, rain and storm. After a few years grandma Karenza's solicitor advised her to make a decision to renovate, or sell, before the cottage became too dilapidated. Carl again expressed his opinion that it should be sold and the proceeds shared with Amy and Ruth.

'You've really touched a raw spot, Carl, in saying I should share the money with my sisters. It makes me feel as guilty as if I'd robbed them. But I won't sell, and grandma left money in her will specifically for renovation of the cottage.'

The rift in Zillah and Carl's relationship became wider, and their entrenched views deeper. Eventually, it was decided they would each pursue their own dream. Carl had suffered a further blow. He had been made redundant. They would each take their portion of the money from the sale of the flat. Carl would go to Bristol to stay with relatives. Zillah would visit Cornwall and repair her cottage. They would keep in touch and still be perfect friends. But this ideal solving of the situation turned a little sour and resentment in both of them meant that their parting wasn't as amicable as they hoped. After a few initial letters, where blame and angry accusations were exchanged, they stopped writing.

Zillah stood at the train window waving until her father and sisters faded into the distance. Time to be going home. Time to forget the dreams she had of her mother being there with her, mending the rift between them, building a companionship. It was too late. She had delayed asking her mother to come because she wanted the place to be perfect; wanted nothing that her mother could criticise.

'A month ago she could have come, even though the garden was a mess,' she scolded herself. 'It wouldn't have mattered, but I had to be so damned proud and beyond reproach. I couldn't have her coming, saying, "Zillah, you'll have to do something about the garden. You'll have to start planting if you want to have it looking good for summer." But, would her mother actually have said that? She doubted it. She never, ever talked of her childhood home.

On the other hand, she'd probably say something about growing things to eat, Zillah thought bitterly.

Her mother was always embarrassing her. She would introduce her daughters, Amy, 'the girl who loves to dance,' and Ruth, 'always smiling and happy,' and my eldest daughter, Zillah, 'who loves her food more than anything, or anyone. You do, don't you Zillah, don't you?' She would laugh in a wild manner, leaving people to wonder at the mad outburst of inappropriate laughter.

Arriving at St Ives station, and before getting into her car for the drive home, Zillah inhaled the warm air blowing off Porthminster beach. In Zennor the air would be fragrant with the scent of yellow gorse, smelling of coconut, and the garden would be exhaling other perfumes from the warm sunny day. She wanted to be home before dark to see the last rays of the sun glinting golden on the sea and glimpse the light fading in the west.

Home was the countryside of many generations of Pender. As a little girl, she had been shown the gravestones of so many of them by grandma Karenza at Zennor church. It was a pity that her mother wasn't buried there. Everything would have been so right; a place to have been born and died. The latter piece of the pattern was missing. She would take flowers to grandma's grave and try to explain her mother's absence. Dad had followed his wife's instructions that, 'On no account am I to be scattered in Cornish soil, or in the Cornish sea.' Zillah had wanted to question her mother's attitude, but her father was too upset to offer explanations.

Sitting in the window with a cup of hot chocolate,

Zillah watched the big ball of red sun slipping over the horizon and into the sea. It was a sight she had always loved as a child, really believing that the sea swallowed up the sun, and that it swam to the east and arose in the morning, coming up in St Ives bay and lighting up the harbour and the cottages in the town.

Gorsemoor Cottage was always destined to be hers. Grandma Karenza had long been a widow and Zillah spent most school holidays with her, travelling on the train by herself from an early age. She had believed this was a privilege, being the eldest of the sisters, but soon learned that Ruth and Amy, 'couldn't be spared,' so their mother said. But she was happy on her own. In those early years grandma met her at St Ives station in a horse and trap. They struggled up the steep hill out of St Ives and again up past the slow incline of Rosewall Hill with its crumbling mining chimneys, and when they reached Trevalgan Hill, the land and sea opened up before them. They let out their usual cheer and tipped down the road in jaunty home-coming gladness.

Zillah drew the curtains to a bright morning sun. Beyond the garden were the fields leading down to the sea, which used to be part of the farm but had been sold off, with livestock, after grandpa Jack died. Grandma Karenza kept the farmhouse, a field, and land around the house for her garden, and long before farmers were told to 'diversify' she had done so, turning the stable block and barn into several self-contained units for holiday-makers.

Over the last five years the holiday lets had remained unused and, like the cottage, had fallen into disrepair through neglect. Zillah had visited as often as possible, staying at Brown's B and B on The Terrace. There was parking behind the house, and it was so convenient for the centre of town. She and her landlady Lyn had become quite friendly. They often shared meals together, especially in the winter when Zillah was her only guest, or they would eat out at the many excellent St Ives restaurants.

'Come and see the cottage, Lyn, see what you think,' Zillah said. They drove out on a misty evening just before it got dusk. The cottage was looking its most forlorn.

'Go for it!' Lyn advised. 'It's what I did, and it does work, as long as you love the place.'

It had taken some years for Zillah to decide to move into Gorsemoor Cottage. During one of her frequent trips to Cornwall she stood in the quiet, neglected cottage garden and looked at the green front door, stripped and faded by the sun and battering storms blowing in from the Atlantic and there came to mind the lines of a poem, which so expressed the way she felt about her lonely house. 'Is there anyone there? said the traveller, knocking on the moonlit door.' She turned the key in the great lock and of course there was no one there. Every time she stepped inside she was hurt by the sorrowful feel of the place and the silent blame from its deserted rooms.

'This time,' she said aloud, 'I'm doing something

about you.' She pocketed the key and drove back to St Ives. It was while walking along the Wharf that she glanced up Bethesda Hill and saw a sign, which confirmed her decision to renovate the cottage. On a red and white lifebelt she read the words, Poynton, Bradbury, Wynter, Cole architects. Without a phone call or an appointment, she walked up the cobbled lane and entered the premises of what had once been four floors of sail lofts, all with separate entrances and now converted into one building, with access to all floors via a specially built spiral staircase. She was reading the history of the premises, The Old Sail Lofts, displayed on the walls of the entrance hall, when down the stairs came the first architect to set up the practice. He introduced himself as, Joe Poynton.

'I've often wondered about that farm cottage,' Joe said, when she had explained her purpose in coming. 'I've got twenty minutes to spare before my meeting but we'd be delighted to come out and look over the place. Indeed, we have already discussed some proposals, out of interest, although we had no idea who owned the property.' At that moment two other partners arrived on the scene who Joe introduced as, Cedric Wynter and Philip Cole. 'Ah!' they said in unison. 'We've had a special interest in that cottage.'

'There, you see,' Joe said, his colleagues words confirming his statement.

'In fact,' Cedric added, 'we have a client who is looking for a farm cottage in Zennor.'

'She is willing to pay the purchase price, and above, for the right property,' Philip said, 'which is why we took a look at it. If you wanted to sell …'

Zillah interrupted at this point. 'No. I certainly don't want to sell. I know I've neglected it for a few years, but now …'

'We'll be only too happy to draw up plans for you,' Joe assured her.

The idea of someone wanting to buy her cottage finally strengthened her resolve to claim her inheritance. Zillah found it comforting that concern had been expressed about the place and anticipated a good relationship with the partners. She arranged to meet one of the architects, on site in a fortnight's time. It was a great relief to be engaged in definite plans. It was only on the drive home that she worried about the effect her plans would have on Carl. Their flat had been sold and Carl had already moved to Bristol.

Zillah had been renting her firm's company flat, usually reserved for visiting overseas directors, to complete the editorial work on a novel. Sometimes she spent a tense weekend in Bristol with Carl. He had hoped that their separation would be temporary. He confidently believed Zillah would sell and then they would set up home again in Bristol and resume their perfectly loving and agreeable life

Guilt had made her delay taking up her inheritance. It surely belonged to her mother. She, after all, had been born there. Mary had shown an odd lack of interest, saying, 'My mother wouldn't have left me the cottage under any circumstances. Her thoughts were for you. There's nothing for Amy and Ruth.' She had given her wry little smile and disparaging look that somehow

22

seemed to be saved for Zillah.

'Dad,' Zillah asked for the umpteenth time, 'Should I sell the property and at least share the money? It doesn't seem fair that I should get everything.'

Without hesitation her father had squashed the idea. 'Your mother wouldn't change her mother's will. You must remember, you were the most important person in grandma Karenza's life. She left you the cottage, and the money for repair work. Your mother wouldn't take the money, believe me, whether for herself, or the girls. There's too much resentment there already.'

'What do you mean?' she demanded.

'Well, Mary and her mother never quite managed to be good friends. Something happened in the early years, which never quite got mended.'

Zillah was alarmed at this news, and then things began knitting together; her holidays with grandma, always alone; the infrequent telephone calls and letters to and from Cornwall. Zillah had been the main correspondent to grandma. Her mother, Amy and Ruth only ever, grudgingly, wrote birthday and Christmas cards.

This remark of her father's that Mary and her mother, Karenza, had never quite been 'good friends' had made Zillah examine her own relationship with her mother. Finding it deficient, she had determined not to allow things to slip into silent resentment, but it came to nothing with Mary's death. She always had been, and would remain, the least of her mother's children. Zillah often thought it was because of the red hair she had inherited from her grandmother and great grandmother. 'You should get it died,' her mother advised, 'or people will think you're a witch and bring them bad luck.'

Some two weeks later, Zillah drove down the unmade-up road to Gorsemoor Cottage. Sitting on the wall was Mike Bradbury, the second architect of the company, taking photographs of the cottage. 'Just a few more shots for reference,' he said, as he introduced himself. He had already made himself familiar with the building and showed a computer print-out with dormer windows and extension for a kitchen and bathroom. 'You have some very useful out-buildings. Are we to draw up plans for those?'

'No,' Zillah said, as she pushed open the front door, now swollen with the rain and grating on the flagstone floor. 'I'm uncertain about them at the moment, but hope some idea will come to mind when the cottage is habitable and I'm living here.'

'There's nothing structurally wrong,' Mike said, as they toured the building. 'Bringing it into the twenty first century, without totally destroying its character, won't be too much of a problem. It's a charming house, a small project, but something we'll enjoy doing. We'll keep an eye on it. One or other of us will drop in to oversee the development, and keep it on schedule. We're often travelling this road to see clients.'

'Many thanks,' Zillah said, feeling happy with their discussion.

They said their goodbyes, with promises of plans in the post the following week. She was driving away to return to St Ives when she heard the horn from Mike's car. Feeling something was wrong, she stopped, and he came running up. 'Car won't start,' he said. 'I'm due to meet a client at the Tinner's Arms and ...'

'I know. There's no signal from a mobile so you're stranded. Get in. I'll take you there,' she said, throwing open the passenger door.

'That's very kind of you. Thanks. Are you sure? I could telephone for a cab.'

'Not until you get to Zennor for a land line. And anyway, there's method in my madness. I can ask you questions about my cottage, and it won't cost me an architect's fee.'

'Right. Fire away. I reckon you've got ten minutes free time,' Mike joked.

Looking at her watch, Zillah said, 'I reckon I can stretch that to twenty minutes, if I drive slowly.'

There had been just a couple of months of travelling to Cornwall to check on progress, often meeting up with one of the architects on site. She usually caught the sleeper from Paddington on Friday night, stayed with Lyn on Saturday, and travelled back on the Sunday night sleeper from Penzance, going straight to the office from the station.

Once her plan was operational she timed the ordering of furniture, and Lyn was there to see everything safely installed, arranging for curtains to be made locally and finding a gardener. Zillah concentrated on establishing a work base from the cottage, installing a computer and watching the conversion of the pigsty into an office, with a door through from the house. It had all gone according to plan.

She was now working freelance for her firm, but if the work dried up she would be in trouble and might have to sell the cottage after all. The architects, trying to be helpful, said their client would be interested in buying the property if she couldn't cope with the move and the expenses. 'You can name your price,' they told her, hoping to relieve her of financial worries. Zillah didn't find this reassuring. It only strengthened her desire to make her scheme work. The idea of someone lurking in the background with designs on her home was abhorrent to her.

Putting aside these disturbing thoughts, she made toast and coffee and sat at her table looking onto the garden. She was now at Gorsemoor Cottage permanently. 'There's no going back,' she repeated aloud over and over as she settled into her new life. She had work to catch up with waiting in her office but for the moment her view through the window captured her attention. Immediately in front was the courtyard, then part of the garden, behind that a field, then another, and beyond, the sea. Her eye rested on the huge, flat, rock lying in the grass of the near field like some prehistoric monster.

'We can get a bulldozer to remove that if you want?' the gardener said.

'Oh no, that's part of the history of the family and the area. It is much older than the house. It's part of the landscape. I crawled over that nice smooth rock as a child. My mother played there, and grandma and great grandmother lived with it. I couldn't lose my rock.'

'Nothing terrible would happen if we dug it up'

'No. It's not superstition. I just can't part with it.'

The gardener laughed and ran and stood upon the stone, then he did a backward flip and landed on the grass. ' I think it must be magic,' he said.

'Oh yes,' Zillah agreed, amused at his athletic leap. 'It's certainly magical. It's like a fairy castle. I believe that in the moonlight the knockers come from the mines and dance round it. I think I may even have seen them as a child.'

The gardener laughed again, and continued rebuilding the dry stone walls that the cattle had dislodged. 'I expect they eat their pasties sitting on the stone.'

'I'm sure they do. I used to have picnics sitting up there with one of grandma's big white tablecloths spread over, with heavy cake and lemonade, and my toy tea set. My dolls sat with me. The cows would pass either side on their way for milking, but I was safe on top of my castle.'

Zillah turned reluctantly from the window and walked through the kitchen to the door of her office. She had several office emails and must print out the latest chapter of a book she was editing. Working at home in Cornwall was now a reality, but she had come to depend on ringing St Ives library, seeking advice. If Jane or Greta answered the phone they knew to put her in touch with Christina, their computer wizard, who would talk her through the occasional difficulties she experienced with the computer; emails failing to open and disks reluctant to disclose their secrets. She did not wish to reveal her weaknesses to the London office, since she had convinced them of her competence to work from home at this great distance. Lyn and her library friends, and computer literate Christina were a lifeline.

The only people she had actually met in her new environment were the builders who came to work on the cottage, and for whom she provided endless cups of tea, while they supplied a never-ending fount of local gossip and knowledge. She hoped, now she was here permanently, to settle into her new life and make friends. On several occasions she had glimpsed a woman, roughly her own age, passing in the lane to a farm and group of cottages a few fields away, and wished fervently for her to knock on the door.

2

Zillah, sitting at her computer, considered all that had led to the break-down of her marriage. Perhaps she had been selfish, but the desire to surround herself with the feeling of safety and magic she had experienced in those early years of childhood had beckoned her, and she felt the pull of Cornwall. 'Well,' she said aloud, pushing the buttons on the computer and printer, and plugging in the telephone for the email. 'I must get on with my new life.' And down the lane came the woman she had caught glimpses of, carrying her bags of shopping. She disappeared behind a high hedge. She had missed her again.

At the sound of the post dropping through the letter box, Zillah got to her feet and rushed to open the door, catching the postman as he reached the garden gate. 'Hello,' she called, anxious to gain his attention. 'How many deliveries are there a day?'

'Only one, I'm afraid. Not like the old days. My uncle used to walk from St Ives to way out beyond Zennor, delivering post. Midday another postman would set out on the same route. My van can only manage one trip a day. My uncle used to stop here at the farm for a cup of tea.' The postman walked back down the path to continue his story. 'He used to be called the singing postman. I don't need to explain that.'

'No. Would you like a cup of tea?' she asked tentatively. 'I haven't started work yet.'

'I'll say yes, but I usually have coffee with Beatrice Paynter. She passed here a few minutes ago. I'll have a second cup with her.'

'Come in, and tell me about my neighbour. I haven't met her. Tell her I'd love her to pop in and say hello when she's passing.'

'She'll do that, I'm sure,' he said, heaving his postbag to the floor and easing his shoulders. 'Junk mail. That's what we deliver mostly these days. You've done it up nicely. Overhead natural light is great in a kitchen,' he said, looking up at the skylight. 'And you've got the view out to the sea. All these old cottages need an extension for today's kitchens and bathrooms. Two sugars please.'

A pleasant few minutes passed, where Zillah learnt more about the young postman, than about her neighbour. He had studied civil engineering at college in Manchester, but had so far not been able to get a job, so he had returned home to Cornwall.

'Better to deliver post here than in a town. I can get to the beach and surf in the afternoons. It's a great life.' He waved a cheery goodbye, and Zillah set herself the task of once again sitting at her computer, but there was the post to deal with.

There was a letter from Bristol, which she put aside, in case some harsh words from Carl upset her day. There were, 'good luck in your new home' cards, from former work colleagues, and a letter from the solicitor in St Ives.

'*Dear Zillah*

I have recently gone through your grandmother's documents and come across an item which I seem to have overlooked. It was a handwritten note, tucked away and easily missed. It says, "I have left a parcel at the local bank which Zillah can claim at any time. Please tell her to collect it. Karenza Pender." I think it would be a good idea to follow this up. Tell the bank to telephone me if there's any bother.
Best wishes, Simon.'

Zillah presented the solicitor's letter at the bank and waited while a search was made into the whereabouts of the parcel, and checks were made on her identity. It looked an old parcel, with crinkled brown paper, roughly folded. A young woman in an immaculate white blouse handed it over the counter, as though it contained stale fish, and an attitude that questioned why she should be handling such an undesirable item. Zillah took it with an apologetic smile.

She couldn't wait to see what object was in this precious parcel. She walked down the High Street and Lifeboat Hill to the Alba restaurant, where she ordered a cup of coffee. She settled herself in a corner and unwrapped the parcel. There to her delight were two hand-written diaries. Written on the covers were the names Loveday Godolphin nee Care b.1882, and on the second, Karenza Pender nee Godolphin b.1902.

'Mother and daughter,' Zillah told herself excitedly.

31

She chose a book at random.

Diary. Karenza. Age 10. 1912
Dad and Dickon, our farm hand, went down to
Pendower cove. They collected lots of coal from the
boat that was wrecked on the rocks in last night's
storm. They spent all day bringing it home. Mother
wanted them to plant the high field with potatoes
before it rains again. Dad and Dickon came back from
Penzance very late and very jolly, with an empty cart,
and money from selling the coal. They woke me up and
I opened my window and looked out, and they threw
pennies up and laughed a lot. I caught quite a few of
them and in the morning I hurried out to the yard to
pick up the ones that had dropped.

These were treasures from her family, part of the
history of people living at Gorsemoor Farm Cottage.
The diary was written by her grandma Karenza, as a
ten year old girl. Her mother's mother. The woman
who had loved her. Zillah's face flushed with excitement. What stories would unfold from her grandma,
and her great grandmother? She would put the diaries
in her basket and continue to read them at home.

In a reverie that excluded everything around her, she
remembered grandma Karenza talking about a 'pirate's
treasure' that one day would be hers. Zillah had imagined a brass bound box with a skull and crossbones on
the top and inside a gleaming hoard of jewels and silver
and gold coins, just as in the books from her childhood.

'Can I see the treasure, Grandma?'

'You're too young my girl. You'll have it all one day when you're old enough to appreciate such things.'

Grandma Karenza put her finger to her lips, 'Don't you go saying a word about the treasure to your mother.' And the child that she was put it from her mind because she and grandma shared many secrets, but today, the adult woman knew that these two books were part of the pirate treasure grandma had promised her. What was the other? She ordered another cup of coffee, hugging the promise of reading and uncovering the secret lives of people who were close family.

Walking along the Wharf she noted how few boats there were moored in the harbour; not the bigger fishing boats she had known as a child, but boats suitable only for inshore fishing for mackerel, or for carrying passengers to Seal Island, or trips round the bay. She had remembered catches of shark-like dog-fish thrown up on the quay from the bigger boats, and the fish aborting, spilling the precious, small, perfectly complete babies. No wonder there were no fish, with such wretched and careless disregard for the next generation.

There should have been men mending nets on the pier, or scraping down the bottoms of boats and paint-ing them, ready for the season. There was one man she recognised from her childhood. He limped, just as he had done as a child, and one leg was stiff; the long knee length boots hiding the injury. She remembered the incident that had caused his lameness.

Grandma had come to buy fish direct from the boat and, as they stood there waiting on the quay for it to be unloaded, a toddler of three years of age, unnoticed by his parents, had fearlessly jumped off the end of the pier at high tide. A young boy of about twelve had jumped in after him, just as a fishing boat entered the harbour. In rescuing the child from the still rotating propeller, the boy's leg had been severely gashed. The wound had not healed, gangrene had set in and the leg was amputated below the knee. It was a strange irony that he remained alive when many of the boys with whom he went to school and swam and fished with in the harbour, had lost their lives in merchant ships during the Second World War.

She wondered how many other faces she would recognise from the past, and as she walked along the pier, a flock of pigeons flew up from the roof of a cottage on the harbour beach, and a woman came out with a basket and began throwing bread and seeds on the sand. She was the little girl who had performed the same duty of feeding the pigeons with her mother; she was a dark vibrant, skipping creature. Now here was that person, grown up, and of a similar age to herself. What sort of life was she living in that same cottage?

It was a rather sad business seeing these two remnants of her childhood. It made her question her decision to move to Cornwall and witness her memories of things past. She rang Lyn and met her at Bumbles, in the Digey. There was always an excellent pot of tea to be enjoyed and Tammy, the young woman who owned the café, attracted quite a crowd of regular locals. Zillah was pleased to be greeted as a familiar customer. Holiday-makers too appreciated the simple but varied menu.

They lingered over tea and scones and Zillah shook off her feeling of melancholy. 'I'm off home now,' she said, closing the café door and parting from Lyn.

On the drive home to Zennor the road became swathed in mist, with swirls of rain obliterating the fields and the view out to sea. Sea and sky became one leaden dark, threatening, grey. Her returning mood of sadness and loneliness was heightened with the rain and sea mist. She began to cry. The windscreen wipers were just coping with the downpour, but couldn't wipe away her tears. She stopped the car beyond the turn to the hamlet of Towednack, sitting miserably in the drizzle and mopping her face. She couldn't risk driving along the narrow zigzag road with blurred vision, meeting oncoming traffic that was unfamiliar with the hazards of country lanes.

What had she given up to come to this place? This morning, in London, she would be engaging with her colleagues in a bright, warm office. They would be enjoying coffee. There would be laughter and companionship, and talk of their lives. They had pretended an envious admiration of her decision to 'give it all up;' 'get out of the rat race;' 'escape the chaos of London;' 'swop living for life;' all those clichés had somehow contrived towards her decision, had persuaded her that she was doing the right thing. And at what cost? She had sold her London flat, which she had loved and shared with a lovely person, her husband. And what of

Carl? She had let him go, to follow her sentimental dream.

On such an evening, after work, she and Carl would eat at their table by the open kitchen window, looking over the trees and discuss how spring was late, or early this year, depending on the growth of the green canopy spread out below them. At this time of year they would still be able to catch a glimpse of bright water through the new leaves, and watch the boys fishing in the pond at Highgate.

In summer they would open their windows and the music from the concert at Kenwood would float through into their rooms. They might prepare a picnic and invite friends to bring wine, and with a proprietorial air, they would gather up cushions and rugs and walk down the road to enjoy music in the park, sitting on the grass overlooking the lake, where the orchestra played in its brightly lit island shell.

In autumn they would shuffle through the leaves on the Heath and fly kites on the high ground in the more blustery weather at Parliament Hill. Winter would find them testing the lakes and ponds to see if they were frozen over to allow skating, and when the snow fell they would be careering down the hills on an old wooden tray, shouting 'Oly, oly, oly,' as they bounced over the rough hillocks and were spilled out, laughing, along with others on their real toboggans.

This morning, in Cornwall, Zillah had only come upon things past, which had saddened her. But there was no turning back, or was there? There was the woman who would buy her cottage at her asking price.

This would take away her problem. This was her lowest point. She turned on the ignition and continued the journey home. And suddenly, the sun streamed through a hole in the clouds and lit up the landscape. There were the hills, rising steeply, with outcrops of rock, covered with moorland heather and gorse. And there towards the sea were the patchwork of small fields, encircled by Bronze Age stone walls. The clouds dispersed, and over the sea two rainbows appeared, bright and sparkling, rising out of the sea, settling and spotlighting a group of farmhouses lying in green fields. 'Ah,' Zillah sighed, remembering that Cornwall did that sort of thing, exerted its magic, and lifted you out of the black mood it had plunged you into moments earlier.

The sun burned fiercely, drying up the narrow path in front of her, leading down to Gorsemoor Cottage. As she turned into her drive the young woman who lived somewhere down the lane, was walking past.

'Oh, don't go,' Zillah greeted her, desperately. 'I've done a bit of shopping in St Ives and I'm ready for a cup of coffee. Do join me, and we can be introduced at last.'

'Everybody knows me. I'm Beatrice.' She beamed a friendly smile. 'Love some coffee.' As they walked round to the garden door, she pointed at a farmhouse, beyond the two trees in the courtyard. 'That's me. Dove Farm. I believe my parents bought some of the fields, which used to belong to the farmer here.'

'Yes. My grandmother. Are you a farmer?'

'Parents are. I'm on and off, as required, shall we say.

I'm a painter. Turned our hen-house into a studio. Look at those rainbows. Glorious aren't they? Wonderful colours. Beautiful. Couldn't paint it. Difficult to capture nature, really. But one tries. One certainly tries. Oh this is nice.'

They walked through into the kitchen, Beatrice chatting all the time, and Zillah's spirits lifted as she listened. She liked her neighbour. She judged she would be a good, hopeful companion, a bright spirit. She smiled at her, inviting her to sit down, but Beatrice wandered around, touching things, making comments.

'Our kitchen is old and lumpy. Great granite walls. Great walk-in fireplace. Great old house, altogether. Older than yours. Rickety stairs, you'd think each one was carved by a different chap – have to remember which ones are steep, and which narrow, to save yourself falling down; and they're worn away on the treads. We've got a huge old dresser, must be seventeenth century, built with the house. You'd have to demolish the place to get it out, or I suppose you could cut the thing up, but ... '

Zillah interrupted the flow, 'How d'you like your coffee. Milk? Sugar?'

This stopped Beatrice, and she asked for both.

'Let's go into the courtyard. The sun seems to have dried everything and it's quite warm.' Zillah led the way. They sat on the newly paved patio area with a view over the fields to the distant sea.

Beatrice continued her stream of chatter. 'I'll give you an invitation to my private view. It's in a newly opened gallery in Penzance. My work's sort of semi-abstract,

38

with recognisable objects, but it varies.'

'I'd love to come, and to see the work in your studio, if that's permissible.'

'You can see the paintings before they go. I'm not one of those precious artists who hate people invading their studio space. You can help me make a decision on the last couple of pieces. Now, tell me about your fascinating life,' Beatrice demanded.

After talking and laughing, and generally enjoying one another's company, they set off across the wet fields to Dove farmhouse, avoiding the longer walk down the lane. They were of a similar age, mid thirties, but Beatrice was small, with short-cut dark hair and a vital, bubbling personality, a contrast with Zillah's more sombre outlook and her long legs and long auburn hair. Beatrice had studied art in Bristol and ran a gallery, which also sold her work. She had returned to Cornwall to paint, more or less full time, when she wasn't helping her parents with their farming chores. Zillah felt lifted in her presence. She drew her out of her solemn, serious self. She knew they would be friends.

They were almost at the house when Beatrice stopped suddenly. She turned with her back to the house, facing Zillah. 'Ooh, the nosey old devil,' she said. 'She wants to see who I'm bringing to the house. Take a sly look at the upstairs window on your left.'

Zillah, hearing the caution in her voice, did as she was told.

'There's a woman sitting in the window.'

'Right. That's Dulcie. She thinks she lives here, but she's long gone. I've told her to go many times, and when I hope she's taken the hint, back she comes again.'

When Beatrice turned around, the woman was gone.

'You mean she's a ghost?' Zillah had understood immediately, but doubted.

'Yes.'

'You are joking, Beatrice. You don't really mean ...'

'Oh, but I do. Dulcie inhabited the house before our family did. She's always in the window. Probably looking out for her son, or husband, returning from the sea, or the mines. Poor soul.'

They continued to walk towards the house, looking at the empty space in the window. 'And she's not the only wraith in the corner. You'll find the past is very close to the present here. Folk are very loath to leave Cornwall, even when they're dead. Be sure the person you meet on the shore, or the cliffs, has substance.'

Before Zillah could question her about other ghosts, or explain her last remark, they arrived at the farmhouse. Mr and Mrs Paynter proved to be as welcoming and cheerful as their daughter. Sylvia was making pasties and wiped her hands on her apron. 'We've been meaning to come round. I've got things for you. Beatrice should have taken them this morning.' She walked into a huge larder off the kitchen and came out with a bowl of eggs, a dish of butter, a newly baked loaf, a jar of honey, a cauliflower and a bunch of primroses and violets.

Arthur Paynter, coming in from the yard, washed his hands at the butler sink and dried them on a roller towel behind the larder door. 'Coffee, Arthur, please,' his wife demanded. Arthur winked at Zillah, 'His master's voice,' he said, laughing, and filled a black iron kettle and put it to boil on a black Cornish range.

Zillah sat at the scrubbed wooden table watching Beatrice mother's skilful fingers cutting rounds of pastry, filling one half with meat and vegetables, folding the other half over, and crimping the edges with thumb and forefinger. Had her mother ever made pasties at the kitchen table at Gorsemoor Cottage? Certainly, grandma Karenza had. She had taught Zillah to make pasties. 'My mother, Loveday, was a famous pasty maker,' grandma told her. 'I was never as good as her, but your mother refused to make pasties, or even eat them.' Pasties were essential Cornish fare, but it would be just like her mother, Zillah thought, to take against something because it was traditional.

'Stay to lunch,' Mrs Paynter said.

It wasn't an invitation. She did not expect a refusal. She put a tray of pasties, liberally plastered with egg, into the oven. Zillah watched Mr and Mrs Paynter moving deftly about the kitchen, their footsteps sounding on the flagstone floor. She seemed to be smiling permanent approval at their movements, as they criss-crossed paths, mother clearing away the baking dishes, wiping down the table, father setting up mugs, fetching a white jug of milk from the larder. It was a co-ordinated dance, familiar and lovingly performed every day.

Zillah was pleased and amazed by being transported back through the years in this old farmhouse kitchen. It

41

was a bigger house than hers with a vast flag stone kitchen and yet it was comforting and nest like, not like her very tidy kitchen extension, added on to the old kitchen, where everything was clean, bright and sparkling. This kitchen had bowls of onions and apples sitting on the dresser. It was like grandma Karenza's kitchen, which she had known as a child, but this one had not fallen into disuse and neglect through the years like Gorsemoor Cottage. A great number of keys hung from hooks on the dresser along with an assortment of blue and white cups, plates, and dishes of various sizes. A ginger cat was curled up among a cluster of ragged cookery books, magazines and bills. Great dusty silver-domed tureens and various sized pottery pitchers and jugs sat upon an open bottom shelf.

Everywhere she looked there were signs of vibrant living. A grandfather clock stood in a dark corner. It had a deep-throated pendulum tick. Overhead, a light blazed down on the table, putting the rest of the kitchen in shade, except for a pathway of sunlight that slid across the floor as the door to the yard was opened. The big butler sink, was flanked by a great wooden plate rack. The kitchen overlooked the cobbled yard and several outbuildings. Chickens picked and clucked outside and wandered in at will if the door was open.

'Coffee's ready Sylvia. Now, at once please. Beatrice, stir yourself and get the sugar for our guest.' Her father pulled out a chair for his wife to sit down. 'Now then, young lady,' he said with candour. 'I want to know exactly what you intend doing with those buildings your grandmother turned into holiday units.'

'Shame on you Arthur,' Sylvia chided. 'Let the poor girl breathe.'

Zillah was jolted out of her comfortable reverie.

'Well, I ...'

'She doesn't know herself yet, dad,' Beatrice interrupted her father, seeing the flush of embarrassment that had travelled up Zillah's face, and hastening to release her from having to answer an unanswerable question. 'Give the girl a break, dad. She's only just moved in.'

Zillah shrugged and smiled, and everybody laughed.

'Did you know my grandmother, Karenza?'

'My father bought the animals, fields and barns from her. I was farming up north, as a tenant farmer, knowing that one day this farm would be mine, but at the time, it couldn't support two families. When dad died, we moved back. I remember seeing a young flame-haired girl walking through the fields with Mrs Pender. I thought they were mother and daughter with that same colour hair. That must have been you Zillah. Beatrice rarely came here for holidays because my mother had died and there was no woman in the house to look after her, only women who came daily to cook and clean for my dad, or you two would probably have met before now.'

'Yes. I've only known the farm as an adult. I feel quite cheated,' Beatrice said.

'Farmers can't be holiday making and moving about the country as other folk,' Sylvia added. 'It's one of the disadvantages of the job. There's always the animals, you see.'

'But I remember your mother, Mary,' Arthur continued. 'She was a bit of a trial to your grandma. We went to the village school in Zennor, walking through the fields, with our lunch satchels. We weren't friends, just lived near one another. Most children stayed in school for dinner. The teacher would put the pasties on the big round stove, and we had hot pasties most days, except your mother. She always had sandwiches. The school room smelt like a bakehouse. Lovely, it was.'

'Why was my mother a trial?' Zillah wanted to know.

'Mary was always complaining about the stink in the yard from the animals. "I'm going away from here, and never, never coming home," she told me. 'I remember it so well. Even as a boy, as far as I was concerned, a farmer was what I wanted to be. We argued and fought and were never great friends. Our ideas were too different.'

'My mum hardly ever visited after she left home. I've got two other sisters but I'm the only one who came to stay and I suppose that's why grandma left me the cottage. She and I were very close.'

Zillah walked home through the lane, passing the granite gateposts of the old farmhouse, and the giant granite millstone propped against the side of the house. Half way down the lane, she took a covert look at the window where the figure had been sitting, looking out; but there was no one there.

Back in her own kitchen, she put the primroses and violets in two separate vases, set one on the table and

44

the other on the windowsill. Already, it began to look more lived in. The eggs she put in a blue and white bowl and placed them on grandma's big table, one of the few items she had retained of her furniture, before the cottage was modernised. The butter she placed in a cheese dish, on the coolest slate sill. The loaf, still warm from the oven, was left on a breadboard on the table. I could do a painting of this scene, she thought with pleasure; if I could paint.

Having lunched at Dove Farm, she went to her office to begin work on the chapter of the novel she was editing, but her thoughts and interests were not in the job. Her mind began questioning what she would do with the outbuildings in the yard. Her neighbour, Arthur, probably wanted them, since he had clumsily approached the subject this morning. She would examine them more closely.

One of the doors was hanging off its hinges. Inside, it was spacious and empty. The other four units were also empty. Grandmother, or the solicitor dealing with the will had sold the furniture. The overhead Velux windows poured light into the space, and the flooring was quarry tiled. She was quite impressed with the pleasant feel of the area. They were certainly useful buildings, but for what?

A number of unsettling elements had happened this morning. There was meeting Lyn for tea at Bumbles. That was nice. There was the meeting with Beatrice, and her parents. That was pleasant too. The farm-house they lived in was delightful, but there was the ghost in the window. Well, that wasn't too bad. The thing that disturbed her was Arthur Paynter describing her mother in uncomplimentary terms; why was her mother's childhood so unhappy in this seemingly idyllic place? What prompted her to leave home so soon? Why had there been a prickly relationship between mother and daughter? Why had this carried on into her life? These thoughts reminded her that her mother had recently died, and there was no mending the many years of anguish and distance that had grown steadily and pushed them further apart.

Going into the cottage, she reached for her jacket, changed into boots, and stepping over the style, set off on the footpath to the nearest cove. She and grandma had picnicked there, but never swam, because of the dangerous currents swirling around the rocks. There was a fairly hazardous descent along a crumbling, narrow path, onto a sand and rock strewn beach.

'Lawrence and Frieda used to bathe naked here,' Grandma Karenza told her.

'Who are they?' asked the ten year old Zillah.

'A writer, David Herbert Lawrence, and his German wife. They lived in a cottage near us and he wrote one of his great novels in Zennor. He loved Cornwall,' grandma said, and pointed out the cormorants drying their wings on the flat rock in the bay.

'What was the name of the book?' Zillah wanted to know.

'It was called *Women in Love*. He was a very scandalous man, by all accounts, and his wife Frieda used to walk to the village singing her German songs and, considering it was the First World War, it was a very unwise thing to do. Her husband just laughed about it when people complained to him.

It wasn't until Zillah came across the name D H Lawrence and his books when studying literature in senior school, that she remembered those few brief words spoken to her as a child, and understood. *Women in Love* became one of her favourite novels because of its association with Cornwall.

On the cliff top it was quiet and calm. The sun warmed her; made her feel sleepy. She sat enjoying the silence and the soothing air, with her back resting against a rock. The swishing whisper of the sea against the stones was mesmerising. Out of the corner of her eye she caught a movement down below in the bay. To her surprise, she saw a man and woman enter a cave. He was a tall, thin figure, with a dark beard; she, a stocky woman, with blond hair. She watched until they emerged from the cave into the sunshine. They were naked. His thinness and pale skin emphasised his nudity, her robust figure was a healthy contrast.

The man took the woman's hand, pulling her, and making her run towards the sea. The woman screamed and pulled back, but he was relentless in his rush to the waves. Now they were both submerged, laughing, and swimming towards the flat rock rising out of the sea. He reached it first and clambered up. The sea washed her up closer and giving her his hand he hauled her alongside. They stood embracing. The woman enfolded

him in her arms, warming him with her voluptuous
flesh as he shivered on the rock. She gave his backside
a loud smack, which echoed around the cliffs.

Zillah smiled at their playfulness. 'If they see me,' she
told herself, 'I'll just wave. That'll stop them being
embarrassed. I'll stand and wave, and they'll wave too.'
Now the couple were both shivering. They lowered
themselves into the water, sliding down the smooth
rock launching themselves towards the shore. The
woman was ahead but the man appeared to be slipping
away. She turned to see him struggling and coughing
and immediately swam back with powerful strokes.

When the woman reached him she turned him over
on his back. Zillah could see his arms and legs stretched
out to keep him afloat, but the fit of coughing was
making it difficult to lie quietly. She took him again to
the rock, where they clung and held on.

'Will he have the strength to swim?' Zillah wondered. The woman was holding him, in case the sea
should snatch him. The tide had turned and they found
difficulty swimming against it. This time the woman
swam behind. It was a slow and painful progress
against a strong current. When they reached the beach
the man crawled forward and collapsed. He lay face
down on the sand shivering and coughing. The woman
immediately covered him with her body, warming and
sustaining him.

When he recovered a little the woman ran to the cave
and returned with their clothes and a bath towel, with
which she rubbed the man's back vigorously to warm
him. She dried his legs, arms and hair. He turned over

and she was careful not to chaff him with the sand that was clinging to his chest. He sat up, snatched the towel angrily, and finished drying himself while she dressed, tying her wet hair in a scarf.

They stood facing each other. The man looked dejected. He had been impotent in this adventure. 'He doesn't know whether he can forgive himself, or her.' Zillah thought, reading the thoughts and feelings of the protagonists as though watching a play. The woman is all sympathy, yet can she pretend his failure doesn't matter? Truly, it doesn't matter as far as the woman is concerned; if one of them is in trouble and the other is able to help, what matter who it is? But she knows about this man's ego, his pride. His philosophy is that woman should be beholden to man. And she has witnessed his weakness.

Their moods begin to change. They both get angry, yet say nothing. The man, having recovered his strength, now suddenly strides off, leaving her to pick up their belongings. She is hampered by her burdens as she tries to catch up. 'Lawrence,' she called, desperately, 'Lawrence, Wait for me!'

'Damn you, Frieda,' he shouted.

Zillah is alarmed that the couple will reach the cliff top and find her there. She puts distance between them. She runs and constantly looks behind, expecting to see them emerging over the cliff face. Her fear that the couple might discover she was spying on them, makes her flush and sweat with anxiety. Her legs are heavy and she has difficulty running over the rough terrain.

Zillah is suddenly startled. To her surprise, she is still

sitting against her rock on the cliff top. She is breath-less and anxious as though she has been running, but realises she has been sleeping. There is no sign of the couple. 'It was so real,' she said aloud. 'D.H. Lawrence and Frieda. Just as grandma said, bathing naked in the sea.' And the words of Beatrice came back, 'Just make sure the people you meet have substance.'

She looked down into the cove, and over the cliffs, as though eventually expecting to see the couple, but of course, they were only a dream, but a dream based on the fact that in their lifetime, they had indeed walked among the rocks and swam in the sea. This is what Beatrice meant when she said the past was never far away from the present. She shivered a little with shock and, feeling chilly, rose to her feet and began the half hour walk to the cottage.

When she arrived home, she made tea, and comforted herself by slicing the new bread and buttering it liberally with the farmhouse butter. Next, she rang her father. She could no longer wait to find the answers to so many problems to do with her mother.

'Dad. When are coming to stay with me? I've got lots of question to ask you. I want to know why mum didn't like me as much as Amy and Ruth, and ...'

'Darling, of course she liked you,' he interrupted. 'She loved you. What a thing to say. You've upset me. I'm missing her so much and then you ...' His voice broke on a sob.

'Oh dad,' she said, full of remorse. 'I'm so sorry. I didn't think about how you must be feeling. I didn't think. How awful.'

'Ring me again when you feel better, and when I feel better,' her father said. 'I don't think I can chat. I'm feeling particularly bad. It comes and goes.'

After saying goodbye, Zillah burst into tears. She had offended her father. How could she have done such a thing? Her father had always been her ally. Now she had mortally wounded him; had not thought about his grieving, and hurt his feelings.

When she put down the phone, it immediately rang again.

'Hello,' she said meekly, preparing to apologise again. It was Amy.

'What ever did you say to dad, Zillah. He's left the room crying his eyes out. The first time he's cried since mum died. Tell me, so I know how to handle it. Though it's probably not your fault and he had to cry some time. He has been too hard on himself. Not let himself grieve, really.'

'Oh God, Amy. I'm so sorry. I asked him why mum didn't like me; well, I mean as much as she liked you and Ruth.'

'Couldn't you have waited? No. Don't take that to heart. I understand how you feel and only dad can answer your question, but not just yet, Zillah.'

'I know. I should have waited. I've waited for years, but a little longer wouldn't have hurt.' Even as she said this, she noticed that Amy didn't deny there was any truth in what Zillah felt about herself and her mother.

51

Her sadness filled her soul. 'I can't talk anymore Amy. I'm upset too. Tell dad I'm sorry. Bye.'

She sat at the table feeling drained of energy. It was five o'clock. She would go upstairs and lie on her bed. She was obviously overtired and overwrought. Didn't they say a death in the family and a house move were two of the most stressful events in one's life? Not to mention separation from her husband and the loss of her job and work mates. Everyone and everything was out of sympathy with her.

The physical and mental tension in her body didn't allow for easy resting, and she took up a book. It was D H Lawrence's short stories. She opened it at random, and read a story, which he based on himself and a relationship with a young woman. It was typical of Lawrence's good opinion of himself, his strength, and his control of the situation, where the woman's will bent to his own superior force.

'Well,' she thought wryly. 'He wasn't all that strong and heroic down at the cove,' and was then shocked to remember that it hadn't been real; but it certainly happened, she told herself. It was more of a time slip than a dream.

When she woke, it was dark. The curtains weren't drawn, and there was a half moon riding in clouds through the window. It was three o'clock. She had slept all that time, and hadn't even woken for her evening meal. A doze, lying on the bed, had turned into a deep dreamless sleep. Even so, she was still tired, and undressing and putting on her nightie, she fell back on the pillows and continued sleeping until woken by the early morning chorus from the cocks at Dove Farm. She made tea and toast and took it back to bed.

Zillah was anxious to carry on reading the diaries and immerse herself in the past, but she was surprised to hear footsteps in the yard below and startled when someone knocked on the door. She pulled herself back to the present day, hurried into her dressing gown and bounded down the stairs.

'You must have been hiding behind the door,' laughed Beatrice.

'What time is it?'

'About eight. Is this too early for you? Only I'm driving in to Penzance this morning and wondered if you'd like to come. I'm taking some more paintings to the new gallery. They don't think they've got enough for my show.'

'Yes. I'd like that, but have some coffee while you're here, Zillah invited, and was pleased when her new friend walked in and sat at the kitchen table.

'I've been doing my Tai Chi this morning down at the cove. I breathed in so deeply that it brought the ocean rushing in and soaked me up to my knees. The power of a breath. You wouldn't believe it.'

Zillah laughed. Beatrice was amusing and nice to be with. She felt a thrill of excitement at the prospect of going out with her and meeting up with some of her friends. 'I'll buy you lunch for the ride,' she said. They set out rather later than intended, having breakfast together and chatting over the odd sequence of events that led to their not meeting in childhood, although such close neighbours. Both of them recollected seeing their childhood selves at some distance away, and ended up convincing one another that they had been friends forever.

The car rumbled up the unmade drive, leaving the hamlet of houses nestling in their hollow and came upon the magic road that wound its way through fields and carns and scattered farmhouses and cottages, until it reached Land's End. Long before then, just past the village of Zennor, with its famous bench in the church and the story of the mermaid luring the vicar's son to her watery lair in Pendour cove, they turned up a steep hill. On their left was the vast stoney outcrop of Trewey Hill, and right were more verdant fields and the remains of a fogue, an ancient tunnelled structure, built mostly below the surface and whose use has long been argued over.

The high moors over which they travelled could be dour and forbidding in wet and stormy weather, the wind blowing the grasses of the moor and revealing gleaming patches of boggy water. It was a place haunted by prehistory, its stone menhirs and quoits, its very feeling of a grim past. But when the sun shone, and hawks and kestrels swooped out of the sky it revealed its softer and more welcoming features, like delicate orchids and wild flowers sheltering in clumps of tough grass, looking for the warmth of the sun and bravely surviving the harsh environment.

Arriving in Penzance they left the car and walked

along the harbour front. There the Isles of Scilly passenger boat gleamed white against the quay. They rounded the bend onto Penzance promenade and looked over the wall at the newly decorated art deco swimming pool. In the road behind was the gallery called Space. The venue was huge and barn-like and Anthony Frost's large colourful chevron paintings in their primary colours of mostly yellow, red and blue, boldly faced the challenge of adequately filling the walls and attracting attention.

'I don't know how I'm to compete with these pictures. Mine will fade into the background by comparison. I wonder if they've made the right decision in choosing me? Oh dear, perhaps they could get someone else quickly.'

Zillah didn't know what to say. She wasn't entirely new to artists and exhibitions, so she said what she thought was right, that Beatrice's paintings would look fine with each other, as long as they weren't in competition with the vibrant paintings of Anthony Frost.

'They shout from the walls, and yours whisper Beatrice, but they still have a powerful statement to make. My sister, Amy, who runs a gallery in Richmond, believes you can make a point equally from quietness as from boldness.'

'Well, what a diplomat you are, and what a very nice compliment to us both as artists. I couldn't be more pleased. Come on, help me get these into the store and then we'll have a cup of coffee. Oh look, there's Anthony. I'll introduce you.'

Anthony was an ebullient young man, full of energy,

charm and bonhomie. He kissed Beatrice on both cheeks, offered a large warm hand to Zillah and, at the same time, produced an invite to the opening of Porthminster beach café in St Ives, and his annual seasonal show at that venue on the beach, flooded with light, and both venue and paintings complementing one another.

Zillah was delighted.

'How did this show go? What do you think of this place?' Beatrice asked.

'Great space,' he said, looking around the gallery. 'Perfect for my work, though I can imagine some paintings would get lost. It really invites large pictures, but mine made a bold statement and, so I'm told, created just the right atmosphere for the opening of a new gallery.'

Beatrice groaned aloud. 'See. How can I follow you? Your work is so dynamic, powerful …'

'No, no. You don't have to follow me,' he said, concerned for her anxiety. 'Your work is totally different and has a softer approach, a quiet appeal. You can hang your paintings in a double line. They'll look great. Believe me.'

As Anthony began removing the last of the unsold paintings, the walls and space were denuded of their vibrancy and colour.

'Now I can see why paintings are so important. They bring life and pleasure to people,' Zillah said.

'Especially when you sell some,' Beatrice said with a laugh. 'Anthony's done well. What if I don't sell anything?'

'Come on, Beatrice. I didn't see any of this self-doubt while you were painting. Wait till you see the impact they make when they're all hung and people are looking at them.'

While Anthony and Beatrice crossed paths taking their paintings in and out of the gallery, they occasionally stopped to introduce Zillah to several of the artists, who dropped in for coffee and a chat. They were friendly and approachable and completely unjudgemental; a refreshing change from the people who worked in offices and were governed by time and their ambitious achievements in reaching deadlines and targets in their day-to-day work.

In Rainyday gallery upstairs in Market Jew Street, another character, Martin Val Baker, offered a relaxed and quiet welcome. Anthony and Martin had been friends from childhood and couldn't be more different in outlook and personality. Martin Val Baker was unobtrusive. The paintings he hung in his gallery showed his eclectic taste. Anthony had filled the Space gallery, not only with his paintings, but with his voice and personality, Martin was as silent as the paintings on the walls of his gallery. His demeanour was laid-back. He was unimpressed by any proud boasts of success by artists who came storming in to say how many paintings they'd sold at a one-man show, or how well other galleries were doing.

'Of course I'll come to the private view,' Martin said, in response to Beatrice's plea. 'Don't I always? And if some major London art gallery hasn't bought the whole show and carted them off to Cork Street, I'll have a couple for my next exhibition, but I fully expect you'll have a complete sell out.'

'Oh, shut up, Martin,' Beatrice said, hoping to stop his teasing.

Zillah watched them laugh, both taking some pleasure in the preposterous idea and unlikely event of a sell out. Martin held an ironic view of the world.

'Stranger things have happened,' he said.

Martin seemed content in operating within his own orbit. He absorbed information without envy, or comment, or desire to emulate examples of success achieved by others, a half smile always flickering behind his questioning, enquiring mind. He jogged along, following his own course and achieving what he intended to achieve, seemingly without effort. Zillah judged that nothing moved Martin to aspire to anything other than what he was, and what he did, and admired this very different personality, as much as she had been impressed by Anthony.

Zillah began to realise there was a lot to discover in this world of artists, and she looked forward to her adventure in learning about them.

3

Meeting the artists, and having lunch with Beatrice in Penzance, had dispelled the ennui Zillah had been suffering from since returning from London and her mother Mary's funeral. She still felt sorely cheated, and cruelly deprived of the chance to win her mother's approval, and establish an adult friendship with her. She had planned meals in her head, rather on the frugal side that would prevent her mother calling her a greedy pig. This was often the label pinned to her as a child. A label in which there was some justification Zillah thought, since she loved her food, and always left her plate clean.

Her sisters, Amy and Ruth, were picky eaters. Their mother never chided them for leaving their meals but criticised Zillah hurtfully for her good appetite, 'You should eat everything, just like greedy pig. She doesn't have a problem. It's munch, munch, gobble, gobble, and there – it's all gone.'

Mary had sometimes gone to extremes and made Zillah eat the left-overs on her sisters' plates, even if she didn't want them. And very soon she refused such tit-bits, knowing that her mother would be looking at her with a grimace of dislike. 'But Mum, I don't want any-more,' she would protest.

'Nonsense, child, you've always eaten everything.

You like eating other people's food. You've grown big and strong because of it. You were a great, big, greedy, baby.' At this point her mother's voice would rise and the three girls watched her becoming hysterical, and angry, but realising the anger would be directed at Zillah.

'Look at you, twice the size of Amy and Ruth. Twice the size. Now eat up. You two can leave the table.'

The two girls would slide off their chairs, and creep out of the room, while Zillah was left miserably contemplating two plates of half-eaten food. Her own clean plate earned the scorn of her mother. 'There used to be a pattern on this plate, but Zillah has licked it off,' she frequently told her two sisters, who wondered at the bizarre situation of making Zillah responsible for their poor appetites. It didn't make sense to either of the girls, but there was no questioning their mother's odd behaviour.

Zillah shook off this childhood memory. It didn't do to be constantly going over those painful circumstances, and trying to understand why her mother treated her with such scorn. The girls had never discussed it. For Zillah it would have been an embarrassment, and for Amy and Ruth it felt like scheming with their mother because they escaped the punishment.

That morning over lunch in Penzance Beatrice had put forward a proposition to Zillah for the use of the units in her courtyard.

'Look, I think you and I could put ourselves to good use, and earn some money.'

'Oh, yes,' Zillah replied with interest.

'I've always wanted to set up a painting school, and teach people in my studio. There's a huge space for several people to work, and there's the countryside and sea for inspiration, but I haven't got accommodation.'

'And I have.'

'Exactly. You could rent your units to the students for sleeping, and maybe provide meals. I mean I haven't thought it through, but what's your initial response?'

'Sounds like the opportunity I've been looking for. Not sure about providing meals though.' Zillah had sounded both pleased and downcast. The idea of cooking food and taking some pleasure in doing it wasn't appealing. It would bring on those guilty feelings about eating that she'd had since childhood, but she couldn't tell Beatrice this.

'I think you need someone to cook with more professional culinary skills than I have, or a genuine rustic, country cooking, type.'

'Well, if you like the idea of accommodating students, that would be a start. I wonder if Mum would do food; a genuine rustic cook if ever there was one. Great chunky casseroles, beef steaks as big as a plate, half chickens the size of a pullet, lamb chops that require a bushel of mint to cover them, tureens of soup, monster apple pies – well need I go on? Anyway early days. Lots to talk about. Come on, let's find the car before it rains.'

61

They rushed through the new shopping centre to the harbour car park and sat in the car breathless and laughing, while a sudden squall pelted the roof with hailstones and set the rigging of boats ringing and clattering against their masts. Beyond the bus and train station, St Michael's Mount disappeared in a fog in its island in the sea. 'I hope the mermaids can find the Mount in this fog, and not swim out to sea and get lost,' Beatrice said, 'Or the fishermen will have to set out in their boats to rescue them.'

'What a romantic you are,' Zillah exclaimed. 'Are you in the habit of making up stories?'

'Oh yes. I always used to believe that mermaids lived on the Mount. In fact, I still believe it. We need new legends and stories, just as the church needs new saints. We must keep everything going. I make up stories, but never write them down, but I do have the illustrations. I must show them to you. Now there's another idea, you write the stories and I'll do the drawings.'

'Come on, stop dreaming,' Zillah said, 'and drive towards the rainbow that's appeared over St Michael's Mount.'

That evening, Zillah was tired after her day out and meeting people. It had been a lunch time of shaking hands, and cheek kissing in the Arts Club café in Chapel Street, and she relived the experience of meeting Susan and Sam, both artists, who had met at art school and been companions with widely different opinions on modern and traditional modes of painting. The source of their arguments kept the spark in their marriage.

'I am constantly experimenting. I don't stand still,'

Susan told her, showing the evidence on her torn and paint daubed jeans.

'I allow her to do that by selling paintings,' Sam, a neat figure in a smart suit, retorted. 'I find it more important to please people, and sell work. I make a living. Susan plays around.'

Their banter was good humoured, and without rancour from Sam, who smiled indulgently, if perhaps a little patronisingly, at Susan's protests.

'I shall net myself a big exhibition at some time, and be hailed as the most innovative painter of the West Country,' Susan laughed, 'And you will be there Sam in your bow tie and neat shoes, and people will say, 'Is that dapper little man your agent? and I'll deny ever having seen you before.'

'Agent!' exploded Sam. 'I'm as much an artist as you, only less paint spattered.'

The club café was a great meeting place for artists, writers and musicians. It was a place to display their paintings, read their poems, or play their music to an appreciative audience. People knew each other and tossed remarks across the room. The staff knew their members and clients and this further added to the friendliness and happy atmosphere of the place.

'See you at my show Beatrice on Saturday. Sent you an invite. Bring your friend,' shouted a woman as Zillah and Beatrice exited, and she entered the café with a group of young people from the Penzance art school, who seemed to be carrying her into the place, in spite of her protests. 'Help. I believe I'm being abducted!'

'That's their tutor,' Beatrice said. 'She doesn't believe

in fraternising with students, but they have other ideas, don't you think? I used to be a student of hers, and she never came out for coffee with us, but they don't seem to care what her ideas are and whether she wants to mix with students, or not. Good for them. Nice one. The young get braver, don't they?'

Beatrice dropped Zillah on her doorstep and proceeded down the bumpy lane, waving her hand from the car window and calling, 'See you!'

Zillah made herself a cup of tea and, resisting a biscuit, carried it upstairs to where she intended sitting on the bed reading her grandma's diary. On the table by the bedside was the Victorian lamp she remembered from her childhood. It was grandma's lamp. It lit the bedroom and made pools of light on the ceiling. She sat in bed daydreaming and recreating scenes from when she lived in this cottage with grandma Karenza. It was strange that the same lamp still comforted her, but downstairs there was no grandma sitting writing in her diary, with the lamp creating a pool of light on the table. It was only now that she remembered the scene when she came downstairs in her nightie to ask for a drink of water, and there was grandma leaning over the table, dipping a pen in a bottle of ink.

'Can't you sleep my child?'

'No Grandma.'

'Come, sit at the table. I'll just finish writing this page, and then I'll make you hot milk and a biscuit.

That'll be nice won't it Zillah?'

'No Grandma. It's too greedy.'

'Too greedy. No. I don't think so. When you're with me, we play by my rules. I'll make you hot milk, and you can have a special biscuit. I only buy them when you come down, so they're my treat. And it'll be our secret.'

Zillah remembered being told to look at the clock on the mantelpiece and tell grandma when the two hands met on twelve, until then she was to sit at the table and be as quiet as a mouse and watch the clock so as not to miss the magic hour.

'It's twelve o'clock Grandma,' she would say urgently.

'Oh. Time for our midnight feast. We must celebrate with the magic folk.' She closed her book, with the brown wrapping paper neatly folded over the cover to keep it clean. 'There. That'll do for today.'

The midnight feast became a ritual where Zillah and grandma Karenza were allowed to enjoy themselves at that quiet hour. Sometimes grandma would wake up the fire with the poker and they would sit with their feet on the brass fender and talk and tell stories. It was something treasured, and safely secret to the child who had so many bewildering questions in her head that she couldn't even ask grandma.

Zillah looked at her digital clock. It was midnight. She went downstairs and took out the biscuit she had put back in the tin before coming to bed. 'Magic time

grandma. I'm allowed to enjoy this because of you.'
And she heated a glass of milk in the microwave.

Settling herself in bed, she opened a diary. It was written by her great grandmother, Loveday. She wondered how mother and daughter, Loveday and Karenza, got on together. Was there any tension between them, like there was between Karenza and her daughter Mary, and Zillah with her mother Mary?

Diary. Loveday. Age 14. 1896
Today I had a letter from my friend Hope Lindner from Chy-an-Porth, St Ives. Dear Loveday, I hope you will be coming to the meeting at Porthminster beach this afternoon. Mother's friends will be coming. Emmeline Pankhurst will be giving a speech and many fashionable ladies will be at our house before they march off to London. Wear something green, white or purple, or all three. Your friend, Hope.

Loveday had always wanted to see some of these famous ladies that had meetings in Hope's house. Her father said he would go to market via the St Ives route. He had business in Penzance and would drop her off at the top of the town. She walked down the Stennack and turned up Tregenna Hill and into the Terrace. Groups of women were outside Chy-an-Porth house and in the garden. She couldn't find Hope anywhere so she wandered around admiring the ladies' dresses and beautiful hats they wore. They didn't look like St Ives women, except for Sundays when aprons reeking of fish were put away and their smartest dresses, coats and hats were worn for chapel and gloves covered work-worn hands.

From the Terrace Loveday looked down to the railway station. A train was arriving, and a great many more ladies, with lovely wide-brimmed, flamboyant hats, got out of the train and were led down the station steps to Porthminster beach. They were carrying banners and flags and she watched them setting up a platform on the sands. She could hear the noise of their laughter and talking all the way up the Terrace, where a party of smart women swarmed out of the Porthminster Hotel. There was an infectious, tense air of excitement.

Loveday arrived at the front door at the same moment that Hope and her mother Augusta walked out. They were wearing white muslin dresses with a wide green sash around the waist, and a purple sash across one shoulder. They looked very elegant. Many of the ladies had white hats decorated with green and purple. Hope's mother told them they were the colours of their special women's group.

It was a different and thrilling event taking place in a town more used to male voice choirs, singing on the newly built West Pier, than anything to do with women, let alone women with such a militant agenda.

Mrs Lindner gave the girls a banner to hold which read Votes for Women and flags with the letters NUWSS on them to distribute among the crowd. 'It means National Union of Women's Suffrage Societies,' Hope's mother told them. Normally, the girls would have felt silly but there were so many flags and banners that they didn't mind. They were caught up with the excitement of the crowd. Loveday's mother, Annie, would have come to the meeting, but she was busy on the farm. Her father, Henry, didn't approve of Annie's interest in the women's movement, but Annie had her own ideas. She would have liked to hear the ladies making speeches about voting in Parliament. 'You go Loveday, and tell me what happens.'

There weren't any local women there. The Bal Maidens were out of town at the mines, wielding hammers to break the mined rock into smaller pieces for crushing in the stamping machines, or sorting the ore from the waste. They would be working in grimy and wet conditions alongside boys who were carting off the waste in heavy wheel barrows. In town, the women were gutting fish on the harbour, or salting them into barrels, or with their salt cracked hands, mending nets, or looking after the children in their large families.

The local women didn't have time to parade about in their Sunday best. Loveday was angry for their sakes that they couldn't, or wouldn't, listen to speeches. She didn't want to be like them, to be too busy, and have cracked hands from handling fish and salt. She didn't want to wear an apron covered in fish scales, and stinking. Even more she disliked the idea of cracking stones with a hammer, working out in the open in all weathers and having nowhere to shelter. She felt lucky to be born on the farm, but knew that some of her aunties in St Ives would like her to live with them, to help look after her young cousins, or with the sorting, stacking, or pressing of pilchards in Maid Betsey's yard for export to Italy. She was certainly going to avoid that.

'Hope, Loveday!' called Mrs Lindner. 'Oh there you are girls. We're going back to the house. Come along. I don't want you wandering off and following the march. Run along and tell Molly and Sophie to have tea ready. We'll be a party of ten.'

Porthminster beach was well trodden with the hundreds of shoes of women who had attended and listened to the speeches about standing firm in their desire to have the vote. The words of Mrs Mary Phillips were still ringing in their ears.

'If we have to have men only in Parliament, then we want to vote for one that knows about women's needs, and children's needs, and family needs. What is the point of having political parties when they represent only one half of the population?'

A great unladylike roar went up from the women standing closest to the temporary platform, who could hear the speakers. But there was general approval from ladies who couldn't quite hear, but knew the gist of the speeches. They were repeated over and over, to keep alive the enthusiasm and determination to state their case for the vote in every possible way, and at every opportunity.

'There will come a time when a woman will give her maiden speech in Parliament, and she will not be laughed at. She will not be ridiculed. She will not be thrown into jail for her desire to have political status, because she will have equal rights with men'

An even bigger cheer went up. But many of the women in St Ives didn't feel the need for a vote. They had equal shares in the boats, alongside the men, and equal shares in the fish, and more shares in the nets. If their husband captained the boat, that would be another share. What more could having a vote in the London Parliament give to them? They laughed at the women who had nothing better to do than sew or embroider tiny handkerchiefs, while they knitted useful things like fishermen's jerseys and socks, made from oiled wool. 'See how dainty their fingers would be after making one of these,' an old dame remarked, as she sat outside her cottage door, with her big knitting needles and a heavy half finished garment tucked under her arm.

Hope and Loveday left the beach and toiled up Primrose Valley to Chy-an-Porth, the house overlooking the bay and Godrevy lighthouse. They entered a large hall where Hope rang a bell on a hall-stand, and Molly, one of their maids appeared from the basement. She bobbed a brief curtsey when the message for tea had been delivered, and ran back downstairs.

Loveday rather disapproved of women twice the age of fourteen showing deference, and was even more embarrassed when Molly included her in the curtsey. She was a woman from St Ives and Loveday felt she was being facetious, but Hope, used to servants all her life had no such qualms. She was the daughter of Moffat Lindner an artist, and his wife Augusta, who had come to St Ives to study with the artist and seascape painter, Julius Olsson.

'Mother gave up painting because father was more successful, but she is very important because father relies on her good judgement of his work,'

Hope explained.

On the stairs Hope pointed to a painting of her mother. 'It's by Philip Wilson Steer, one of father's artist friends. He was teaching at the Slade school of art and came to stay during the vacation to paint the portrait of mother.'

Loveday was familiar with some of the artists who were living in St Ives because they opened their studios to the people of the town to view the paintings destined for the Royal Academy, in London. She said she hoped that some day one of the artists would ask her to sit for her portrait. 'But most of them are only interested in painting pictures of the sea,' Loveday moaned.

'Perhaps mummy will do a sketch of us together,' Hope said. 'But daddy is going to ask Augustus John to paint my portrait when he comes to Cornwall. In fact mummy was going to ask if you'd be in the room at the same time. Apparently, Mr John cannot be trusted with a young lady,' Hope giggled.

'If he can't be trusted with one young lady, how will he manage to cope with two. And shall I be able to pro-tect you?' Loveday and Hope laughed aloud with embarrassment at the absurdity of a possible romantic confrontation with Mr John.

'Anyway, he'll be more interested in you Loveday, than me. He likes strong women, with long, dark red hair and lovely eyes, not little mice, like me.' It was the nearest Hope ever got to paying Loveday a compli-ment, and putting herself lower than her friend. But there was still the great divide of class between them, and a different way of life that marked their attitudes and characters.

It was the Suffragist connection that united Hope and Loveday in friendship. It was unlikely they would have met, Hope coming from a rich middle class background and educated at a private school, and Loveday from farming stock, attending the village school. They had met after a meeting at the Drill Hall in St Ives a year ago, where Mrs Bolitho had been speaking to an audience of women, trying to form a committee to work towards recruiting for the National Union of Women's Suffrage Society and establish a branch in the town. Loveday had been taken there by her mother, Annie, to report on the meeting, which she was unable to attend. She was now waiting for Annie to pick her up in the trap.

Hope's mother had stayed behind to talk to the organisers, and most of the crowd had left for home. The girls found themselves together outside the hall, surrounded by a group of boys intent on causing trouble. They blocked the door, and effectively cut off the girls' escape back into the hall. There was no one to appeal to for help.

'Think you're better than us, do you?' they taunted.

'Gonna have the vote are you? Well I vote we give you what for, little maids.'

'Come on boys, run 'em down to the sea in their petticoats.'

'See how big and strong you are then, shall we?' taunted the ringleader.

They found themselves herded along at a run, with occasional pushes. Loveday took the girl's hand, thinking they were better together than apart. Hope was smaller and frailer than herself, and obviously terrified. They couldn't escape the circle of boys and outrun them. They were now near the crossroads at the library corner. At the pace they were going down Street-an-Pol, Loveday feared that they would indeed find themselves pushed over the wall near the Arts Club and into the sea. The boys would easily manage to herd them the next few yards.

'I know you Charlie Ninnes,' Loveday shouted, and stood her ground, while Hope cowered behind her. 'And your mum'll give you what for when I tell her what crowd you're mixing with.'

This made the boys laugh. His little mother was a tyrant with a slipper, and though twice her size, he took his beatings manfully, knowing she only wanted to teach her son right from wrong, and for his dead father in heaven to look down on him with pride.

'Would your father be proud of you, son. Would your father be proud?' Mrs Ninnes would question, if she thought Charlie might be involved in any wrong doing.

Big Charlie Ninnes paused for thought. 'I aren't with 'em, so!' he said, and slunk off down St Andrews Street.

Loveday realised it would have been better if he'd stayed, and maybe she could have appealed to him for help. She had seen him use his strength to help the underdog. He was something of a simple hero. There was a temporary lull, while the boys directed their scorn at the retreating figure of Charlie Ninnes, but cautiously, in case he should defend himself from their taunts. Loveday wished her mother would appear riding down Skidden Hill with Soldier and the trap. She would soon deal with these stupid boys.

They were moving again towards the wall. There was a high tide. The sea would be thrusting against the rocks and if the threat to toss them into the water was real, they would find themselves caught in a swirl and thrown helplessly around until they drowned. The girl at her side was stumbling in terror, clinging to the hand that held her. She looked up at Loveday, tears in her frightened eyes.

'Don't cry,' Loveday whispered, 'it'll make them worse.' She was used to dealing with the rough boys from the town and knew you had to brave it out whatever punishment they intended for you. She probably would have fought the boys, but for the figure clinging to her.

'I can't swim,' the girl stammered.

'What's your name?'

'Hope. Hope Lindner. I live up on the Terrace.'

Loveday had never seen the girl before but if she lived on the Terrace, she was from one of the rich families. The boys from the fishing quarter in Downlong wouldn't know her, though Loveday herself was a familiar figure, and she recognised many of the boys from the fishing families in the town.

With Charlie Ninnes gone attention once more homed in on the two girls. They could hear the slap of water against the rocks and feel the spray in their faces. Still they held on to one another, fighting off the hands that grabbed at them, protecting themselves as best they could.

'Come on. Let's see them swim. Let's drown them in their petticoats.'

'They can float, instead of vote,' laughed the boys.

Loveday stood her ground, once more, and faced the six boys. 'Have you seen my friend before?' she said.

'No, we 'aven't my 'andsome.'

'And we 'aven't seen a witch with copper knob hair.'

'Oh no, not likely,' they chorused. 'And we don't know the other one neither.'

'Well, she happens to be the daughter of the new master at the Board School at Island Road. Take a good look at them, and you'll be able to tell your father which boys are in need of the cane.'

Loveday shook Hope's hand to make her look at the boys. She wished Hope would rise with more courage to her scheme for getting them out of this dangerous situation. She was being too timid, but this sudden shock forced the boys to hide their faces behind their sleeves, and then turning swiftly, they ran up the Warren, and disappeared.

Hope nearly collapsed with fright after they'd gone and Loveday held her up, half dragging her back towards town. 'Hope, come on. Walk. They've gone. We're safe,' she said, trying to sooth her and stop the shivering that was shaking Hope's little frame. And then down Skidden Hill came Annie Care with her horse and trap to rescue them. 'Now then, my girl, what's happened here?' she asked her daughter, and when told, she was prepared to go looking for the boys with her horse whip, but Hope was still in danger of fainting away so between them they lifted her into the trap and drove to the hall.

In the lighted doorway of the hall, Hope's mother was looking in the street trying to locate her daughter. It had been the intention of Augusta Lindner to walk home with Hope, but she was grateful to accept the offer of a lift home after Loveday had explained the circumstances of Hope's distressed state.

'You're more than welcome, my bird,' said Annie, showing her sympathy for the poor young woman, by relapsing into the vernacular; much to the embarrassment of Loveday, who had begun to notice the difference in speech patterns between the native St Ives people, and the incoming artist folk.

Next day Loveday, as planned, answered the summons to Chy-an-Porth house to receive the grateful thanks from Hope's parents. She travelled rather grandly from the farm in a Landau and arrived at the house just as Dr Nicholls was leaving. 'Ah Loveday,' Mrs Lindner said, 'you're just what the doctor ordered. There's nothing Hope needs more, apparently, than a companion to sit and talk to. I'll send you up some lunch. Try to coax my daughter into eating something.'

A maid showed Loveday into a large, bright and comfortable room overlooking Porthminster beach. Hope looked very pale and held her hand out to Loveday, who took it and patted it, not knowing what to say or do. She was alarmed that such a trivial event could have such a dramatic effect upon someone. Loveday had hardly thought about the incident.

'I'm so glad you've come. I told mummy how brave you were. I'm sure those boys would have drowned me if you hadn't been there.' Hope's eyes filled with tears.

'Well, it's all over and we're safe, and it's a lovely day, and the sun is shining, and I'm staying to lunch, and we can talk about it, and soon it'll be something to laugh about.' Loveday gabbled on in her anxiety to prove useful and help her through her anxiety. Hope smiled weakly and dried her eyes.

Hope spent the next few days in bed recovering. From that time on Mrs Lindner favoured Loveday as a friend and protector for Hope, and encouraged visits to the house, especially when the parents were absent and their child only had the servants for company. At these times Loveday would sleep at the house. An extra single bed was now a permanent feature in Hope's very spacious bedroom. Although the girls' parents never mixed socially, there were frequent messages sent from Chy-an-Porth to Gorsemoor Farm via a servant, asking permission for Loveday to accompany Hope to various meetings, or to parties and events held at the house.

It was an uneasy alliance because Hope was a young woman, who was prone to histrionics and fainting fits and always had her own way with her parents. Loveday was chosen as a friend because she had a calming effect upon Hope, and they thought her a sensible and well-behaved companion for their daughter. However, Mr Henry Care couldn't help but be flattered by the attention paid to a farmer's child, from an obviously well off artistic family. Mrs Augusta Lindner was a suffragette, which endeared her to the heart of Mrs Annie Care, though she saw no reason to be overawed by people because they were educated and rich.

The girls saw much of one another at Chy-an-Porth house, and had their own patch of flowers in the Italian designed garden. Loveday dug, watered and did the heavy work, while Hope designed the shape of the beds, and chose seeds from a catalogue. Both were happy with the division of labour. They picnicked on the beach. They shopped in Penzance. The Landau was always available for their jaunts into the countryside to pick wild spring flowers. However, there was the embarrassment of refusing the first party because Loveday didn't have a party dress. Hope sent a note demanding an explanation of why her new friend couldn't come.

'I won't accept a refusal. I need you. You make me strong. I don't have bad tempers when you're with me. Please come. You will stay the weekend.'

Loveday wrote, 'I can't turn up in my pinafore to be shamed in front of your friends.'

When the true reason was discovered Hope was indignant. She couldn't understand how such a simple thing as a party dress would prevent Loveday accepting her invitation. She appealed to her mother to remedy the situation.

Thereafter, Mrs Lindner made a point of having dresses made for both girls as a matter of course. They enjoyed looking at patterns and material with the dressmaker and being fitted for new outfits, and Loveday came to accept this as the normal procedure. The only worry was that none of her friends from Zennor, or St Ives, were ever invited to these occasions. Only the children of artists, and other rich families visited Chy-an-Porth. And yet, with all her privileges and wealth, Hope was not a happy girl. She was not popular and had very few real friends.

At fifteen, Hope was a small frail girl, while Loveday at fourteen was taller and much more grown up. Loveday soon realised that Hope was unreasonable and very spoilt. There were many occasions when calling at the house that she was obliged to wait in the drawing room, while screams and temper tantrums from upstairs indicated that Hope was in one of her demanding moods. However, when she emerged to greet her friend, there was a smug smile on her face and no evidence of the drama she had created. She had obviously won the battle. Neither Hope nor Loveday referred to the incidents.

If Hope was using her as a protector and because she had no friends who would tolerate her infantile behaviour, then Loveday was using this friendship to learn how more privileged people lived and, apart from Hope, learn from their good manners how to behave with confidence in society.

Having passed on the message about serving tea, the girls ran upstairs to change into afternoon dresses. Hope said, 'I'm going to a finishing school in Switzerland in September, when I'm sixteen. When I'm away, I won't miss you so much. I'll show you my new wardrobe.' Without waiting for a reply, Hope threw open the double doors of her wardrobe, and there, hanging between sweet perfumed lavender bags, were dresses designed for every occasion. Loveday fingered the silk, satin and cotton dresses, admiring the colours and patterns and the petticoats, chemises, hats, bags, gloves, coats and shoes that complemented each outfit.

She remembered her own sparse wardrobe, but she was not envious of the clothes, having benefited many times from Hope's desire to have a new dress for a special occasion.

'I don't have such pretty clothes for my work on the farm, only aprons and overalls, and hats to stop my hair falling into the milk, or sticking to the butter.'

'Ugh!'

'But it's a good life, when you get used to getting up at five in the morning.'

'Oh, I couldn't. I simply couldn't get up at five. If they dare to make me do that at college, I'll tell daddy to send me somewhere else.'

'But I've passed my dairymaking course. It took a few weeks. We had a teacher come to our farm to teach me and five other farmers' daughters about dairymaking. She used our dairy like a classroom. You could have joined us Hope.'

Hope's shocked expression made Loveday burst out laughing. Hope, who rarely saw anything funny, laughed too.

'We've all got a certificate.' Loveday said, 'But there are going to be agricultural colleges soon to teach everything about farming. I've been really happy learning, in spite of the hard work. I'll be able to get a job on a dairy farm up country and live with the farmer's family, and get paid too.'

'I should hate it. I should really hate all that mess. Do you really have to get a job Loveday? I always want you to be here. I was hoping you'd work on your father's farm, then we could be together during the holidays.'

'Well, it's somehow difficult getting paid by your own parents. We could write, I suppose, though we work such long hours that I hardly get time to write letters.'

'I know all about that, you only sent me three cards while you were learning about your dairy stuff.' Hope complained. 'It's a good thing I was so occupied with my dress fittings, or I would have come to the farm to find you myself.'

'Well, that would have been an adventure for you,' Loveday said, thinking of Hope stepping daintily through the slush and cowpats in the yard.

'I cried at least twice and Mummy nearly wrote to you herself when she saw me so upset, to tell you to come and see me. She can't bear to see me upset.'

'Nevermind. You'll have a big adventure in Switzerland, and we'll see one another in the holidays. You'll make new friends at college.'

'They won't be as good to me as you are. Nobody is as good as you.'

There began to develop an awkward silence between them, with Hope beginning to sulk because she expected an apology from Loveday for neglecting to write to her. Loveday was determined not to apologise for a perfectly legitimate reason for not writing. It was about time that Hope knew what it was to work. But the moment passed

when the bell sounded for tea, making the girls hurry
into their dresses, and they entered the drawing room
like good friends.

It was a warm summer night when Zillah woke to the
bark of a fox in a nearby field. It was such a new sound
to a town girl that it disturbed her. She went to the window and saw the field flooded in moonlight. The sea
beyond had an inviting moonlit path. She saw the fox
slink into the hedgerow, and it was gone. From Dove
Farm, a few fields away the dog, who slept outside in
the yard, was aware of the fox and began barking. This
set off a cacophony of sounds from their chickens, and
Mr Paynter shouted at the dog to be quiet. The only
thing to do, she thought, was to make a cup of tea and
sit up in bed reading one of the diaries until she was
ready to sleep. There was a yellowing newspaper cutting
and the diary opened with an intriguing entry.

4

Diary. Loveday. Age 16. 1898
'The artist Laura Knight is looking for girl models.
Please write or call at Oakhill Cottages, Lamorna
Cove.'
  I saw the advertisement in the local newspaper and,
without letting my parents know about my interest in
the advert, I took the paper upstairs and copied out the
address in my private diary. I don't see anything wrong
in wanting to have my picture painted. I don't feel in
the least proud, or conceited, I just want to do some-
thing nice. I shall write to Laura Knight. If Hope can
have her portrait painted, there's no reason why I can't
too. I wouldn't say it to anyone, but I'm much more
attractive than she is. My auburn hair is naturally curly
and long; Hope's is straight, thin and short. I'm tall and
slender; she is small and skinny. I don't mean to be
unkind, only to justify to myself that I'm worthy of a
portrait, if looks are to be considered.

Loveday could hardly conceal her excitement. She had
heard of the artist, Laura Knight, who was spoken of
mostly in uncomplimentary terms by her parents,
Annie and Henry Care, and other local families from St
Ives and Newlyn. These villages were where the artists
had chosen to live and work, alongside fishermen, min-

ers and farming folk. The indigenous population con-
demned the free and easy attitude of the artists to nudity, and the posing of local girls in provocative states of
undress. Such were the objections of parents, who tried
to keep their daughters firmly in place, observing the
proprieties expected of decent, modest girls, from the
strict Methodist dominated fishing communities.

However, Laura Knight at Lamorna did not restrict
herself by any moral or religious edict and imported
girls from London, who were likewise not inhibited in
their thinking, and would throw off their clothes and
romp on the seashore in gay abandon, showing no
modesty to a passing stranger, who might come upon
them unexpectedly. Indeed, such were their wanton
ways that they were known to laugh at the
embarrassment caused by their state of undress.

Some of the local women had complained to the
landowner, Colonel Paynter, that there was a great
immodest showing of flesh on the seashore, and girls
were undressing behind rocks, and discarding their
clothes for all to see. 'It is highly immoral and is a bad
example to the young women of the district,' their
spokeswoman said.

'We can't have that,' the Colonel stoutly cried. 'We'll
have to remedy the situation.'

Misunderstanding the complaint, or perhaps choosing to do so, he built Laura Knight a weatherproof
wooden studio on the cliffs, where she could paint on
rainy days and where the models could change and
leave their clothes.

'It's not what we meant at all,' complained the ladies.

'He's encouraging them. It's outrageous. It's objectionable. It's disgraceful. Such behaviour is appalling,' said the middle class lady, who had been chosen to put their case because of her great regard for words that would show the true indignation of their grievance.

Colonel Paynter merely shrugged off the criticism, and came by to admire the models and the artist's work. He was a great supporter of artistic endeavours and was favoured by being invited to their parties. 'Artists who are painting on my private land may do as they please,' he told his critics. He had clearly shown whose side he was on and was not to be trusted to uphold the view of the community.

The villagers were afraid their innocent girls would be lured into depravity by the rich, sophisticated lifestyle adopted by the artists, with their wild parties; where the demon drink would promote outrageous and debauched behaviour by both men and women. The name Alfred Munnings, was especially talked of with keen disapproval. Some of the fishermen from Newlyn had threatened to waylay the artist on his drunken way home from a party and throw him into the harbour, but he was a popular man and roared his way through the village surrounded by groups of equally raucous companions. But someone had to be taught a lesson. It was clearly a question of waiting for the opportunity to arise. The Cornishmen were used to waiting. They waited for the tide. They waited for the season. They waited for the fish to arrive. They waited for God to provide. They were a patient people.

Loveday had no qualms about posing for Laura

Knight. She was a tall, well-built girl of sixteen and did not doubt her appeal as an attractive model. She would put her trust in the artist Laura Knight to look after her. Her friend, Lilian, had posed for one of the students of the Stanhope Forbes School of Art, who was lodging at Minnow Cottage, the home of two of the Newlyn artists. The painting was of Lilian lying in a hammock in the cottage garden. It had drawn criticism from the girl's family, and the village folk because one strap of her dress was pulled down to reveal a bare shoulder.

The painting was shown in the Newlyn Gallery, built by the philanthropist, Passmore Edwards, for the artists to display their work locally. Both the artist and model became the object of talk in Newlyn. Many matrons had denied their daughters friendship with Lilian, who they felt had brought the village into disrepute. Lilian was sent away to Devon to stay with an aunt until the indignation of the villagers had subsided. Loveday did not want to invite the censure of her family and friends.

Now, Mr Stanhope Forbes, they believed, was an entirely different artist. A gentleman. He respected the local people and showed their true lives. His painting *Fish Sale on a Cornish Beach* had been much acclaimed at the Royal Academy in 1885, and the people of Newlyn had been celebrated as representing the Cornish nation. None of the Newlyners had seen the painting on the wall at the Royal Academy; such working people did not go to London. They had the privilege of visiting the studios of the gentlemen artists on Show Days, and saw a great number of pictures, for which so many of them had modelled, before they were sent by train to London. They were proud of themselves, and proud of Mr Forbes, who wasn't rowdy, like some of the artists, who gave more time to parties than they gave to their art, and behaved badly as the result of too much drink.

However, the artists paid the local people to model for them. They, and their students, rented their net lofts as studios in times of poor fishing. They built houses. They rented rooms in their cottages, and needed people to cook and clean for them. The local people were aware that these itinerant folk could take up their easels and paints and vacate the place, as easily as they had arrived, taking their money with them. An uneasy alliance existed between them, and a modicum of respect.

On a warm June morning Loveday was up early deciding what to wear for the meeting with Mrs Knight. She had a number of good dresses, made for her by Hope's dressmaker, but subterfuge was needed to avoid alerting her parents, to her real intentions for the day. It was because of her friendship with Hope, and mixing with her educated family, that she had gained a degree of confidence in making decisions for herself, which is why she had dared to write to the artist to say she would call on her.

Loveday left her address off the letter in case Mrs Knight replied. She hoped everything would turn out all right. If she had found a model, she would cycle back, and no one would know anything about it. Her mother turned a surprised look at her daughter when she offered to cycle to Newlyn to take some farm produce to her aunt and uncle. Usually she needed persuading to do the journey, but when she was there she enjoyed staying over for a few days, when she could be spared from work on the farm.

'I might cycle out to Lamorna while I'm there,' Loveday said.

'Mind you watch your step then, my girl. And if you should happen upon any of those artists setting up their easels, and showing off as though they owned the place, you walk right on by, and take no notice.'

'Yes mother.'

'I don't want you getting into the wrong company. They say some of those young men at the painting school can click their fingers, and the local girls will come running. Mind you run the other way, or your father'll want to know the reason why.'

'Nobody's ever clicked their fingers at me. I wouldn't take any notice. I wouldn't know what they meant anyway.'

'Well, you do now, because I'm telling you. Just keep your distance. Don't be led into talking, and don't go walking, because that's how you'll land in trouble. I heard as one of the girls down Falmouth way got persuaded to go to one of the artist's studios. He gave her a glass of wine - and she from a teetotal family – said he wanted her to pose as Mary Magdalene, and when she saw the picture it was called The Lost woman. And there she was lying on a couch, wrapped in a leopard's skin, with her feet on a lion's mane, her hair loose, and her head in a heap of jungle ferns.'

'Perhaps the artist meant lost in the jungle,' Loveday

88

said ingenuously, hoping to draw the heat out of her mother's disapproval.

Her mother dismissed her with a click of the tongue and went back to her task.

Loveday set out early to cycle into St Ives from Gorsemoor farm and took her bike on the train to Penzance. From there she cycled to Newlyn arriving at aunt Care's cottage with a good supply of farm produce. After lunch she pushed her bike up the steep hill of the Strand and came upon Mr Stanhope Forbes, standing before his large canvas and easel, paintbrush in action, stepping forward and making a dab with his brush, and stepping back to see the result. On the corner of the Fradgen a woman stood on the cobbles posing in her stiffly starched white apron and cap, bought especially for posing. Loveday knew better than to stare at the scene, not that the artist minded, but usually the sitter, or subject of the painting objected. Everyone was happy to pose for Mr Forbes; and he paid well too.

The village had adopted his wife, Mrs Elizabeth Forbes, who was also an artist. Loveday first saw Mrs Forbes when she was an infant. She had been staying in Newlyn with her aunt and attending the local school. The children were delayed going home while Mrs Forbes made quick sketches of the children in the classroom. Loveday had been the child standing on a bench taking her hat off the peg. The other children were in various stages of preparing to leave school for the day.

Some weeks later the children were invited, with their teacher to Higher Faughan, the Forbes' grand house, where a maid had served them tea in the garden. They were then taken into Elizabeth Forbes studio and shown the finished painting called *School is Out*. The children were overawed and impressed and stood shyly looking at themselves and thanking Mrs Forbes, who smiled fondly down at them. The painting was then exhibited at the Royal Academy in 1889, the same year as her husband's work *The Health of the Bride* was shown. It was an exciting time for the village of Newlyn.

Not only were the artists famous, but also their sitters, the fishermen, their wives and their children, and the village itself. Newspapers sent reporters from London to interview the artists and take photographs. People came to see the place that had created such a stir at the Royal Academy. Strangers were seen drifting around the fish market and walking along the quay, attempting to get into conversation with the locals.

Loveday's uncle Josh, with his short beard and long sideburns, had been stopped and asked if he was a model for the artists.

'Well, I'm no model. Not one of they professionals, but I am a fishermen, and no model could stand on the beach with a catch of fish and hope to look like a professional fisherman. We're all fishermen, who happen to make good models.'

'Perhaps you'd like to join me for a pint at the local inn, sir?'

'And why not young man. And my crew alongside. Come along lads.'

And uncle Josh, with a delighted chuckle, had told

how he and five others had joined the stranger in the local pub and answered such questions as they were prepared to answer, and evaded those for which they had no safe reply. It was usual to protect the integrity of the artists and their subjects. The people praised the artists –

'They are gentlemen and lady artists, Sir, and we do respect them. They paint us as we really are, fishermen, and working people.'

And the artists praised the people –

'The fishermen, and their wives, are perfect subjects, so natural and good natured. They make ideal models for our mode of painting out of doors in their natural surroundings.'

There was an unwritten law that safeguarded everyone's reputation. It was one thing to complain among themselves, but definitely out of order to make those same complaints to nosey strangers, who could destroy the close working arrangements that artists and models employed, and largely enjoyed.

As Loveday mounted her bike to set off for Lamorna, and her meeting with Laura Knight, she convinced herself that posing for Mrs Knight would be a valuable experience, and bring no shame on her parents, herself, or her village. She would be following the tradition of the families in Newlyn and St Ives since the 1880s when the artists began to arrive and discovered Newlyners ideal subjects to paint, and in St Ives there were ideal seascapes and scenery. Studios were available, and they were perfect places to live.

With this comforting thought Loveday arrived at Lamorna, noting Oakhill Cottages on her right, before the road leading down Lamorna Valley to the cove. She dismounted, pushing her bike, and composing herself after her journey. She was now prepared to meet Mrs Knight. The front door to the cottage was open, as though expecting her. Loveday suddenly took fright and thought of mounting her bike and cycling away from the temptation to pose as a model. As she hesitated, Mrs Knight appeared in the doorway. 'Ah! You must be Loveday,' she said, and then threw up her hands and, much to Loveday's surprise and alarm cried, 'My dear, a reincarnation of Lizzie Siddal. How splendid. Come on in my dear. Delightful. I couldn't be more – well - delighted.'

It was too late. It would be ridiculous to back away now, especially as the artist was so pleased with her. Loveday walked up the garden path, and couldn't help the words that spun in her head. 'Come into my par-lour, said the spider to the fly. I've the prettiest little parlour that ever you did spy.' Again, doubts confront-ed her. What if Mrs Knight asked her to take her clothes off? Would she dare to refuse? Who was Lizzie Siddal? How much risk was she taking in entering the world of these exotic free minded artists, who were afraid of nothing, and feared neither the wrath of God, nor needed the approval of man?

Watched by Mrs Knight Loveday parked her bike in the front garden under the window sill. She felt her fate was sealed, whatever the consequences. She couldn't make a fool of herself by turning and running away. It would be childish. Loveday followed the artist over the threshold and into her sitting room and soon found herself the subject of critical appraisal.

'I think you will make a good model, tall, lovely hair, just the right colour, young, strong. Could be even nicer, if you smiled and forgot to be shy. Now, I saw how shocked you were when I mentioned Elizabeth Siddal. Do you disapprove?'

Loveday shook her head.

'Do you know who she was?'

Loveday shook her head again.

'Ah, she was a lovely girl, a red-haired beauty, just like you. A favourite of the Pre-Raphaelite Brotherhood. Sat for many of them, modelled especially for Dante Gabriel Rossetti's paintings; eventually married him.'

Loveday turned away with embarrassment, not knowing anything of the model or artist, but Laura Knight carried on talking, leading her out of the room.

'I have some very nice dresses upstairs in my bedroom for you to try on. I want to paint a bright picture of a young girl, full of hope and looking to the future. That dress you're wearing is very nice, but does not quite fit my idea. We'll choose what seems to give the right mood. Does that sound acceptable to you?'

Loveday, unused to being asked her opinion, said quietly, 'I think so.'

'Well, I'm glad you think so,' said Laura Knight, treading heavily up the narrow stairs. She had stopped and turned on hearing the shy reply. She looked down severely at Loveday's upturned face.

'Don't look so worried. Nothing bad is going to happen to you. The clothes are beautiful, and you must enjoy wearing them. You must also address me as Laura. I will of course call you Loveday. Will that suit you?'

'I think so,' Loveday said.

'Let's have a little less thinking and more positive replies,' Laura said, decisively. 'I asked if that would suit you?'

'Yes, Yes,' Loveday said, and followed as Laura continued walking upstairs. They entered a bright room looking out to the lane and the fields opposite. On the bed were laid several dresses, and skirts and blouses in bright modern colours.

'We'll try the blue stripe first. I'll leave you and make some tea. When you're ready, stand on the top landing and call me.'

The artist disappeared downstairs and Loveday was left to dress herself in the blue stripe cotton dress. It fitted her tall figure very well and she admired her looks in the cheval mirror. Moving to the top of the stairs, she called timidly, 'Mrs Knight. I'm ready.'

At once, Laura Knight came from the sitting room. She was holding a cup and saucer. She stood at the foot of the stairs and looked stern. 'If you remember, I asked you to call me Laura. Is there something you object to in my name?'

Loveday stood wildly shaking her head. She did not wish to offend the artist. She did not wish to take liberties with her name. It was not polite. Neither did she wish to appear so ill at ease in the situation. She took a deep breath and tried to relax.

'Now my dear. That looks very nice indeed. Give your hair a good brushing. I've left everything ready for you on the dressing table. Try the next one.'

Laura Knight disappeared with her teacup.

Loveday tried on a white long-waisted dress with a sprinkling of rosebuds. The material felt and smelt nice. She brushed her thick red hair and prepared to dare calling the artist. She took a deep breath.

'Laura!' she called, too loudly and cringed with embarrassment. She stood on the landing waiting for approval.

Laura appeared at the bottom of the stairs carrying a plate of buns.

'Very nice Loveday, but too delicate. Try the next.' She carried off the buns.

Wearing a bright yellow dress, which set off her red hair to perfection, Loveday called Laura, this time more confidently. The artist, holding a jam covered knife, looked up the stairs and gasped in approval, 'A vision, but I think I prefer the blue and white, much bolder and more in keeping with my idea. Change back to that one and come down for tea. We'll have a little chat.'

At the tea table Laura tried to relax her terrified sitter, but was herself so impatient, that it made matters worse, so that the process took some time, while they drank their tea and ate the buns.

'You look very pretty, and I think you could make an ideal subject, but you see Loveday - that's a very pretty name too - we need to be friends if my picture is to be successful. I cannot paint a scared rabbit. I do not wish to see terror in those beautiful eyes. You are a modern girl, confident, and looking forward to a bright future. Do you understand?'

'I hope so,' Loveday said, and then corrected herself. 'Perfectly,' she said, and remembered to smile.

Loveday was pleased and flattered by the compliments. She was unused to anyone passing favourable opinions on her appearance, but she was dismayed by the criticism and felt she was failing to live up to the artist's expectations. She was, after all, brought up to be modest and self-effacing. It was difficult to become a confident adult in one afternoon. She was angry with herself. Had she learned nothing from her association with Hope?

'Let me pour you some more tea, and please tell me something about yourself, and I'll tell you a little about my husband Harold and me.'

'Well,' Loveday began tentatively, 'Father has a share with uncle Josh and cousins in the fishing boat Our Sarah. They fish out of St Ives and Newlyn. Mother has the farm at Zennor. Father mostly works on the farm. We have family in both places.'

'I was born in Derbyshire. Harold and I met at Nottingham School of Art. We are both painters, and perhaps one day we will be famous.' Laura gave a little laugh and turned the conversation once more upon her young guest.

'What work do you do, Loveday? Do you have anything to do with fishing?'

'I don't want anything to do with fishing.' Loveday said defensively. 'I want clean hands and I want to wear nice clothes.' She looked down at the dress she was wearing, as though it fulfilled her ambitions. 'But I have to work on our farm.'

'So what would you really like to do, given the choice?'

'I want to work in a shop in Penzance, and ride to work on a bike.' She sighed as though talking of some remote, impossible, dream. She looked up and smiled at Laura who, much to her surprise, commented.

'That sounds perfectly reasonable.'

'Mother says I'll need a letter of recommendation.'

'Perhaps I could help. I could have a talk to your parents sometime, but let's see how we get on with the painting first, shall we?'

Laura Knight began packing up a basket with pencils, sketch pad, paints, brushes, and rags. Finally, she took hold of a large canvas standing against the wall, and instructing Loveday to take the other end, they marched out through the door, leaving it wide open to the elements.

In the lane they turned downhill to follow the route through the wooded valley to Lamorna Cove, carrying the tautly stretched canvas between them, and being buffeted by the wind. At one point they both went sailing towards the woods, unable to counter the strength of the wind. A moment before they were toppled into the undergrowth, they managed to right themselves, and laughingly went on their way. The laughter, and the many near misses of being swept off

97

their feet, created a shared amusement, which brought them closer together.

'If you think this is dangerous, wait till we get to the cliffs,' yelled Laura, as the wind intensified.

'I know exactly what you mean,' yelled back Loveday. 'I can handle canvas on a boat, but not on land.'

Laura Knight found this amusing, and both women careered off down the lane, holding their wildly flapping canvas between them, laughing at their near mishaps. It was a long, struggling effort.

The artist, leading the way, yelled back to her battling companion. 'I thought I'd pay you every day, then we can decide if I need you the next day, or not. You can let me know too if you are available. Will that suit you?

After a moment's thought Loveday yelled into the wind. 'Yes. That will be very good.' She almost dropped the canvas at the uttering of such a bold statement, but she had learned her lesson and her reply was positive, as demanded by her employer.

At the mouth of the cove, where the wind blew strongest, they came upon a young man sitting sketching on the rocks. He looked up when he saw them approach, and seeing their difficulties, packed away his sketch pad and pencils in a rucksack, and came to their aid. 'Let me help you,' he said, and reached up and held on to the top of the stretcher. The three of them proceeded precariously along the cliff path, until Laura found the spot she had picked out for the painting. The canvas was placed behind a huge rock, where it, and everyone, was partly protected from the wind blowing off the sea.

'Well, thank you young man. We're very grateful to have you on board,' Laura said. They laughed at the reference to a ship and began introducing themselves.

'I'm Nicholas Godolphin. I'm at the Stanhope Forbes School of Art. We were given the afternoon off to find a subject for ourselves. I walked along the cliff path from Newlyn and found myself here, where I've been sketching sea creatures and stones found on the beach. I like the intimate subject, rather than something big and bold.'

Loveday was amazed by the young man's ease of conversation and realised this came about through his education, and the confidence that gave him.

'I'm Laura Knight. This is my canvas...'

'And I'm her big, bold, subject,' Loveday interrupted, and had the pleasure of hearing Laura and Nicholas laugh at her wit and temerity. She liked the feeling of being equal with these people, and remembered how Hope acted in company, confident and sure of herself, but not, Loveday remembered, sure of herself in Loveday's environment.

As suddenly as it had arisen, the wind dropped. The sun blazed out from behind clouds, and Laura was ready to begin her picture. She began methodically organising her materials, storing some of them in the wooden shed near by recently built for her by the admiring land owner.

'Do you mind if I watch?' Nicholas asked.

'Let's see if Loveday minds, shall we?'

She looked quizzically in her direction. Loveday shrugged her shoulders in dismissal of the idea. She would normally object to someone staring at her except that, for Laura's sake, she wouldn't dare object. But more than that, she wanted Nicholas to stay even if he crooked his finger at her in the manner her mother had described as dangerous.

Laura took Loveday's hand and they walked towards a rock overhanging the sea. There she planted her on a spot, tweaked her dress a bit, turned her slightly, angled her this way and that, and stood back to approve of the pose. Satisfied, she returned to the path, and propped up the huge canvas, and with Nicholas's help, arranged her brushes and paints. She began immediately, calling to Loveday to 'hold still.' Taking up a pencil she began drawing swiftly, sketching and outlining the figure.

'I'll tell you when you can have a rest. I'll work as quickly as I can. Fix your eyes on a certain point, and remember it after you've had a rest. Very important to get the tilt of the head right.'

Loveday was to remember that afternoon for the rest of her life; the sunlight sparkling on the sea below, the sound of it washing against the rock, and her almost nymph like feeling, as she stood there, tall and reaching out, feeling a vitality of strength and power, such as she had never experienced before. 'That's right,' encouraged Laura. 'Now keep that pose.' When allowed to relax, she jumped up and down on the rock to relax herself, not wanting to leave her throne in case the magic feeling wore off.

'Wonderful Loveday,' Laura said, laughing at her

antics, and pleased that she could be so relaxed, and in keeping with her idea of young womanhood.

And there was Nicholas, looking at her, admiring her Loveday thought. She'd never seen a young man with such light blonde hair, and blue eyes. He was delicately built too, and moved gracefully. She liked that difference in him, the contrast with the rough, awkward young fishermen and farmers, with their bold swagger, and taunting remarks. He was sketching her too. She felt beautiful for the first time, and blossomed under the artists' gaze.

And then another extraordinary thing happened. A man appeared along the cliff path, leading a horse. A handsome man. Another fair, blue-eyed, good looking man. A gentleman, Loveday thought. He stopped and stared hard at her. 'Relax,' Laura said. 'Have a rest.' Loveday, mesmerised by the stranger, returned his bold stare.

'Laura,' he yelled. 'My dear woman, what are you doing risking that young lady's life. She'll be blown over the cliff.'

Loveday was startled by such a remark, but both Laura and the handsome man were laughing, so she realised it was just a joke. When he came alongside he and Laura had an intimate and quiet conversation, excluding the two young people, who looked on in questioning silence.

'This is Mr Alfred Munnings,' Laura said suddenly, breaking away from the ardent look he bestowed on her, 'a poet, a painter of horses, and jockeys, and race-courses. A man to beware of young Loveday.'

Alfred Munnings again stared at the figure on the rock, then handing the reins of the horse to Laura, he stepped up to Loveday, who could step neither backwards nor forwards on her precarious perch, and took her hand. He held it to his lips and kissed it. He took her other hand and kissed that too.

'Delightful. Delightful. Laura, you have chosen the most beautiful sprite, the most charming of sirens, a fox, with a beautiful mane. You must bring her to my party. Can you dance?' He did not wait for a reply, but lifted Loveday off her feet and danced round on the narrow pinnacle of rock, humming a tune. She caught glimpses of Nicholas's scared and stricken face. There was no protest that could be made; a struggle, a sudden movement could have them both tumbling down the steep cliff into the sea.

Loveday was a victim of this man's fierce embrace. His arms held her close. His breath brushed her cheek. As he danced, the sea sparkled below her as she was twirled again and again over the edge. She relaxed into his arms, giving him complete control over their movements, in order to ensure the safety of both of them.

'Put her down, Alfred,' commanded Laura, smiling. 'I need a live model.'

He released her, and without steadying her, or saying another word or look, he and Laura walked a little way towards the cove together, leading the horse, and laughing all the time. Loveday, watching their retreating figures, noticed his limp, and wondered at the man's audacity in attempting such a dangerous action.

Loveday, sat down dizzily on the rock. Nicholas

hastened to join her.

'Are you all right?' he said, concerned, holding her arm, in case she was giddy and tumbled over the edge.

'I suppose so. I'm still here,' she said, shading her eyes and peering at the sea swirling among the rocks. 'It's a good thing uncle Josh wasn't passing in Our Sarah, or both of us would be in trouble. He would probably have brought the boat over, anchored off shore, waded through the water to the rocks, climbed up, biffed Mr Munnings on the nose, thrown me over his shoulder, and into the boat, and sailed off back to Newlyn, where I would be scorned by the local population,' Loveday said in one breath.

'It wasn't your fault,' Nicholas protested.

'I'm only joking, Nicholas. I'm making a scene of it, that's all, but it was a bit scary at the time.'

'He should be more careful with other people's lives. He's known for his mad escapades. He'll probably write one of his lengthy rhymes about it, and read it at his next wild and silly party.'

'Well, wouldn't that be exciting,' Loveday said. 'And there's Laura coming. Don't make a fuss. I don't want to mention it.' Nevertheless, there was a thrill attached to the gentleman lifting her off her feet and holding her close, and being so free with his compliments. She could understand how girls from the village would be overwhelmed by the romance of such encounters.

'Are you fit to carry on Loveday?' Laura called. 'I hope that wicked Mr Munnings hasn't upset you too much and set your head in a spin.' She grinned, and Loveday grinned back.

103

Only Nicholas seemed disgruntled by the whole affair, but he carried on with his sketching until he had rid himself of the ill feeling towards Mr Munnings, someone he usually admired for his wit and his paintings. Really, he thought to himself, he was taking too much of a proprietorial interest in this young girl, and lovely and lively as she was, he felt a great need to protect her.

Loveday, on her throne of rock, felt Nicholas's gaze as something physical. It was persistent and intense. She was conscious that she would not like this young man to disappear out of her life. She wanted him to look at her, it made her feel special, and dare she say, loved. It was an extraordinary feeling.

5

Zillah watched from the kitchen window as the rain spattered on the courtyard. It was a good day to begin decorating the first unit, and turn it into an attractive and liveable space. She intended to apply the paint on one wall to be sure about the colours she had chosen, before handing it over to the decorator. She was wearing a huge pair of white overalls, already paint spattered, that she found hanging up in the converted dairy.

Paints, brushes, rags and ladders were already installed. All she had to do was run across and get started on the decorating. She picked up the radio, opened the kitchen door, and made a dash through the rain. She turned on the radio for Woman's Hour. Jenni Murray was interviewing a woman who had written about her experiences on a farm at the turn of the century.

'All the children in the family worked. The littlest ones collected eggs and fed the chickens. The boys often dealt with the goats and pigs, because the animals were lively and needed a bit of handling. Mother and I milked the cows. We took our stools and pail out to the fields in the summer. The cows knew we were coming, and some liked to tease and move away just as we were settling. Others would even meet us halfway across the field and stand still and ready. Father would be mucking out and cleaning down the yard. It went on relentlessly, morning and evening.'

The woman could have been talking about farming in Cornwall. It must have been very like Gorsemoor, when it was a farm, where her great grandmother, Loveday, and grandma Karenza, lived and worked Somehow, she couldn't imagine her mother being here. Mary had left home at an early age and not returned. In an unusual show of intimacy with the girls, their mother had talked about her job in an office, 'I preferred city life with a nine to five lifestyle, rather than a twenty four hour grind.' What had happened to make her so disillusioned? But then she supposed it was often the desire of the young to escape the confines of their parents' lifestyle.

Painting was a good reflective activity and Zillah indulged in the thoughts about her mother, now occupying her mind. She turned off the radio. She marvelled at herself for being so incurious in her younger days. Why hadn't she talked to her mother, asked questions, learnt something of her childhood, and braved the snub that she invariably received from her.

Grandma hadn't talked of her daughter either. When Zillah spent the long summer holidays with her there was an opportunity to listen to tales of Mary as a young girl, but when she asked grandma Karenza a simple question about her mother, she would often say, 'Ask no questions and I'll tell you no lies.' And that's how it was between them. Why hadn't she been more insistent? Why this secrecy, this unwillingness of her mother and grandma to talk to, or about, one another?

There was the instance when a man had called at the cottage one summer evening. Zillah, aged ten, had been having her tea. Grandma always set a pretty cloth at one end of the huge table, with everything Zillah would need, jam, butter, milk and sugar, and her own special small teapot, with cup, saucer and tea plate decorated with roses, a biscuit tin and a glass cake dish standing on short stubby legs. It was very special and grandma would sit in her armchair by the stove, ready to top up the teapot with boiling water. It was a cosy time and the interruption was unwelcome.

Through the half-open door Zillah could see a man in a grey suit. He took off his trilby. 'Good evening Mrs Pender,' he said, and told her his name, which Zillah didn't hear. 'I'm so glad to see you're still here. I heard the farm had been sold, I thought perhaps you had moved.'

'No. As you see,' said grandma with a short and snappy reply. 'We had to sell most of the animals and the fields – no money to pay wages, and keep things going.'

Zillah expected the door to be opened wider, and the man to step inside, but instead, grandma held the door and leaned against the jamb, so that Zillah had difficulty in trying to see his face. Then grandma almost pushed the man outside and closed the door behind her. Zillah slid off her chair and peeped out of the window, but they were nowhere to be seen. She knew instinctively that this was something secret, something grown-ups kept from children, so she hurried back to her chair and sat waiting for grandma to return. She was surprised at the look on her face, of embarrassment and triumph, when she came in. She locked the door after her and came to the table. She held a bundle of notes in her hand, which she counted out on the table.

'Never be too proud to take what's owing to you little one,' she said. 'This pirate's treasure will go into the bank, and one day it'll be yours. For myself, I wouldn't touch it. But I'd no reason to refuse. Now don't mention it to anyone at home.'

Zillah was used to such statements. She carefully shielded Cornwall and London from each other; her two secret societies. When she got home even Amy and Ruth only got cautiously filtered information about picnics down at the cove, flying kites on Zennor Head, swimming from St Ives safe beaches, and shopping in Penzance.

Who was that mysterious man who had appeared at grandma's door, and to whom she had reacted so strangely, and hostily? And was her inherited money the very same that grandmother had promised her as treasure, and carefully counted. And if so, how had this come about?

These recreated memories and disturbing thoughts meant that she had almost finished the painting task she had set herself, without even noticing. Perhaps she would call on Beatrice, whose parents had known grandma Karenza. Maybe they would have some answers. She quickly tidied away, leaving her overalls hanging on a peg behind the door, firmly pushed home the lids of the paint tins, steeped the brushes in a can of cold water and made for the shower.

Her hair was still wet as she hurried across the field

and made for Beatrice's studio. She was surprised to find her not alone because very few people came to her studio. She was introduced to Ethan Doyle, a young Irish painter, whose present mode of painting was to create a black canvas. He made no acknowledgement of Zillah, until Beatrice repeated, rather forcefully, 'This is my friend, Zillah Brook. I'd be pleased if you would say hello. She is the one person I allow in my studio. I especially don't invite other painters, and if you had wanted to see me, you could have phoned, rather than turn up on the doorstep.'

Zillah was surprised at the chilly tone Beatrice used towards the young man and prepared for a conciliatory smile that she would aim in his direction to alleviate his pain, which she was sure he must feel, coming from a usually happy, kind and sympathetic Beatrice.

Ethan turned his head in Zillah's direction, gave a brief, cool, dismissive nod, and then back to Beatrice. Zillah realised at once that he had no interest in making her acquaintance and needed no sympathy from her. He continued talking to Beatrice.

She was unnecessary in this two-way conversation.

'I've this painting I want you to see. It's troubling me. You could come over right now. I don't mind your friend coming. It's only a couple of miles across the field,' Ethan said. 'You could be back here in no time.'

Beatrice, unable to hide her impatience, replied, 'I am busy with my own work at the moment. I have an exhibition, and must have enough work to hang. I can't spare the time. My need to work on my paintings is greater than your need to have me glance at one of your works, which I know intimately, and cannot understand anyway.'

'There's nobody interested in what anyone else is doing. Everyone's totally self-centred. You're just like the rest of them. I thought you, at least, would have some fellow feeling.'

'But you haven't heard what I said. I am busy. Have you even taken a glance at my work? No. And if there's one person who is totally self-interested, it's you. I have seen your work. I am not prepared to make a judgement on it, but may I ask what colour it is Ethan?'

'Black.'

'Then it's the same as all your other work. Quite honestly, I'm tired of your bloody black pictures, and I don't want to see any more, however many shades of black you paint them.'

Ethan glowered fearsomely at Beatrice, totally ignored Zillah, and executed a swift, surly exit. They watched him striding across the fields swearing to himself and throwing his hands into the air in a fury. Beatrice sighed with relief.

'That man is a disaster. He refuses to exhibit – not that anyone would show his stuff – and is under the illusion that when he dies, the art world is suddenly going to discover his genius. Honestly, to have such an ego, yet at the same time he is so dependent upon someone's opinion, mostly mine. I don't give him any encouragement at all, whether it's about his work, or his passion for me. Why won't he back off?'

'Oh dear,' was all Zillah could say. 'He's not dangerous, is he?'

'Well, I don't know. He could be I suppose. He's so egotistical. He also thinks everyone is ganging up against him. He could be right there. We're all fed up with him.' Beatrice gave a short laugh.

'I think you should be wary of him. You did give him a bit of a bashing, and he does appear to have problems,' Zillah warned.

'Trouble is, I'm one of his problems. I know his type. Wants me to solve his life's difficulties and make him feel better, and do you know what, you get blamed if you can't. Well I am not his mother, nor his mentor, and he can go somewhere else for comfort, and a bit of ego polishing,' Beatrice said. She smothered her annoyance and turned a welcoming smile on Zillah.

'Oh goodness, let's get rid of his doom laden spirit.' She turned on the radio and began dancing to the tune of Good Vibrations by the Beach Boys. 'Very apt,' she said. 'Come on Zillah, dance.' And the two girls danced, and opened the studio door to let out the gloom, and replace it with the gaiety, which they were creating between them.

'Now, what can I do for you?' Beatrice asked, coming to a standstill.

'I'd rather like to ask your parents what more they can tell me about my grandma, and under what circumstances she sold the fields and animals to your family. And is there anything more to learn about my mother, who seldom, if ever, talked of her childhood on the farm. Were there friends and neighbours who visited?'

'From what I know, friends and neighbours met at church, or chapel, or during farming and harvesting.

Public holidays. That sort of thing. They were so caught up in the daily grind that they didn't visit each other socially, except if anyone was in trouble. But I understand that everyone helped out when there was a crisis, because animals had to be fed, and milked, and harvests had to be gathered. But what about the diaries you got from the bank, haven't they provided some useful background information? Have you finished reading them?'

'Good Lord! I'd forgotten about the diaries. I'm sorry Beatrice. I'm going straight home to dig them out.' Zillah smacked herself on the side of the head and went off muttering about her ineptitude.

Beatrice laughed. 'I'll call round on you later to see what secrets you've uncovered.'

'Lunch is at one!' Zillah called back. 'I'll expect you.'

Back at the cottage, Zillah ran upstairs, reached under the bed and picked up a diary labelled, Loveday. She sat on the bed to read.

Diary. Loveday. Age 16. 1898
I had a wonderful day at Lamorna Cove. Laura Knight worked for hours. I was standing on my rock for ages and had to keep my head in one position, and remain still, but I could feel my skirt blowing against my legs in the warm breeze, and my hair lifting. I think the wind kept me awake. The sun sparkled on the water and threw bright diamonds into my eyes. I could hardly see for the brightness. It was lovely meeting Nicholas Godolphin, who made lots of sketches of me and stayed with us all day. We were exhausted by the time Laura

said she'd finished, late afternoon, but we cheered up when we ate soup and bread in Laura's kitchen. Aunt and uncle, in Newlyn, had been worried about me being so late back. I'm expected at Lamorna tomorrow for more posing. I'll have to start out really early because Laura wants to finish the drawings and get started on the painting. Nicholas said he would join us again too. I'm not sure how I'll feel if Mr Alfred Munnings turns up again!

Loveday, Laura Knight and Nicholas Godolphin walked down Lamorna valley carrying the huge canvas, dozens of pencils, tubes of paint to dab on for colour, brushes, and all Laura's paraphernalia for another day's sketching. The canvas could have been stored in her little hut on the cliffs, but she needed to study her work closely in her cottage studio.

'I shall be able to finish off in my studio tomorrow and begin painting,' Laura said, 'so I shall pay you for two days modelling Loveday. Let me have your address so I may write to you, in case I need you again. Will that be all right?'

'Thank you Laura. Yes, that will be fine.'

Loveday decided that when she got home to Gorsemoor Farm she would tell her parents that she had cycled down to Lamorna and had posed for Laura Knight who, she would tell them, would be a famous artist one day. It was done now, and they couldn't raise any objections. Besides which, she had met Nicholas and tomorrow she had invited him to cycle back with her to Zennor and see the farm. She wondered whether he was more interested in the farm than her. He seemed to have abandoned his studies at the Stanhope Forbes School of Painting, though he had made several sketches of Loveday as she stood posing on her cliff top for Laura, which both women had praised and approved. Nicholas had given them to her as a gift.

Uncle was already out fishing when Loveday appeared for breakfast next morning. Aunt had her coat on and was on her way to market, with her basket over her arm and her black straw hat, pinned to her head with a huge hatpin of a large round pearl ball.

'Uncle's wrapped some fish for your mother in a bit of his old oilskin apron. Keep it in there till you're ready to cook it. It'll keep nice and fresh.'

'Yes, thank you aunt,'

'And there's a boy out there with a bike. Been here this half hour. Says he's riding to Zennor with you.'

'Oh goodness. I hope he hasn't gone!' Loveday got up to rush to the door.

'Don't worry. He looks as though he'd wait there forever. Nice boy; not one of the folk from Newlyn. I know everyone of the boys from fishing.'

'No. He's come to study painting.'

'Well, you gotta be rich to study painting. Rich is he?'

'I don't know aunt.'

'Can't be working then. Where'd you meet a chap like that?'

'He's a student of Stanhope Forbes, aunt. He was sketching at Lamorna.' Loveday dived into her bag and brought out several lightning sketches done by

Nicholas, to stave off further questions. She hoped her aunt would think a whole group of students from the school were there. Aunt was a great admirer of Mr Forbes, having posed several times for him on the beach with white apron and big black boots, surrounded by fish. She was one of his favourite models, 'Mr Forbes said I was a natural,' she said proudly, 'but I told him, there's no skill in holding a basket of fish. I've been doing it all my life.' Loveday had heard this tale several times, but she smiled fondly at her aunt's pleasure in the artist's praise.

'Must be in the family, then aunt, we natural artists' models,' Loveday said.

'Well, don't get too proud, my girl. You're not a London model, thank goodness, and not likely to be. You're not in the way of taking all your clothes off. Wouldn't do for a young woman from around these parts.'

'Of course not,' Loveday said, hearing the warning in her aunt's voice.

'Now don't keep the young man waiting, and I gotta be going meself. Don't leave it too long before you come again. And give my love to your mother.'

Loveday swallowed down the last of her bread and butter, and cup of tea, and kissed her aunt's cheek.

Outside, Nicholas was pleased to see her emerge from the cottage door.

'Let's walk a little way, and we can talk. Tell me about the farm. What animals do you have, and what food do you grow?'

Loveday was irritated by his questions about the

115

farm, and district, and how people lived in Zennor. She would rather he asked questions about her, or be told where he lived, and about his family.

When they arrived at Penzance Nicholas decided they should stop at a teashop in Market Jew Street for a cup of tea and a buttered bun. This was a bold thing to do for a Zennor lass, but Nicholas seemed to regard it as perfectly ordinary to have tea with a young lady. They left their bikes against the railings and went upstairs to a café overlooking the High Street, where the horses and carts were milling around outside. It was a busy scene and interesting to watch from the window.

'That's the statue of Humphrey Davy. He made the miner's safety lamp. He was a great engineer. He saved many lives with that lamp,' Loveday said, 'Before that the miners only had tallow candles, and they had to buy them out of their wages, and all their tools.'

'I'd like to work down a mine and be involved in doing some real work.'

Loveday laughed to scorn his idea. 'It's like going to hell,' she told him.

'I think working as a fisherman, or farmer, or a miner, is doing a man's job. I know I'm not built for such hard work, but I would become stronger, and I would love to be part of a group of men who relied on each other, shared their happiness, and their sorrows. It must be like being in a family.'

'But Nicholas, you must continue your education and your painting. You don't know how lucky you are. There are too many sorrows in those jobs you seem to admire. I can't understand anyone wanting such a life.'

Loveday learned that Nicholas lived in Brighton. His mother had died at his birth. His father was a shareholder on the railways, and on a management committee for extending branch lines into the countryside. Nicholas was able to travel anywhere in the country, which is why he had travelled so far for his painting lessons. His father had suggested he study painting, after he had left college because he seemed to have no direction.

Nicholas had been to the Royal Academy Summer Exhibitions and seen the work of the Newlyn artists, which featured the working lives of the villagers, and which sparked his interest in visiting Newlyn and St Ives. He hadn't yet been to St Ives. He wanted to see the work of the seascape painters and was especially pleased when he learned they would be travelling through the town to get to Zennor.

'You can find somewhere in St Ives to stay tonight, and cycle out to Zennor tomorrow morning,' Loveday suggested.

It was late afternoon when they eventually arrived at St Ives station, along the picturesque branch line, which Nicholas fell in love with. 'I remember I wanted to be a train driver,' he said, 'but my father wouldn't hear of it. He couldn't approve of his son starting as a greaser and cleaner, then a fireman, and years before one could become a train driver. He said he would have to disown me because the Board of Directors wouldn't sanction such a division of class.'

'Well I suppose you can't blame him,' Loveday said, having much more understanding about how class worked.

Nicholas delighted in the journey on the St Ives branch line. He marvelled at the great stretches of white sand along Porthkidney beach, creamed at the waters edge by a softly lapping ocean. He admired the lighthouse and the humped backed stones that were revealed at low tide. 'Many a ship foundered on those rocks before the lighthouse was built,' Loveday informed him. 'One was a ship, carrying the King's wardrobe and precious objects.'

Nicholas was enthralled with St Ives and its busy harbour of fishing boats, but he insisted on accompanying Loveday all the way home to Zennor, in spite of her protests that she was used to riding alone, and in the dark, and he would have difficulty returning, not knowing the road.

Loveday was anxious about introducing Nicholas to her parents, especially to her mother, who had warned her about artists crooking their little fingers and enticing young girls to pose for them. But somehow Nicholas's own easy manner and way of introducing himself, and explaining his association with Stanhope Forbes, helped smooth the situation. Usually, introductions were much more formal.

'Well, thank you Mr Godolphin for bringing our daughter safely home.'

'It was a real pleasure, Sir, and I am delighted to meet you, Mr and Mrs Care,' Nicholas said, with enthusiasm. 'I am hoping to stay in St Ives tonight, but may I call on you tomorrow. Loveday has promised to show me the farm, and countryside hereabouts, with your permission.'

Loveday was amazed at his cheek. Nicholas had already endeared himself to her mother and father. His polite manners and obvious good breeding pleased her parents. They were happy to accommodate him in the barn for the night, promising he would be warm and dry with blankets and pillows that they could provide. Nicholas was more than pleased with his makeshift bed. From the window, Loveday watched her father, Henry, show the young man to his quarters. They were chatting quite amiably.

Next morning at seven o'clock, Loveday woke Nicholas and brought a tousled, still sleepy lad into the kitchen.

'Go and wash,' commanded Annie Care, 'then sit yourself down to breakfast.'

Nicholas ate his breakfast with relish, savouring the new laid eggs, the home cured bacon, and the rough homely bread.

'I've never tasted anything so delicious,' he declared, 'and I've never had such a wonderful night's sleep. Everything is so fresh and marvellous here. You are so lucky to live and work on a farm. I can't wait to try some more of that lovely morning air.'

Loveday's parents were more enchanted with the boy, than she herself. They laughed with pleasure at his delight in everything. And he seemed more enthralled with his surroundings than with her, she thought resentfully.

They were given the task of driving the herd to the fields after milking, then were free to range over the farm, Loveday taking him to her favourite spots for blackberrying, or the best place under the trees for picnics, and showing him the field by the cliff's edge where the daffodils were picked whilst still in bud and were sent by train to London's Covent Garden. He was surprised to learn that the fields had names. Lastly they took the slippery slope down the cliff path to the tiny cove. The tide was out and the sand clean washed. They held hands like two young children, and paddled happily in the clear, cool, water, relishing the tingling cold of the sea on their feet.

'This is paradise,' declared Nicholas. 'I love this place. I love you Loveday.'

Loveday looked at him with some alarm.

'No. Don't be angry with me,' he pleaded. 'I know this is my destiny.'

She was too amazed even to reply to this fantastic statement. In a dreamlike state the two of them walked back to the farm in time for lunch.

Nicholas spent lunchtime asking her parents about the animals, crops, seasons and the working of the farm. They appreciated his interest and Loveday was surprised at how jealous she felt of the attention he was claiming from them. He was very impressed when her mother told him about the dairy course they had initiated for her and other local girls. Nicholas spent the afternoon trailing around after her father, questioning, and eagerly helping out where he could. In fact the two men were so occupied that they had to be called when dinner was ready and waiting on the table.

Nicholas stayed a few more days and nights learning the routine of farm life, rising early to begin work, and impressing her parents with his good manners and enthusiastic attention to the smallest detail of farming practice. In the evening Loveday and Nicholas walked to the many coves below the fields, exploring the area, and getting to know each other. Nicholas felt especially privileged when Henry Care introduced him to other farmers and friends in the Tinners' Arms, the local inn.

Annie Care eventually became concerned and made Nicholas walk to Zennor village Post Office to telegraph his father and ask if he could stay and work throughout the busy harvest time at Gorsemoor farm.

'Wouldn't you rather be studying your painting, Nicholas? Laura Knight said you had talent. And what about the painters you want to meet in St Ives? Wouldn't you like to visit some of the studios? Perhaps you could study seascape painting. There's lots of studios on Porthmeor beach, plenty of artists. I'm sure some of them would welcome a good student. Shall I come to St Ives with you?' Loveday asked.

'No,' he said. 'I'm happy being here, on the farm, with you and your parents. I never had a family life. I was sent to a boarding school from a very early age because my mother had died. It was lonely. You don't know how lucky you are to have people you love, and somewhere you belong.'

'Poor Nicholas,' she said, giving him a hug and understanding his interest in the farm and his keenness to learn everything; to please her family and earn their good opinion. How shallow she was to be jealous of such well-meaning intentions. She kissed his cheek by way of an unspoken apology.

Over several weeks of working in the fields, Nicholas had become stronger, and more robust. His skin was pleasantly tanned. Suitable clothes for manual labour had replaced his smart city attire. He had acquired a working rhythm, labouring alongside Henry Care's family and neighbours, who gathered the harvest on the local farms. Nicholas could not have been happier, exchanging his canvas and paints for field and pitchfork. He loved the farm animals and he enjoyed every aspect of working on the farm, not minding rough, hard labour, because it was countered by good weather and sunshine, the freedom of the countryside and the sea.

Meanwhile the development of a serious relationship between Loveday and Nicholas was very obvious. Mr and Mrs Care gave every encouragement to the young couple. By this time Nicholas had moved into the farmhouse and showed no intention of ever leaving the farm again, or going home.

But Loveday couldn't entirely believe that someone with Nicholas's education and privileged background could be satisfied with her rough way of life. His father was a gentleman with money to invest and a house in the city. His friends and neighbours were people of wealth. How could he leave such comforts for the hard, dirty life in a farming community? She must question Nicholas again.

'Aren't you homesick Nicholas?' Loveday wanted to know.

'I've got you, and I've got my work on the farm. If I left you, and Cornwall, I should be homesick. This is where I want to be.'

'Are you sure Nicholas? But what about your painting lessons with Mr Forbes, and the good times you had with the students and artists at the painting school. Don't you miss that?'

'I can draw and paint any time.'

'Except you don't have time Nicholas, now that you've tied yourself to this way of life. I worry that you'll suddenly realise it's not what you really want. People like you don't forget their education and become farm workers. You've got such a funny idea about working with your hands, about doing a proper job. You weren't born into this kind of life and I find it very difficult to believe that you could be happy here.'

'I'm completely happy, Loveday. I think this is the happiest time of my life. I think I'm so lucky to have met you. And you love me, as I love you. What could be better? How could I have anything to compare with you, your parents, and this wonderful farm?'

Loveday looked long and hard at this beautiful young man, who had fallen in love with her, and she with him, while she stood upon a rock looking out to sea. It was the sort of romance that didn't happen in her world. It was wonderful. She was satisfied by his expression that he really had chosen this life, and her. She smiled at him and he positively glowed in smiling back so she was completely happy, contented, and convinced he knew his mind.

At Trewey Farm on a fine day in August, the traditional ceremony of Crying the Neck and thanking a deity for the good harvest, was a yearly celebration, with jugs of beer and cider to celebrate in the fields.

Loveday saw the delight on Nicholas's face as he was included in the company who had worked to gather the harvest. The farmer prepared to capture the corn spirit. He held aloft the traditional scythe to show the company that he was about to perform his task and mow the last strands of corn from the centre of the field. He worked rhythmically and slowly, savouring the moment. When the sheaf was cut and tied he held it above his head and cried, 'A neck! A neck! A neck! We have a neck!' The young men and girls threw their hats and caps into the air and cheered. Cornish prayers were offered to the divine being who had ensured a good crop and the harvesters shared a picnic meal in the field with pasties, saffron buns and heavy cake.

Life at the farm continued at a steady, relentless pace. The local harvests had been gathered in record time and in perfect weather. A harvest tea and entertainment was provided by invitation from Mrs Westlake and friends on the flat grassed area in Eagle's Nest garden. Loveday and Nicholas walked along Church Path from farm to farm over stone stiles and cattle grids and up by Tregerthen Farm to the big house on the hill, where the thermometer in the glasshouse read over 90 degrees. It was indeed a glorious summer.

Zillah was fascinated to read about her great grandfather, Nicholas Godolphin, and looked closely at the sketch he had drawn of himself and presented to Loveday. His features were fine and delicate, Loveday, her great, grandmother, was like herself, tall, red haired and robust. Grandma Karenza followed the same pattern, and Annie, her great, great grandmother, if she could judge from a black and white photograph, appeared to have the same stature and colouring.

Zillah's mother, Mary, was smaller and dark haired. Her other two daughters Amy and Ruth were in her image and acceptable to her. Zillah, according to her mother was 'the odd one,' 'the copper knob,' 'the Zennor witch.'

Surprisingly, in spite of the many derogatory remarks about her appearance, Zillah was proud of her inherited red bronzed, luscious hair, and the close resemblance to the Cornish women in her family. She treasured her father's name for her, 'flaming beauty.'

6

One evening, when the mist seemed settled over the countryside and each house was isolated and withdrawn into itself, Zillah drew the blinds in the kitchen, settled herself at the table with grandma Karenza's lamp and, more importantly, her diary; she wanted to know more of the woman who was the most important element in her life, who had never really talked of herself as a young woman, or revealed her thoughts and feelings, or explained what it was like to live in Zennor as a child.

Diary. Karenza. Age 15. 1917
Today I leave school. Mother is sending me to college to learn about agriculture. I already know about farming and looking after the animals. We've got a dairy herd and make butter and cheese and Cornish clotted cream. We have several pigs, chickens, grow potatoes and cauliflowers, and even have a field of daffodils out on the cliffs. Dad thinks he's taught me all there is to know. He's quite offended that I'm going to college, but mother insists, and so off I must go. I have this small legacy that my grandmother left for my education. Grandmother Annie, believed in education and equality for women. She supported the women's movement, and believed in votes for women. I can't let her down.

My friends are getting married, not going to college.

Karenza, and her mother Loveday, drove Soldier and the trap over the moors to Penzance, taking with them several wicker baskets, some containing butter, others eggs, to sell at market. The previous day they had been to St Ives to deliver a regular order of butter, eggs and cheese to the grocers in Tregenna Place. Soldier enjoyed prancing along, showing off his trot, stopping to munch grass along the way, while his mistress had a chat at the gates of neighbouring farms. If neither the farmer, nor his wife were around, Soldier would always stop for a snack, often offered by someone waving Loveday down and requesting she take an order for goods to a merchant in town. It was part of the ritual of the journey.

When they reached Zennor, Loveday turned right and halted outside the Tinner's Arms. Very soon several women arrived with baskets of produce for sale, or a note to buy goods; some had baked bread, others had picked early mushrooms. The women cooperated in taking it in turn to sell their neighbours' goods. There was a ready market in Penzance for produce from the villages. Everyone helped load the cart with the baskets, which they all hoped would return empty.

The women knew Karenza was about to go to college. Many of them didn't approve of women leaving their village, and getting a bit above themselves. Although they had no experience themselves, the women seemed to know what was required for a farmer's child about to leave home, and offered their advice and wished her luck.

'Don't expect to buy clothes for best. You'll have no time for dancing or going to parties.'

'Good sensible shoes, some warm jumpers and long skirts, are what you'll need.'

'You'll be lonely among strangers and want to come home, but you'll soon make friends.'

'It's not a ladies college. It's for folk from working farm families, like ours,' Loveday advised her daughter.

'I know mum. I've read the pros... pros...'

'Prospectus. Better practice saying that word when you're on the train. Learn it before you get there or they'll think you're too ignorant for their college. It'll be hard work.'

'No more than I'm used to.'

'We let you off light my girl; you'll see a difference when they get you up at five for milking. And you'll have exams. At least you didn't have to write everything down at home. It was all practical. Your dad's a good teacher. Won't get much better than him, even with those college people.'

'Anything I don't know I'll ask you. You're the one who taught him everything he knows about farming.'

'You'll ask your father. Remember, he manages the farm now.'

Loveday had married Ned Berryman a year after the death of Karenza's father.

Karenza sighed, enduring her mother's unceasing advice, all the way over the moors, through Newmill, and into Market Jew Street. 'Take note of your education, it'll outlast people you meet, and places you visit, and everything you do.' She always had a good many lectures from her mother, who wanted her to make the best use of her life.

'You can't be sure of anything, Karenza,' her mother warned her. 'Your real father, Nicholas Godolphin, and I were sure we had a wonderful life ahead of us, but it went horribly wrong. It would have been better for him to have made use of his education, instead of trying to fit in with life in Cornwall.'

'But you told me he loved you, and he loved Cornwall,' Karenza reminded her mother. 'And he didn't want anything else.'

'Well, Nicholas was mistaken. You see, he had an unrealistic view of what it was like to be a working man. He was very sadly disillusioned.'

After shopping, Loveday and Karenza would go to a café and have lunch. It was a town that gathered folk from the villages around and invariably you met up and exchanged news with any number of people. It was an event to travel to Penzance and take butter and cheese, and chickens to market once a week. This trip was even more special. It was a shopping outing for Karenza. Her stepfather, Ned, had given her extra money in case she saw anything she fancied, which wasn't on the shopping list of clothes for the college.

'I don't know how you could leave your mother and father, and the farm. You'll miss the sea,' a friend had told her.

'I'm quite looking forward to seeing a bit of the world over the Tamar Bridge. I haven't even been to Plymouth.'

'Truro is the furthest I've been and that's enough for me. And who are you going to meet in a school for women? You could use your grandmother's money for a trousseau. You'll end up an old maid, and that's not for me. Soon as I can I shall be looking out for my man.'

'Well, I hope you find him.' Karenza said, tartly.

Altogether, it had not been a pleasant experience to part from the friends she had grown up with. Girls she had walked to school with over the fields when it rained, and clothes were dried on the round stove in the middle of the Zennor schoolroom. And when the sun beat down, they would find a cove and swim in their knickers, and picnic on bread and jam, or home-made pasties.

It had rained heavily late afternoon and on their drive home from town Soldier was urged to perform his smartest gallop. He was the third Gorsemoor horse called Soldier. He was a large horse for the small vehicle and the cart rocked and threw its passengers about round the curves of the road, until they feared it would tip over, so they endured the rain and a slower pace. Over the fields they could see the merchant ship still anchored in the lee of the shore. It had been sheltering from the south westerly gales for a few days.

'Could be a good harvest there,' Loveday remarked to her daughter. 'Carrying wood, so the postmistress said. And the sea's no calmer now, and the wind's getting up to a good blow. We'll see what tomorrow brings.'

At supper, Ned, told them with some excitement, that the boat in the bay had dragged her anchor and was listing dangerously. Some of the cargo had slipped into the sea. It was already washing up in the coves along the coastline. The crew had been taken off by breeches buoy when the weather worsened, and were being cared for at the Seamen's Mission at St Ives. The captain had been made aware that last month a steamer had gone down one mile off shore with a crew of 25 all drowned.

'They're keeping a watch on the cliffs, taking it in shifts,' Ned, said. 'The boys from Trevail will let us know what's happening. Down at the Tinner's Arms they reckon she'll not last the night. Karenza, see the lamps are filled and ready. We could be called out. I need that timber and we'll have to get to the cove before the tide turns and takes it to St Ives and on to the stones, to be smashed to matchwood around Godrevy light.'

Karenza did what was needed, leaving three lamps on the stone flags by the kitchen door and sorting through the mound of clothes hanging there, ready for a quick departure. She fell asleep to the murmur of her parents' voices from the kitchen, and the increasing howl of the wind rattling at the window.

From the depths of sleep Karenza awoke when the sound of the wind changed to a hammering on the great wooden door and men's voices shouting. 'She's going!' and then retreating footsteps clattered over the cobbles. It took no time at all for Ned, Loveday and Karenza to dress in their oldest clothes and light the lamps from the Cornish range. As the outer door was opened, the wind rushed into the kitchen and almost blew them back inside.

Ned pulled the door shut, heaving until the heavy latch held it in place. Ahead, they could see the swinging lamps of their fellow wreckers, making for the cliffs and further afield there were others intent on salvaging what they could from an act of God that put opportunities in their way.

Loveday had made them cloaks with hoods from heavy sacking but the fierce wind would have blown them out like sails if Ned had not tied rope around their middles. They plodded along the field paths, their lanterns barely lighting the way, and always in danger of the flame being blown out. Over towards the sea and the west, the sky was pitch black, but behind them the eastern sky was brightening, and dawn and daylight would bring the customs men to guard the boat and its cargo.

The path to the cove was running with water and Ned and Loveday slithered down on their haunches. At the top of the cliff Karenza was left to guide her parents up the path and to safeguard the gradually growing pile of wood. She crouched down to prevent the wind from blowing her over, and below, on the beach she could see several figures with lanterns scurrying around, picking up planks of timber.

Loveday and Ned made several trips carrying the long lengths of wood between them, always hampered by needing their lamps to guide their footsteps. After an hour's hard struggle, her parents had carried what they could and sank down exhausted on their bounty. The light from the east was growing and people were gradually fading away. Ned returned to the farm and tethered

Soldier to a low sledge-like carrier, which he pulled with ease equally through the meadows as over the rough terrain of rocks, gorse and wild wind-blown heath.

The timber was unloaded at the farm and hoisted up by pulley to lie over the rafters in the barn. It made a floor and a room, where none had been before, and apart from the timber being wet and looking new, there could always have been a floor there.

'I'll paint some bitumen on that when it dries. It'll look as if it's been there forever,' Ned laughed.

They were glad to get out of their heavy wet sacking and soaked through clothes. Loveday opened up the door of the range and they relished the warmth. Karenza was sent up to bed to steal another hour's sleep before leaving home and catch the train from Penzance for her great adventure at college. Loveday and Ned made tea and sat around the fire until their five o'clock hour of rising.

Because of the excitement of the night, and her anticipation of the morning, Karenza couldn't sleep. She lay curled up on her feather mattress, glad of the warmth, and thinking of grandmother, Annie, who had squirreled away a little nest egg so that she should have the opportunity of going to college. The money had been tied up in a trust fund, and even though her mother and grandmother sorely needed the money at a crucial time on the farm, it wasn't available to them.

Karenza looked around her room. She wanted to memorise its contents and bring them to mind whenever she felt homesick. On the fireplace opposite her bed were several watercolour sketches of her mother standing on the edge of a cliff, looking as if the whole world was available to her. They were painted by Nicholas Godolphin, the father who died tragically. The father she never saw.

Karenza sighed for the loss of a talented and educated father. There was a briefly sketched self-portrait drawing of him under the lamp on her bedside table. And a drawing of herself as a baby, signed Laura Knight. There was also a photo portrait of Loveday, with her mother Annie. A woman photographer had called at the farm for a drink of water, while struggling along the coastpath with her heavy equipment, taking pictures of nesting gulls on the cliff top.

The women had talked of the meeting of the Women's Social and Political Union on the slipway to the harbour at St Ives the previous day, when a delegation from Bristol had arrived to stir some interest in the movement. Annie had invited the woman to have tea and discuss the poor response to the hesitant speakers, shouting their messages over the heckling of local fishermen, and the hostility of the fishermen's wives. The photographs were taken in recompense for Annie and Loveday's hospitality.

Karenza sat up in bed savouring the delights of the morning sun shining on a patch of wood floor, where her cat lay stretched out. In the yard was the bustle of morning. She could hear the cattle moving clumsily about in the cobbled yard, jockeying for position for milking. Her father occasionally called to one of his 'ladies' as he named them. 'Come on Betsy. Move along now Jessie. Don't you step on my toes Blossom.' She could hear the slap of his hand on their rumps, and the jangle of metal buckets.

From the kitchen below came the smell of frying bacon and toast. Her mother would be making tea, and when father had finished milking, and turned the cows out into the field, the three of them would sit down to breakfast. Karenza was always excused the early morning starts, her parents believing that she needed her sleep in order to keep awake in school and concentrate on her lessons. Several children fell asleep in class because they were woken early to fetch the cows in for milking. A sharp rap on the head from the teacher soon had them paying attention. She had many friends who were out on the fields in the morning mist, shrouded in sacking, driving the herd to the milking sheds, shivering and trying to hurry the slow moving beasts.

At the end of her bed was Karenza's cardboard suitcase, ready packed for her big adventure. Although she was sad and rather afraid of what lay unknown before her, she was comforted by the new clothes which she hoped would give her confidence. She opened up the suitcase and put inside the framed portrait of her father, Nicholas Godolphin, at the same time feeling disloyal to the man who had loved her and been a real father to her, Ned Berryman. And tucked away, she had a little pot of face cream bought by her mother, to show the other girls that she was quite grown up, although only fifteen.

'Karenza!' her mother called. 'Time to get up.'

'Come on lazy bones,' dad yelled up the stairs.

This morning dad was driving her into Penzance to

catch the train. He was taking pigs to market and the trailer would be pulled along behind, wafting smells around them. She would complain, as always, and dad would laugh and put on a northern accent, and say, 'Where there's muck, there's brass.'

'But dad, I don't want to arrive at college smelling of pigs.'

'Why not? They'll know you're the genuine article, and not one of these genteel ladies who don't know what the inside of a pigsty, or a cowshed smells like.'

'Well, you didn't know what a farmyard smelt like until you married mum, and came to live on her farm. I think you should have been a painter, like my dad, Nicholas Godolphin.' She savoured the name, enjoying the sound, shaping her lips to give quality to the name. 'You could have been famous by now. Dad knew painters like Laura Knight and Stanhope Forbes.'

'Karenza, I was never even a student. I was a model for Alfred Munnings, and looked after his horses. He was a master at painting horses. It was never my idea to be an artist. I can't replace your real father in that way, but I've tried my hardest to live up to your idea of him. When I met you and your mother, I promised I would look after you. She taught me everything I know. The farm is my life, with my Loveday, and you Karenza.'

'But dad, you could still learn to paint.'

'No Karenza. Don't try and turn me into your father. I'm sure Nicholas Godolphin was a fine man but I don't want to paint. I'm too busy and happy as I am. You've got your father's sketches of your mother, and you never know, they could be quite valuable one day. I see the train is waiting for you.'

Leaving her father at Penzance station was hard, but when the train began to pull away, she felt a lift of excitement. He did not stand and wave, but hurried her into a seat and walked briskly out of the station to attend to his business in town. Karenza looked out of the window, filling her eyes with the bright, glinting sea, and a last look at St Michael's Mount standing out in the bay. It would be months before she saw it again.

Zillah thought about the young girl going off to college and leaving her home and Cornwall for the first time. How different were their lives. She could travel anywhere in the world, and Karenza's big adventure was to cross the Tamar Bridge. It was in the smaller room next door that the young girl would have slept and looked down that last morning watching her stepfather in the yard.

Zillah reached for Karenza's diary and turned over the pages, hoping to read of her experiences at college. Some of the writing was smudged, perhaps by the tears of Karenza, finding herself in a strange place. Zillah wondered whether she should be keeping a diary, if only to carry on the tradition by the two previous generations, but hers she thought, would be writing about her life as a failure. A failed relationship with her mother; a not particularly sparkling career, when all the world was open to her generation; a failed marriage.

Altogether, a rather failed person.

There seemed to be everything to strive for, everything to achieve, in the life of her grandmother. Every little step was a way forward towards a better life for women. The journey was beginning and it was an exciting time. Conversely, there was a legitimate excuse in those early days for not striving for a goal. The time wasn't right. No matter how much you beat against the barriers, they were not to be broken. Victories were hardly gains, except to alert the nation to think about the inequalities suffered by half the population. The next generation would take up the challenge, and creep forward into the world of men a little further. It was a life of hope and small triumphs.

Diary. Karenza. Age 15. 1917
This house used to be a monastery. When I arrived last night it was quite dark, and this morning when I looked out of my window there was no sea at the end of the fields. I'm sitting at a long table, with benches at both sides. There's no one else here. I haven't seen any of the other girls yet and there's supposed to be ten of us. Mum said to be sure to get up early and make a good impression, but there's no one here to impress.

Hastily, Karenza slipped her diary into her big pinafore dress pocket. She could hear voices, and the clattering of shoes on the stone floor in the corridor outside, and then there appeared a line of girls holding their breakfast trays and making for the refectory table. She stood up, feeling foolish, and remembered she was to report to the kitchen at seven o'clock. She hurried down the corridor and found the kitchen. When she returned with her tray there was one space left at the end of the bench. She slipped into it and began eating the porridge from an enamel bowl. Beside it was a slice of bread and butter and a mug of tea. The porridge was gruel-like but milky.

At half-past-seven a woman appeared at the doorway, looking intently at the girls. Their chatter gradually reduced to silence as each of them became aware of her presence. Then the woman approached the end of the table.

'Good morning girls.' She stood there and raised her eyebrows until the response came in stumbling disorder from the girls. 'I'm Miss Palmer. I shall no doubt learn your names, as you will learn each others, but for the moment, my name is the important one to remember. I am the housekeeper, and your mother in loco parentis, in other words, you are in my care.'

Miss Palmer walked around the table looking at the dishes of porridge, noting who had left food in the dish, and when finding it, she leant forward and looked enquiringly at the girl, but said nothing. It was a slow walk and made the girls nervous. They couldn't quite decide whether she was critical of them, or critical of the food. Karenza picked up her spoon and finished the last of the porridge, taking care not to scrape the bowl and call attention to herself. The bowl being empty when Miss Palmer stood behind her, she did not receive the benefit of a questioning look.

'I shall try to see that your meals are as appetising as

possible, but you must know that ten people cannot share the same taste. Some of you will be pleased some times, and some of you at other times. The food will be good and wholesome and I advise you to cultivate a good appetite. Please take your trays back and afterwards assemble in the yard outside the kitchen. I will see you at lunch time. Good morning.'

She was gone and marching off down the echoing corridor before the bewildered girls could offer a reply. They gathered up their trays and walked into the kitchen. There they observed a large enamel bowl for scraping food into, another for cutlery. They piled dish upon dish, plate upon plate, and mugs in rows. Out in the corridor they found a door leading to the yard and stood around whispering, learning names, generally assessing each other and wondering what would happen next.

Chickens ran about the yard, picking, clucking, chasing, and expecting food from the assembled girls. They all thought to save bread from breakfast tomorrow morning.

Karenza turned at a touch on her arm.

'I heard you arrive last night,' said the girl. 'I'm Betty. I've got the room next door. I hardly slept. I think I've got the haunted room. They should have got rid of those old monks before allowing ladies into their cells. My candle kept blowing out before I could get undressed, and every time I closed my eyes I imagined a hooded figure in a brown cloak creeping towards me. It was scary.'

Karenza looked into a pair of pale blue eyes. The fair

skin showed dark shadows underneath, as evidence of the girl's lack of sleep.

'I slept very well. I'm sorry about your scary night, but I did notice a draft under those big wooden doors, which was probably the reason your candle blew out. I didn't hear a thing all night, but this morning I got totally lost in those corridors.'

The girls chatted back and forth, exchanging their various experiences They were silenced by the appearance of a very tall woman, who emerged from across the courtyard carrying several baskets on each arm.

'Well,' she said, smiling and surveying the group. 'You're a fine looking lot. Now before we do anything, we're going egg hunting. Take a basket each, look in the sheds, the egg boxes, of course. Follow the hens around and find their hiding places. Look in the hedges, and anywhere you feel a hen would like to lay an egg. I take it none of you are afraid to search under a warm feathered body for an egg?'

Most of the girls laughed quietly, and shook their heads.

'Only, own up if you've never been near a chicken before, because we had one young lady terrified of the creatures. She had to be sent home. I don't know what her parents are going to do with all those chickens she said they were going to buy for their new farm.' She waited while the girls laughed again. 'Now I hope to get you through the poultry course, or my name's not Molly Mason.'

The girls scattered to search for eggs, while Molly directed and advised. They took their baskets into one of the large sheds, placing them on a bench and, as instructed, wiped the eggs on straw and filled up ceramic pottery bowls with the delicate objects. Not one egg was broken.

The rest of the morning was spent sitting in a schoolroom, listening to Molly Mason, who was only a little above their own age, talking about poultry, drawing on a blackboard showing various diagrams of the different varieties of chicken and answering questions. Karenza learnt that most of the girls, like herself, were from farming backgrounds and already well-informed so that the introduction to this part of the course was easy.

They were released half-an-hour before dinner to make their beds and tidy their rooms. Betty and Karenza decided to make the beds together, which they thought would save time, and make a quicker job of pulling up the blankets and tucking in the sides. The sheets were of thick, coarse cream linen, the pillow cases of the same material. The black iron framed bedstead was without decorative features and the mattress was wafer thin, and hard. There were two grey blankets, and no top cover. Their suitcases were stored under the beds.

The rooms were identical narrow cells with a bedside cabinet and a washstand holding a bowl and jug. There were hooks on the wall to hang clothes. These monk cells in the annex adjoining the manor house were ideal for the purpose of housing young women on a short vocational course. The girls did not find the rooms unpleasant and were glad they were not housed in dormitories.

'I could fit this room four times into my bedroom at home,' Betty said.

From her locker, Betty took out a jar. 'Hand cream,' she said, handing Karenza the jar. 'Mother makes it from honey and lavender and other stuff. She said it'll save my hands from getting cracked. It's quite thick, you have to spread it over.'

'I'll let you have some of my face cream,' Karenza offered. 'I bought it from a shop.' The thrill of buying a specially made beauty product from a shop was not lost on most of the girls, who came to smell and admire the cream and its porcelain pot.

They spent some time sitting on the end of the bed rubbing in the hand cream and delicately sparingly applying dabs of face cream, which they were sure enhanced their appearance although they had no mirror to confirm the results.

Facing the bed was a huge oak door and pinned to the inside was a notice for the students. They read it together to learn the rota.

Women Students.
Students will be called at 6 am for breakfast.
Work and study begins at 6.30 am
Dinner at 12 noon.
Work and study begins at 1.15pm
Tea at 4.30pm
Work and study begins at 5.15pm
Supper at 7.30pm
Lights out at 10pm

'I thought we were lucky having breakfast at seven this morning. It seems this is our one easy day. After dinner Miss Palmer is giving us a talk, and then we're to meet the dairy maid,' Karenza reminded Betty. She wanted to ensure that both of them turned up at the right time in the right place and not repeat her mistake of this morning.

There was a knock at the door and a dark haired girl with long pigtails peered round.

'Hello. What luxury,' she said, 'There's a bath. I'm Sarah. Mind if I have a bath this evening at nine o'clock? We have to sort out a routine between ourselves. There's a notice board on the bathroom door where we have to write our name and fill in the time.'

'From the size of that bath, I think it would probably take four of us at a time; it's huge, sitting there on a platform, with its great lion feet,' Karenza said. The girls laughed, and then joined the other girls in the corridor which led into the main house. They ran down the broad wooden staircase as the sound of the bell summoned them for dinner, already feeling more at home in the new environment.

The girls were now familiar enough to smile at each other and claim their seats at table, thus Karenza sat on the end, the only space that was available when she turned up late the first morning for breakfast; fortunately it was next to Sarah. Sitting opposite was Betty.

'Yummy,' Sarah said, helping herself and Karenza to a dish of potatoes and passing a plate, on which she had piled mince and vegetables. 'God helps those who help themselves – if you'll pardon the expression. You'd only get the leftovers from that seat. I'll see we're not neglected.' Sarah immediately concentrated on eating.

The dishes passed back and forth along the table and Sarah was ready to bring the dishes of rhubarb pudding to the table from the sideboard before others had finished the main course. She poured a liberal amount of custard for the two of them, and was the first to sit up and sigh with satisfaction. Thereafter she could be relied upon to serve them both. Karenza repaid the service by making sure her bed was properly tucked in and cornered before Miss Palmer did her inspection of the rooms. Sarah had very little idea about making beds. 'Mother always looked after everything like that, and now I've even got to wash my own clothes.'

'Monday morning's washday,' Karenza informed her. 'The big boiler will be lit and we have to strip the beds and take the sheets down to the washroom. Fortunately, there's someone to look after the washing and hang the sheets to dry, but we have to collect clean linen and make our own beds, but don't worry, Betty and I will help you. You'll soon get used to it.'

Sarah wailed in protest but was heartened by her new friends' offer of help.

'Everyone,' their house mother told the girls, 'must write a postcard home to say you have arrived here safely, before Miss Sutton takes you to the dairy. These have been provided.' She passed cards and pencils along the table. 'But before then I want you to introduce yourselves. We are quite informal at this college, and forenames will be acceptable to begin with; starting on my left.'

Betty, Josephine, Barbara, May, and so on round the table. Karenza was the last to say her name. 'You now have five minutes to write your cards. You will leave them on the table and I will see they are posted.' Miss Palmer walked around the table peering over shoulders, saying, 'Five minutes girls.'

Miss Sutton duly arrived to collect her charges. She was a large woman and stood imposingly in the doorway, waiting for Miss Palmer to dismiss them. Miss Sutton beckoned them and led them on a long walk down the corridor, out to another cobbled yard and into a large building whitewashed inside and out. They entered a cool room, lined with thick slate shelves built up on bricks, on which stood wide shallow pans with a handle each side. The pans were filled with a thick creamy substance from the milk and this was ready to be made into butter.

'This is my domain,' Miss Sutton began, and looked around with pride. 'Here everything is clean and spotless. You enter with dirty hands at your peril. You put on the coats and aprons provided, and you leave them here when you go. Hair will be tied back and caps worn at all times. Is that clear?'

'Yes, Miss Sutton,' they mumbled.

'I said, is that clear?'

'Yes, Miss Sutton,' they chorused.

They put on their white stiffly starched coats and large aprons, tucked their hair into caps, and sniggered at each other's appearance. They scrubbed their hands and nails.

'Hands must be properly rinsed of soap. We do not want carbolic tasting butter. Is that clear girls?'

'Yes, Miss Sutton,' they replied loudly.

'Before any of you use the butter churn, you will make the butter by mixing it in a bowl with your hand. This is hard work but will allow you to see when the butter turns.'

At one end of the dairy two women were rolling and pressing the butter through a muslin cloth and the buttermilk ran down a channel and through a hole into buckets to be fed to the pigs. On another slab salt was sprinkled onto a flat sheet of butter and rolled to distribute it. Two other women were shaping butter with large wooden pats. Another was wrapping pieces of butter in greaseproof paper. These had motifs of a cow pressed into the middle, a large sun was pressed onto the salted variety.

In the corner were huge metal churns in which the milk arrived from the cowshed to the dairy. Some of these were being scoured and cleaned in the yard outside. In the final section were lidded wicker baskets in which the butter was packed ready to be taken to market. It was a noisy, busy place, with the sound of metal buckets on stone floors, the swish of milk in the churns, and the pat patting of the wooden mallets shaping the finished product. The girls were fascinated by the processes.

They each took a turn at winding the handle on a butter churn to feel the weight and substance of the milk inside from its liquid form to when it began to coagulate, and where water was poured onto the solid mass of butter to clean it and wash away the last of the buttermilk. This first day was one of observing the whole process of the dairy, except at the end when the girls were given pats of butter to try their skills at shaping it into patterns to take to the dining table, where they spread it onto buns for their tea. Afterwards Miss Palmer, the housemother, addressed them briefly.

'You've had a busy day girls and I don't want you chatting after lights out. You will have an even busier day tomorrow and will need your sleep. You will be called at six o'clock to go to the milking sheds and watch the cows being milked. Fortunately, you will not be required to bring the cattle from the fields. I shall come round tonight to see that you are all in bed. Now, any questions?'

None of the girls had the temerity to ask a question. It was a time to receive instruction and be initiated into their routine. A time to observe and learn before embarking on their hands-on experience. The newcomers watched the skilled girls working so proficiently in their different activities. They were required to take on one of the new pupils and teach them, under supervision, for the last fortnight of their course. Then they would gain their certificates and be sent out into the world to practice their skills and be paid for their labours. Miss Palmer had not yet finished with the new arrivals.

'Before dinner there will be the basic lessons in reading and writing and in weighing and measuring, as required for the jobs you will do in dairy making. Now, are there any questions?'

Again, no one made a murmur, and Miss Palmer left, satisfied that she had made everything clear and was perfectly understood.

7

Diary. Karenza age 16. 1918
I met Jack Pender down on the quay at St Ives this evening. He was unloading the day's catch. He and his uncle were on the boat loading up the baskets with fish, and Jack was standing at the edge of the quay pulling the baskets up with a rope. His father owns the fishing boat Barnabas. It's the big old wooden one, clinker built. He's been fishing out of St Ives for a couple of years now. He went to the Island Road school, and I went to the school in the village at Zennor. But I remember him when the Sunday schools paraded round the harbour and we picnicked on the Island, or at Man's Head, where the elders could set up the tables. He was smaller than me and quite an ordinary little lad. I remember his curly hair. It was his hair that first attracted me to him. When I saw him today he had grown tall and sturdy, and his hair was still the best thing about him. All the girls wished they had curly hair like Jack Pender.

'Hi Karenza.'
'Hi yourself, Jack Pender.'
'Didn't think I'd noticed you, did you?'
'Can't say I thought about it.'
'Saw you coming along the wharf, wearing that

white dress and the blue hat with a ribbon. Looked as if you might be looking for someone. Was it me?'

'You think too much of yourself.'

'Yeah, but it weren't no one else you was looking for. Must have seen the Barnabas coming alongside from your aunty's window.'

'I did just happen to glance out.'

'When I've had me tea, do you fancy a walk round the Island, along Porthmeor beach, or down to Clodgy? Could sit and watch the sunset from there. You could tell me what you've been doing all day.'

'Well, I might. I'm staying in St Ives tonight. Call for me at aunty's cottage, and bring a couple of fish. I'll exchange for a dozen new laid eggs I brought from the farm today. Then I'll see if I'll go for a walk with you.'

'All right then, Miss High and Mighty, but we're off early again tomorrow. Be away for a few days, so better catch me while you can. Mind you, if we put a candle on the end of the pier and it stays alight, there's not enough wind for a sail, and if it blows out, it's too windy to go to sea. So who knows, you could have my company for a whole day.'

'In that case you'll have to come out to Gorsemoor Farm, because I'm going home tomorrow.'

'I'd like to do that sometime anyway,' Jack said, and because he dropped his teasing manner, he flushed slightly. Karenza, as she turned away replied, 'We'll see.'

Behind her she heard Jack's father and uncle teasing and shouting at him for slowing things up.

'Pasties are for tonight's tea, not tomorrow's breakfast,' his father yelled.

'See that – the red sun's setting full in his face,' laughed his uncle.

Jack Pender had worked on Gorsemoor farm in every season of the year, but mostly when fishing was slow. Karenza had taken a shy interest in watching him pulling potatoes and turnips, or using the pitchfork to pile up the hay on the cart. He had helped her father in the pig killing and mucked out the barns.

'That one's a useful chap to have around Karenza. Mind you, with those handsome looks he might be a bit flighty. Many's the lass'll throw her cap at him, so don't you be too eager my girl. I know you're keen …'

Karenza cut off Loveday's comments with a toss of her head and slammed out of the door. She hated to think her interest in Jack had been observed, especially by her parents. But she was spending more time now in St Ives, waiting for him on the quay. She hurried through her tasks on the farm, getting up early to feed the chickens and collect the eggs. The butter making was made in a whirl of activity, and sometimes left half way through the process when the milk wouldn't coagulate, so that her mother had to finish the job. Nobody complained. This was all in the natural activity of selecting a suitable partner and her parents were well pleased with her choice.

Jack would make a very useful additional hand on the farm in Zennor if he married Karenza. But would he give up his share on the fishing boat and take completely to farming, or would he prefer fishing and take Karenza to live in St Ives? This would mean they would lose the expertise she had learned at college, and the

151

experience she had gained working with her parents on the farm since she was a child.

There was always this ambivalence of competition and cooperation between fishing and farming, and even mining took its toll on the other two occupations, especially when the mine captains tried to persuade the young ones to desert their occupations and 'earn a fortune' in a new mining venture. Some of these mines started on land and then tunnelled out to sea. There were deep shafts with man engines taking the workers to the bottom of the pits, which were dangerous and often not well maintained. There was always water in the tunnels, and the sea could be heard pounding and threatening the men in their enclosures.

In the Sloop Inn, where locals gathered, the fishermen and farmers looked ruddy of complexion and lively. The full time tin miners, whose cottages lined the road leading out of town, were pale and thin. They were stooped, shoulders hunched. Their grey faces and hands were often ingrained with dirt. They seemed naturally morose and would sometimes clash with the more hearty men of the open sea and fields.

It was a fine evening when Jack and Karenza set out to walk to Clodgy along the cliff path from St Ives. They walked a little apart until they reached Man's Head, and then Jack declared he wasn't going to play follow-my-leader along the narrow coast path, and he put his arm firmly around Karenza's waist, and moved her arm to encircle his waist, and they trod the path together. It was the most intimate they had ever been and both enjoyed their closeness. It was sometimes difficult to maintain their balance without toppling over into the ditch, but Jack's strong arm kept them upright, and they laughed at their sometimes precarious footsteps.

They stopped often to look out to sea. There were still little boats coming into harbour from a day's fishing. The quay would be busy with the sound of men's voices as they unloaded the fish, which would be piled up on the granite stones, until sorted into boxes and driven away to market.

'You still smell of fish, Jack,' Karenza said gently, so as not to offend him.

'It's the perfume of my trade,' Jack said, neither embarrassed, nor defensive. 'No matter how many times you wash yourself and your clothes, there's no denying I'm a fisherman. If I worked on a farm I'd smell of shit.'

'Jack! I don't smell, surely?'

Jack turned her to face him and began sniffing at her hair, neck and face, and finally placed a small kiss on her lips. It was the first time they had kissed. Jack looked at her, and knew from her eyes, that he could kiss her again, and he did. They stood a long time hugging, enjoying the touch of bodies, and shaking slightly at the effect it seemed to have on them.

Back along the path, they could see another couple coming their way, and they moved on. They knew this was the beginning of their serious relationship. It was too good to try it with someone else. They must explore each other. There was a lot to discover. And they couldn't wait to begin.

When they reached the grassy cliff top, they sat against a rock looking out to sea at the sunset and over the five bays of the coastline. The south westerly wind was quiet, the sea calm. It was a tranquil scene, but neither Karenza, nor Jack, seemed particularly aware of their surroundings, so intent were they exploring the delights of one another's lips, which progressed to touching. There was so much to learn, but Karenza, although allowing Jack's kisses, kept her blouse firmly in place, and her skirt tightly over her knees. Karenza's hands crept under Jack's shirt, over his chest and back, feeling the muscles developed from his days of hard labour. But that was the extent of this first lovemaking.

The sun had set when they began walking back along the cliff path. Jack led the way, she holding his hand stretched out behind him. Every few yards he would turn and they would kiss. They would have liked to lie on the soft turf and abandon themselves to the magic of kissing, but this was not the way. There were rules. She was not to be compromised. She had a reputation to uphold. Jack had to prove his worth; value her more than just an experience that he could talk and boast about to his mates on the quay. They had to establish a serious relationship; one that was leading to an engagement, and marriage. She had heard how girls had been destroyed by talk of 'going too far' in the early days of courtship. Allowing a man too much too soon, and then he abandoned her and moved on to someone else. It was unfair on a girl who considered herself in love.

There were few lights this side of town, but out to

sea there was Godrevy lighthouse, and Trevose light further along the coast. There were the twinkling lights of boats coming home late, not wanting to come to port without a good catch. At the door of the middle cottage on the harbour beach, Jack reluctantly said goodnight, lingering over the final kiss, until Karenza had to push him away.

'Auntie Millie will wonder what we're doing out so late.'

'She knows I'll take care of you.'

'Will you Jack. Take care of me?'

'I reckon so Karenza. I'm not planning to let you go, now we've got to … well, you know. I can't wait to see you again. I shall be dreaming about you tonight, and thinking about you all day tomorrow. I don't want to sound daft, but that's the truth of it.'

'I'm going back to Zennor tomorrow.'

'I'll come over in the evening to say hello to your mum and dad, and we'll maybe take a stroll down to the cove.'

Karenza was pleased with the way the evening turned out. She hadn't realised quite how serious Jack was about her, he was always so teasing in his manner. She was certainly interested in him, and now they were a pair. Girlfriend and boyfriend.

Zillah was startled by the knocking on the door, and leapt off the bed. She had been engrossed in reading Karenza's diary. 'It was about how grandma met grandpa,' she told Beatrice, when they were sitting down to lunch. 'It was so slow and careful. No jumping into bed. A girl had to mind her reputation. Imagine any girl today being thought a loose woman if she went to bed with a fella on her first date. Then it would have been a shameful thing to do. I think most men and women were probably virgins when they got married.'

'Poor things. They probably only had one relationship, and when it got to heavy petting, they had to get married. It must have driven them crazy not being able to satisfy their sexual urges. I think I would have been a loose woman if I'd lived in those times,' laughed Beatrice.

She confessed to being unable to keep a relationship going. She usually got tired when a boy friend began deciding how she should live her life, and told him she preferred being single, living at home, and making her own decisions.

'As soon as you allow him into your bed, he thinks he owns you.'

'But didn't you fall in love with any of them?'

'Love. Hmmm. I'm not sure. I suppose if I could let them go so easily, I couldn't have loved them.'

'I let my dear Carl go easily enough. I do still love him and miss him terribly but I suppose he's rapidly falling out of love with me. But that's the trouble; when your ideas don't coincide, you tend to fall apart. And we're married too. Now he's in Bristol and I'm down at the very toe-nail of England.'

'I can see you're going to get all sentimental, and we can't have that. Don't give up writing. Keep in touch, and see what happens.'

Zillah sighed. She was finding things hard again and was grateful for having Beatrice as a friend. Her cheerful disposition and honest matter-of-fact nature, helped Zillah through some trying times, and questioning why she should stay in Cornwall.

'Come to dinner tonight,' Beatrice insisted. 'Mum has invited you. You'll love her apple and pear tart. I've asked dad to tell you anything he can remember from those early times on the farm.'

Arthur Paynter had found an old photo album belonging to his mother. In it were scenes of farming folk picnicking in the fields at Dove Farm at haymaking time; of driving cattle to the milking sheds; leading the big farm horses as they pulled a plough, and an intriguing photograph of Arthur's parents sitting at their big kitchen table with their farm workers, eating dinner with the family. Arthur, as a young boy was among them. A vacant chair was next to him.

'It was seeing this photograph that reminded me of an incident at that Harvest supper. Your mother, Mary, who a minute before was sitting in that chair next to me, slipped under the table when she saw the camera, and stayed there for the rest of the evening,' he explained. 'Your grandpa Jack tried to persuade her back to the table, but there was no moving Mary.'

'Where was grandma Karenza?' Zillah wanted to know.

'There she is, with her back to the camera. There was a photographer staying at the Tinners Arms, and he wanted to take pictures of working life in the countryside. I remember your grandmother was cross with her daughter for refusing to be photographed, but there you are, that was Mary. Once she decided on a course of action, nothing would dissuade her from it. I remember her screaming from under the table, 'I'm not a farm animal.'

It reminded Zillah that her mother would never have her photograph taken. This was a further insight into her mother's odd behaviour; to the others it was just one of those sudden childish wishes not to conform. Everyone dismissed the tale, and after an enjoyable evening of reminiscences of life at the farm when Arthur was a boy, and Sylvia's excellent cooking, Zillah made her way home through the damp, dewey grass of the field that separated the two farmhouses. The sun was setting in a golden ball, behind the horizon line of the sea, falling off the edge of the world. No wonder people thought the earth was flat. It was far easier to believe. As she opened the door, the telephone was ringing. 'Carl,' she thought, eager to speak to him, but it was Ruth.

'You'll never guess,' Ruth said, 'but dad's coming to see you. I'm not quite sure when, but he'll be coming by train from Paddington. Will you be able to meet him?'

'Of course!' Zillah yelled. 'Oh that's the best news I've had this week. Of course I can meet him. Whatever made him change his mind? I thought he would never come to Cornwall.'

'He said he's missed you. Apparently, Amy, baby and I are no substitute.'

'Makes a change. Mum could never part with you two girls, but I could always be spared and sent off to stay with grandma.'

'Now Zillah. Don't fret about that. How lucky you are to have grandma's cottage. We would have loved to come to Cornwall but mum wouldn't let us. We thought it was always you having this special privilege. We had to stay at home. We were so envious of you going off to the farm.'

'Grandma never complained, but I think she never gave up hoping you would come. But you and Amy must come. It's looking very pretty, and ... and mum would have loved it. I'm sorry she didn't see it. I'm still sorry it didn't happen.' But Zillah was lying to herself, Ruth and Amy knew it too. She gave a little sob, said goodnight to her sister, but nevertheless, went to bed happy that she would see her father very soon.

The next day was bright and sunny. It was proving a very good summer. Zillah began to feel that things were working out. There was one missing ingredient, and that was Carl. She yearned for him. She determined to write and ask his opinion about matters. Tell him she would love to have him with her. Ask him to come and stay for a few days. In this she failed. She aborted every letter. She felt he may still be in the quiet rage that had made him leave and pursue his own path. But what was happening in his life?

It was at a book launch in Exeter when Carl and Zillah had first met. Zillah had worked on an author's first novel and become friends with her during the long course of editing the book. The whole charabanc of the publishing house had been invited to stay at the novelist's farmhouse in Devon. Publicity had alerted local radio, and Carl turned up to take photos and interview the writer for the local paper. During the party afterwards, to which Carl was also invited, they danced and got to know one another.

They were a couple from that moment. Both had waited a long time to meet the right person. Their commitment was slow and sure. This had to be right, so they had taken the old fashioned route of getting to know one another by courting. A good night kiss was just that. An evening out didn't lead to bed, and flowers meant, 'I love you.' They even wrote letters. When they did commit, it was with the certainly that they had chosen to be with that person.

Carl applied for a photographer's job in London. Zillah had already left home and was working in London and living in a three-roomed furnished flat in West Hampstead, with a drunken woman for a landlady, and lots of other itinerant tenants. Carl came every weekend to stay from his bedsit in Kilburn, creeping into the house when they hoped the landlady was sufficiently drunk to be fast asleep. Sometimes they were sure she lay in wait for them. Zillah would quietly turn the key in the front door and Carl would dash silently through the hall, stepping over the loose ceramic tiles, and without turning a light on, try to avoid stumbling over the cat lurking on the stairs. Zillah then closed and opened the door again, making a noise. She walked loudly on the tiled floor and the landlady's door would open.

'Is that you Miss Ward?' she would call querulously. 'Are you on your own?'

'Yes, it's only me from over the sea, all alone, alone oh,' Zillah would sing-song from half way up the stairs. The landlady's head would peer round the door, as Zillah's leg disappeared round the bend in the stair.

'Only I don't allow guests in the house after nine o'clock!' she called.

'I should hope not, indeed,' Zillah called back.

Together, Zillah and the landlady shouted out, 'This is a respectable house.'

By this time Carl would be safely inside the room, and several doors of other tenants would be opening cautiously, wondering what all the shouting was about.

'Goodnight ladies, goodnight!' Zillah would call in passing, and the doors would be hastily shut. Once again they had breached the defences of the enemy downstairs, and the collaborating spies on the landing. Behind the bolted door, Zillah and Carl laughed with the bravado and cheek of the young. Fortunately, the landlady was unable to climb the stairs, so having safely escaped detection at the front door, they were safe.

They had an uncomfortable but happy time at weekends in a single bed. They began by facing one another and clinging tightly to prevent Carl on the outside from falling out. When they slept they lay folded together, both turning the same way. They had to do it in unison, but this became automatic after a while, though it led to many wakeful moments as they carefully manoeuvred the operation. After a few months they decided to get married. The flat they found in Highgate was affordable, with a joint mortgage. It was a great step up from Carl's bedsit and Zillah's equally insalubrious dwelling. Now they could really start living.

It was a strange irony that Zillah's West Hampstead flatlet, which they found so uncomfortable at the time, should later provide them with many years of amusement. At the time they felt deprived and under privileged living in an unheated house, sharing one bathroom with crazy tenants who strode around the place naked, or drunk; the cat with fleas, the smell of Guiness, the stuffed crocodile in the basement and the danger of being given notice by the landlady for Carl's suspected weekend stays.

'Do you talk to yourself, Miss Ward?'

'All the time. Doesn't everybody?'

'Perhaps. Well, at least more than they laugh. I have heard you laugh, all by yourself, upstairs. Was there somebody with you Miss Ward?'

'Absolutely nobody. Nobody, but me and my radio. ' Zillah said, then seeing the landlady's face light up at the possibility of increasing the rent for extra use of electricity, she very quickly added, 'My battery operated radio.'

It was a time that marked their climb to more successful living, of acquiring savings in order to buy a property. It was a time of growing up and enduring all sorts of privations that the young had to suffer to emerge as adults. In fact, it was fun. But only in retrospect. It belonged to the 'do you remember?' era, and was accompanied by laughter.

'Remember when you and I were invited to tea and

the landlady got out her best china?' Carl said.

'Which hadn't been washed or dusted for years. There was a grey scum on the top, and we had to drink it. Ugh!'

'And she only invited us because she wanted me to go down to the cellar and bring up an old army trunk.'

'There's something in there that belonged to my husband,' the landlady told them, when they had struggled up the narrow cellar steps, carrying the large trunk between them.

'Now if you'll just open it for me and perhaps drape it over the settee in the window. I don't sit there so it's the perfect place to show it.'

Zillah was expecting an Indian rug. The husband had served as an army officer in India. Carl opened the lid and Zillah stepped back in fright. A great tiger's head, with open mouth and huge teeth stared at her from glassy eyes.

'My husband loved animals,' the landlady offered by explanation at Zillah's startled response.

Zillah snorted indignantly, holding back her question, 'Then why did he kill it?' for the sake of peace. Any disagreement on any point was liable to incur, 'Take a week's notice, Miss Ward.' She couldn't count the number of times she had been asked to leave, but when the end of the week came around the landlady had forgotten and was waiting for her rent.

Those days gave Zillah and Carl a proper perspective on life and helped them appreciate having their own flat and being in control of their lives and their living.

Full of the memories of their early courtship Zillah

was at once filled with nostalgia, regrets, and a little sadness.

There were times since moving to Zennor that she had felt so engrossed in the diaries of Loveday and Karenza, that she almost felt she had lived their lives. Certainly, Gorsemoor Cottage contained the embodiment of their feelings, emotions, and the trauma of their experiences. Perhaps that's why her mother had rejected her child-hood home because of the strong personalities that resided with her in the cottage. Though probably, she was giving her mother too much sensitivity, which she didn't think she displayed, except maybe in her strong reactions to Zillah. Her mother would discard anything which encroached on her own life, whereas Zillah wanted to be embraced and enfolded with them.

She was especially close to grandma Karenza because of the years of care and love that Zillah had enjoyed with her. Great grandmother Loveday was becoming a real person too through the diaries and events of her life with Nicholas, and her second husband Ned, and learning about their lives in times past. Her great, great grandmother, Annie, was emerging as a strong personality

Diary. Loveday. Age 18. 1900.
Nicholas is so happy working with mother and father on the farm. It has been a wonderful summer and we are all looking golden brown with so much sun.

Nicholas says it is the best year of his life, and yet it is so simple compared to college and art school and his educated background. Sometimes I envy his previous life, which he dismisses with a wave of the hand. I'm sure if I'd had a proper education I wouldn't waste my time working on a farm. But, then again, as mother points out, there's not much work available for women, whatever education they might receive.

Summer was drifting into autumn for several quiet, uneventful weeks, then suddenly, the fine weather ended in a violent storm, for which everyone was unprepared. The local fishing boats could be seen ploughing their way to the harbour through troughs and great eddying swirls, which threatened to engulf them and sink the little craft. Larger vessels were running for shelter in the bay. Daylight was taken over by huge rolling black clouds, which almost touched the land in their density, and then broke and deluged the entire region.

The great noise of the thunder and flashes of forked lightening caused a stampede among the cattle in the fields. Henry Care, out on his own with the herd, was in an agony of helplessness. He tried moving the herd to the milking sheds and yard, but the sudden onslaught of weather caught him unawares and the cattle were beyond sense and took flight. Fences were mown down by the surge of so many heavy bodies. Some cows, in complete terror, galloped wildly over the cliffs to their deaths. Henry returned to the farm, where Annie, Loveday and Nicholas were sitting cosily in the kitchen, waiting for him to join them, unaware of the drama happening outside where the storm raged, and prevented Henry from driving the cattle to the yard.

'Get your coat Annie,' Henry said, bursting through the door. 'I couldn't get the cows to the shed. They've panicked, and we're likely to lose the lot. I've never seen a storm like it. God help those at sea. Come on. Come on.'

Nicholas jumped up and had his coat on before Annie could remove her apron.

'Those cows can be real jittery and dangerous, Nicholas. Better let me handle them,' Annie advised. But Nicholas was closing the door behind him, deaf to her pleas and running after Henry into the thunder and lightning. Heavy hailstones, as big as mothballs, bombarded the men and scattered the cattle even more.

It took time for Henry and Nicholas to locate some of the terrified animals. They managed to drive several cattle away from the cliff top areas and into smaller stone hedged fields, but in spite of their frantic efforts many cattle were lost over the cliffs. Their carcases were already being washed out to sea by a fast running tide. Most of their herd, and those from other farms, were found wildly floundering along the narrow road to St Ives. When they came upon a group, they cautiously guided them into neighbouring fields, being aware of the power, weight and strength of the frightened animals in their panic driven actions.

It was nearly morning when the accident happened. Both men were exhausted by their night's work, wet to the skin and bewildered by this unexpected wild weather. They found it difficult to stay on their feet as the wind tore the breath from their mouths and lashed their bodies. The storm continued to rage; the cattle were still stampeding. They came upon six cows, milling about and quite out of control. Henry herded them off the road, waving his arms wildly, and driving them towards a gateway to a field.

Nicholas, risking his own safety, pushed his way through that lumbering mass to get ahead of the animals and open the gate. He was considerably bruised for his efforts. 'Open the gate, Nicholas, and stand back,' Henry yelled, over the wind and pelting rain. The thunder rumbled ominously, as Henry stood, arms outstretched, easing the terrified and panicky cattle towards Nicholas, who put his shoulder to the wooden gate. It was stuck fast in the mud. Nicholas sweated and heaved. He tried lifting the gate. It yielded only a slight opening, not enough for a man or cow to pass through. Then disaster struck.

The thunder gathered itself together and clapped several times in loud succession. The lightning shrieked incessantly and screamed across the sky, lighting the fields and the heaving black sea beyond. The cornered cattle spun around several times, threatening to blunder into Nicholas, who couldn't escape through the tiny aperture between the gate and hedge and he saw his fate slipping away into injury or death at the water-logged entrance to the field. But another roll of thunder and bolt of lightening thudded into the field behind him. Nicholas could feel the earth tremor, causing the cattle to change direction. In a wild hysterical rush they turned in flight towards the farmer, who was floundering in the thick oozing mud to get out of their way. Nicholas saw his terrified face lit by the blaze of lightening and heard his final scream as they mowed the farmer down, crushing, turning, and trampling him under their hoofs in their frenzied haste to escape.

Nicholas watched in horror as the cows stamped the farmer into the soft earth. He was by his side immediately, unable to believe the simple act that had turned into a nightmare. Henry's face was pressed down into the mud. His back was crumpled, as though under the jacket there was a pile of smashed loose bones. Nicholas turned him over, and in the soft morning light, he could see that the life had been crushed out of him. He broke down and wept and wailed in an agony of fright and shock. The cattle had galloped off down the road. Nicholas was found by farmers minutes later kneeling and cradling the dead man in his arms.

'There was nothing I could do. Nothing I could do,' he cried desperately.

The farmers in turn repeated Nicholas's plea. 'There was nothing you could do. Nothing you could do.' They lifted Nicholas to his feet and half carried him back along the road to the entrance of the farm.

Loveday and her mother stood on the wall of the farmyard in the pouring rain, anxiously watching the fields for the return of the two men. What they saw in the distance was a party of four men carrying a board between them, with something on it covered in sacks. Their anxiety increased as they recognised Nicholas among their neighbours, trailing behind, looking bewildered and broken. But there was no sign of Henry. Annie Care leapt from the wall and ran towards the approaching party. 'Henry!' she screamed. Already she knew the figure on the board was her husband. The group stopped at her approach, and allowed her to uncover the material over his head, letting Loveday know by another scream that her father was dead. Loveday remained on the wall, stunned with shock, and watched as her father's body passed beneath her, with her mother crying at his side.

The men lay the body reverently on the kitchen table and stood aside while Annie Care covered her husband's face with kisses and wiped the mud off his face, already the iron cold of death was affecting his lips. Nicholas crept quietly away to Loveday and lifted her down from the wall. She sank to the ground and he sat with her, cradling her head on his shoulder.

'I couldn't do anything. I couldn't stop them,' Nicholas cried. They sobbed into one another's necks, clinging tightly. And then, as suddenly as it had devastated the Cornish village and the local farms, the rain stopped; the sun shone mildly like an unspoken apology; many of the cattle returned calmly to their own farms, innocent of any trouble they had caused. The doctor's horse and carriage passed by unheard into the farmyard, while Loveday and Nicholas sat huddled into the wall, totally lost in shock.

It was some time before Loveday realised that Nicholas was trembling in his sodden clothes and needed help. She hoisted him to his feet and led him into the house, through the kitchen, where Annie was washing

169

Henry's face, and the men stood awkwardly around the body. The doctor was writing a death certificate. Upstairs, Loveday removed Nicholas's clothes, and though still muddy, she tucked him into bed, piling blankets over his shivering form.

In the worst storm that anybody could remember, land slides covered roads in mud, trees were uprooted and tossed about, cliff faces tumbled into the sea, houses were flooded, trains were stranded by tracks that were washed away and waterlogged, ships ran aground, and no fishing boats from St Ives, Newlyn, or from any harbour around the Cornish coast could put to sea. The seafaring communities suffered hardships with lack of earnings and many families went hungry. Schools closed as educational establishments and re-opened to serve soup and bread to the needy population.

8

Zennor church was filled to overflowing. As well as Henry Care, two unnamed and unclaimed men were being interred. Their bodies had been washed ashore at Gurnard's Head in the storm and were being buried in unmarked graves. Inside the church the men's voices rose strongly to those outside, as though all the male-voice choirs of Cornwall were singing. In the parish rooms, close by, the women provided refreshments, each bringing the best of their produce to show their grief, their support, their village closeness, to celebrate the life of one who was so recently among them, and so well regarded and to show respect for the unfortunate strangers.

Annie, Loveday, and Nicholas, left the graveside accompanied by the closest of their family and friends, and inside the community rooms, the men continued their singing, but softly and thoughtfully, remembering their friend and neighbour. Gradually, the singing subsided, and people mingled and talked and shared the food among them. The villagers had made their contribution to a valuable lost comrade and now it was time to continue their lives and tend their animals and land at Trewey, Foage, Treveglos, Tremedda, Tregerthen, Wicca, and Churchtown Farms and the outlying farms at Towednack.

Nicholas drove the trap to Gorsemoor Farm, with the good wishes of people left to disperse in their own way. He made Annie and Loveday sit at the table while he put the kettle on and made tea. They seemed inert and incapable of any kind of action, so numb were they by the afternoon's funeral, and the kindness of friends. While he busied himself setting out cups on the table, he said quietly to them.

'I'll be here for as long as you want me.'

Already neighbours were bringing the cows in for milking. They had been sharing these activities between them since the accident, but sooner or later, they had to return to their own duties, which as every farmer knew, took up all of their time every hour of the day, and day of the year, relentlessly.

Nicholas did his best for the next few weeks under the guidance of Annie Care and Loveday, but was called home urgently to Brighton where his father's health had collapsed. His shares in the railway business had suffered great losses when he invested most of his money in a bogus railway company in South Africa.

One fine early morning Loveday and Nicholas loaded up the cart with goods for the market at Penzance. They were also on their way to the train station, where Nicholas would say goodbye to Loveday, not knowing how long he would be away. Loveday wondered whether she would ever see Nicholas again after his traumatic experience on the farm, her father's death and his own family misfortunes.

'I can't blame you for wanting to stay at home with your father, and getting back to a better life; the life that you knew before coming to Cornwall, and the educated people you mixed with. I'm sure things are not as bad as you expect and perhaps you can help your father regain his health, and wealth. If you feel you can do that, I will release you gladly. I only want what is best for you, Nicholas.'

'Loveday,' he said, 'you are always urging me to go, always telling me what you think I want. I shall help my father, if I can, but I shall be back.'

Loveday barely stopped the cart outside the station and Nicholas had to jump down and drag his suitcase from the still moving cart. 'Loveday,' he said, running alongside. 'Say goodbye.' 'Goodbye,' she called, and whipped the horse away, convinced that this would be the last she saw of Nicholas. She didn't want him to remember a distressingly tender scene of their last parting.

The air at Brighton was harsh and cold. It stung his face. The sea was grey and the beach stony. It wasn't a place he would choose to come back and live, in spite of its grand houses, opulent hotels facing the sea, expensive shops and the wonderfully inviting pier and its wide seafront promenade. People here looked prosperous.

He found his father in his terraced house in one of the smaller squares. He was shocked by his diminished appearance, his robust, haughty, confident self reduced to a shambling wreck.

'Thank you for coming, my boy. I'm so sorry and ashamed Nicholas.'

'Hush,' Nicholas replied, following his father along the wide hall, once lined with paintings, but now bare. The front parlour and dining room were stripped of furniture and his father lived in the back kitchen, with a table and two chairs and the barest of essentials for simple living. Nicholas tried to hide his shock at his father's obvious reduced circumstances.

'I'm sorry, Nicholas,' his father told him, 'I have lost money that should have come to you. Indeed, I had hoped to increase your legacy, but I was foolishly persuaded to invest without the proper financial checks.'

Over the next few weeks Nicholas watched his father fall into despair at the ruin of both himself and his son. He spent some time helping to wind up his father's affairs and was dismayed at his sudden decline into old age and his inability to manage his life. He realised that prosperity was enabling. Poverty was disabling.

There was enough money left from the sale of the house to provide accommodation in a guest house in Brighton for his father. Nicholas stayed with him for the first week, to see that his living arrangements were suitable and his finances would support his new way of life, then he thought about returning to Cornwall. There was no reluctance to say farewell from either of them. They had lived most of their lives apart, Nicholas for his education, his father for his business interests.

He did not inform Loveday that he would be coming home, choosing a day when she would be trading her goods in Market Jew Street at the Penzance market. Her face lit up when she saw him. 'Am I taking you back to Gorsemoor Farm, Nicholas?' she said, joy creasing her face in a broad smile. 'Please,' Nicholas replied.

Annie Care had taken on a farmhand to do the milking, while she and Loveday coped with the dairying and chickens, and although Nicholas was welcomed back to the house, there was not enough money to pay for both his labour and the hired hand, John Fanshaw. Nicholas had lost his status on the farm with Annie. She no longer needed him and he had to find a job to pay his way. He had heard talk at the Tinner's Arms that men were needed at a newly dug shaft at Wheal Raven, St Just, and he determined to try his luck in mining.

'It's better money than I could earn on a farm,' he assured Loveday, 'and now I have no money to inherit, I feel I must work and save for our future.'

Loveday was horrified that a man of Nicholas's sensibilities and education should have to consider mining as an option. 'You will die down there in a black pit, even before you begin to work. It will break your spirit and destroy you. It is not for you, Nicholas. I beg you to think about it.'

In spite of the protests of Loveday and her mother, he rose early the next morning and rode his bicycle to St Just. The nearer he got to the town the more the fields and lanes in every direction filled with scattered groups of men, making towards the engine houses and mine buildings. He joined a group waiting to be chosen to climb down the new shaft, which yawned before him. There was great uncertainty among the crowd, waiting to be chosen to descend into Hell. He watched while other men, summoned by a bell, shuffled up close waiting to step into the old mine by the noisy gear wheels of the clanking man-engines, passing men who had completed their shift and come to grass, their heads bowed with exhaustion, their faces mottled with dust from the mine and their own sweat.

There was hostility from the miners at the pithead when they saw Nicholas, this fresh faced youth offering himself as a fledgling mine worker. Many of them worked in gangs and would be taken on as a group of experienced miners. They knew each other and were local to the district. Their clothes, which they had changed into in the sheds, consisted of a hard hat, jacket, shirt and thick trousers. They wore old worn shoes with no socks. Their tattered red-stained clothes bore the marks of their trade, the tin miner. Nicholas wore his oldest clothes, but still he stood apart.

'I reckon this young lady should be wearing a skirt,' they teased.

'Give 'im to the Bal Maids, see what they make of 'im.'

There was loud, raucous laughter, and other men took up the jeering. They spat upon the ground at his feet. They raised their hats in mock greeting. They took dainty steps and walked around him.

'Reckon he's a spy, working for the mine captain. Have to watch yourselves my lads.'

'He's one of the shareholders, pretending to be interested in our work.'

'He won't be back tomorrow, that's for sure.'

Nicholas suffered these ominous jests in silence, flushing at the insults and feeling slightly disillusioned about the supposed comradeship he thought there was among men who performed dangerous jobs, and realising he would always be an outsider. Most of the gangs of men had been dispersed and were descending into the mine. Nicholas was about to turn away when a young man spotted him. 'Hey there, you, the one with the red face, Pinkie. I'm one short. Could do with an extra hand. You'll be better than nothing.'

'Thank you,' Nicholas said, and went to join the group. The men still around laughed at his new name. They mouthed it among themselves, 'Pinkie, Pinkie' and at the idea of being thanked, and at the innocence of the youth. The name Pinkie suited him.

'We're fitting pit props,' Nicholas was told. 'You're about to become a timber man.'

Down underground he was surprised to find it hot and dry, the dust choking as it filled narrow passageways, from the chippings of the miners' tools. Some passages were wet with water seepage, and he splashed along behind the group, eventually discarding his socks, which soon became saturated with water. Whenever they stopped to secure a roof he took instructions, selecting wooden piles of a suitable height for that particular passage. There were a great many variations, from small tunnels, which they had to crawl through, to vast caverns, where there were great rock columns left by the miners as props to hold up the roof, as well as extra wooden props made by the team Nicholas worked with.

They were deep underground below sea level and Nicholas was disappointed when he learned that the men were not leaving the mine for their meal break, but sitting in a dry spot, lit by their own headlamps. 'It'll take time and effort to go to grass,' the foreman told him, 'so we take croust down here.' Nicholas opened his blue spotted cloth and took out a Cornish pasty, made by Mrs Care, and his enamel jug with a lid, filled with cider. The other men had the same sort of fare.

Nicholas sat a little apart from his group, who chose to ignore him. He listened to their conversation, hoping to learn a little of their ways and know how to fit in. He had already guessed the meaning of 'going to grass' and 'croust' and accepted that his embarrassment had earned him the name Pinkie, and that was that. Everybody had a nickname and, at least, he belonged in that sense.

During the period of silence from the working tools of the men and the clattering of trams, he was alarmed to hear the sea flinging boulders and stones against the other side of the wall of rock where he sat. He realised that the mine was partly under the sea. He hoped they were safe, and that the wall would not collapse under the weight of water, but none of the men talked of this fearful happening, and he was more nervous of the scorn of the men if he should mention their safety, than of the sea breaking through into the compartment.

Nicholas didn't like the mine. That first day he emerged from underground bathed in sweat and exhausted. He did no more than wash his face and hands in the changing shed and with others, stand around in the boiler house until he was warm and his clothes partly dried, then he stiffly mounted his bike and rode home. Tomorrow he would wear different clothes and leave these in the sheds to change into.

The men Nicholas worked with never lost their contempt for him, his education, his polite ways, his desire to learn his job and execute it to the best of his ability. Nicholas lost his romantic and heroic ideas of the men who toiled alongside him, and despised their cynicism and suspicion of his non-Cornish background. He got used to working with his team, of earning money and paying for his board at Gorsemoor Farm, but he was anxious to return to working on the farm, when the farmhand's verbal contract of one year's work should be over.

John Fanshaw, the hired hand, whom Nicholas did not particularly like, was saving to buy a sheep farm in New Zealand. Annie let John sleep in the barn, where he was on call for all eventualities to do with the farm. The free accommodation helped build his finances and so furthered his ambitious plans.

Although Nicholas was living in the house, Mrs Care had come to rely on John Fanshaw because Nicholas was working down the mine from early morning to dusk. And apart from his good relationship with Loveday, he was no longer part of the every day life of the farm, or the family. On the occasions when they were able to walk and talk Loveday told of her anxiety about their farmhand.

'I don't like the way he tries to get round mother,' she said. 'He is always flattering her, telling her what a wonderful manager she is. Persuading her that she would love New Zealand. Saying how he knows she would prefer sheep to cows, once she got to know them. There's never been much call for sheep in Zennor.'

'I don't think there's anything to worry about Loveday. Your mother has no intention of leaving her farm. I've never heard him trying to persuade her that she could make a life in New Zealand.'

'That's because he's wary of you. He wouldn't want to set alarm bells ringing by talking such nonsense in front of you.'

'Well, he'll be gone soon, and we won't have to worry,' Nicholas assured her.

In the autumn Loveday and Nicholas were married at Zennor Church, nine months after the death of Henry Care. It was her mother Annie, who insisted the wedding should take place as soon as possible. Henry would have wished it, she told them. It was a simple affair, quite without the usual build-up to a wedding, with no one attending except Henry's brother, second coxswain of St Ives Lifeboat, and an aunt who scorned the idea of a year of mourning before a celebration of any kind could take place in a family.

Nicholas had no relations that he could invite and Loveday, still in mourning for her father, invited only a few friends, but her friend Hope and her mother, turned up unexpectedly, their maid Molly having informed them of the wedding. Hope, being on holiday from her finishing school in Switzerland, insisted that her mother accompany her to Zennor church.

Unexpectedly too, Mrs Lindner invited the newly married couple, the aunt and the coxswain of the lifeboat and the few friends, to Chy-an-Porth for a wedding lunch, when she discovered that nothing had been arranged at the farmhouse. Loveday's mother seemed to be quite over her husband's death, but declined the invitation to lunch because she was dealing with the day-to-day events of the farm. There were essential jobs to be done, she said, excusing her absence.

Outside the church Annie informed the young couple, 'You can live at Gorsemoor Farm for a short time, while you look around for a cottage to rent. I expect Nicholas, that you are well settled into your job at the mine, and are earning good money, better than you could earn on a farm.'

Loveday and Nicholas were dismayed that Annie Care wanted to be rid of them, but neither could question her reasoning, or say they hoped to remain working with her on the farm. What were her plans they wondered?

'You could work in a shop in St Ives, my girl. White's in Fore Street sell furnishings and fabrics. You've always wanted clean hands and I know they are advertising in the local paper for young ladies as counter sales assistants. You could probably get a discount on materials for curtains for the cottage, as you'll be working there,' Annie told them.

Loveday, in spite of her disappointment that she and Nicholas could not remain on the farm began, for the first time, to think about herself standing behind a shop counter, wearing a long black skirt and crisp white blouse with leg-of-mutton sleeves, greeting customers, selling yards of material, sheets, towels, ribbons and buttons. But what if they didn't think she was suitable? They might offer her a position in their curtain making department. She had heard of girls working as dress-maker's assistants in a shop in Tregenna Place, working late, even until twelve o'clock at night when there was a special order which had to be delivered on time. No. She didn't want that.

For a moment, Loveday was carried away by this long held ambition to work in a shop. It was exciting to think of it, and Nicholas couldn't take this opportunity away from her by saying he hoped to go back to working on the farm, so he too was drawn into the deceit. If he and Loveday rented a cottage, she would be free to work in the shop, and with a recommendation from a woman such as Laura Knight, Loveday would be successful in achieving her goal. But Annie Care had her own secret agenda.

After their wedding lunch, Loveday and Nicholas took the trap and drove over to Penzance, where they spent a night at the Queen's Hotel, overlooking Penzance promenade, a spontaneous wedding gift from Hope and her mother. They stabled the horse and were due to drive back the next day, after visiting aunt and uncle Josh at Newlyn.

Uncle Josh greeted Nicholas in a cheerful and admiring manner.

'Well, my lad, you've had a pretty tough journey into our life down here in Cornwall, from the home of a gentleman, and with an education too.'

'I've been very happy on the farm, Sir. I hope to return to farming when the time is right.'

182

'So mining's not for you then, lad?'

'I prefer to be in the open air. I admire those men tremendously, but ... ' Nicholas couldn't finish his sentence for fear of saying something unpleasant about his working conditions and his fellow workers.

'Nicholas thinks the miners should join a union and demand fair wages. And have more checks on equipment and safety,' Loveday said.

'Do you now,' chided uncle Josh, 'and what would happen to the starving families while the mine owners locked the men out? You must be a very popular chap down in St Just.'

'I don't actually talk about such things in the mine. Loveday you shouldn't have mentioned this. It's only something that you and I discuss. It's just an idea of making progress for the working man.'

'It's all pie in the sky, then,' concluded uncle Josh.

'Yes. I suppose so, if you put it like that. I've no intention of putting my ideas forward. I wouldn't dare. I'm not one of them,' Nicholas said dejectedly.

'In that case, young man, and if you wouldn't cause a revolution on the quayside, I'll take you out fishing one of these days. How would that suit you?'

'I would really love to try fishing. You must understand, I don't know anything about it except what Loveday has told me, but I'm very willing to try.'

'All right then my boy, we'll see what can be done.'

With this new offer in mind, Loveday and Nicholas spent a cheerful day in Newlyn harbour, with uncle Josh taking them over the boat and explaining how it functioned, and the equipment for fishing, and what

183

seasons to catch which sort of fish, and where in the ocean they were to be found. Again, in spite of their newly married state, Nicholas showed a keen interest in all the information about this new trade of fishing, and Loveday again found herself resentful of his inattention to her.

Later that evening, Nicholas drove the trap through the village of Ludgvan, on to Gulval and Nancledra, the Towednack turn, and down the coast road to Gorsemoor Farm. Soldier knew the road so only one hand held a light rein, while Nicholas's arm held Loveday closely to him, and she wrapped her two arms around him. It was a slow contented journey home. It would be midnight when they arrived, but they wanted to savour these few hours they had spent together, which had mended a relationship that had fallen apart over the last few trying months, with Nicholas almost too tired to eat when he got home, and Loveday worried about the effect the hired hand was having on her usually very down to earth, sensible mother.

'Nicholas, you must give up mining, you've got so thin. I don't want you ill, or injured, or worn out working.'

'Yes. I want to be out in the fresh air, breathing earth smells, and feeling the sun on my face, but all these jobs have their dangers. You warned me of that some time ago. I've learnt that lesson. Look at our own tragedy of your father on the farm.'

'Oh dear. Poor father. I still miss him.'

The memories brought back the nightmare for them both and the fatal storm that changed their lives.

'In the morning we'll talk to mother, tell her you

want to work on the farm. It's strange that she wants us to leave, especially as John Fanshaw will soon be going to New Zealand. What has she in mind?'

When Loveday and Nicholas arrived home, the farmhouse was in darkness, probably mother had gone to bed. They crept silently to their room, disappointed that she hadn't waited up to welcome them home. It was only on coming down to the kitchen in the morning that Loveday saw the note on the table.

'I'm sorry Loveday, but I am going to New Zealand with John Fanshaw. This is an opportunity for me to start a new life. I will eventually sell the animals and the farm and proceedings will start when I arrive in the country. You have Nicholas and are starting your life together and I know you will be very happy. Love mother.'

'Nicholas. Come down quickly. Mother's gone! She's gone to New Zealand!'

Nicholas tumbled down the stairs, still half asleep but dressed ready for work in the mine. He read the note in some confusion.

There was a loud knock at the door and they turned as though expecting some further explanation for their dilemma. It was Mr Paynter from Dove farm.

'I've come to take the cattle,' he said, as though Loveday and Nicholas already knew about this arrangement. 'I took your mother to Penzance station. She's meeting John at Plymouth, and they're sailing from there.'

Without waiting for a response from the two bewildered people, he closed the door and his feet echoed over the cobblestones in the yard. Soon they heard the cattle passing through the courtyard and watched them moving across the fields to Dove Farm.

They sat at the table wondering what this meant to their lives. If the farm and animals were sold, there was no chance of Loveday and Nicholas taking over. Their mother had pulled the carpet from under their feet and their world had collapsed. No wonder Annie had painted a picture for them of moving into a cottage, and of Loveday achieving her ambition of working in a shop. Loveday had been deprived of her inheritance. How long would it take before they were informed by an agent that the sale of the farm was in negotiation? Should they begin searching now for a cottage to rent?

'I'll have to carry on working at the mine,' Nicholas said, losing any gleam of hope they had conjured by a talk with Annie Care. 'I can't risk losing this job, and with so many mines closing down, it's likely to happen.'

'I know love.'

'The mine is my destiny. I'm sorry I can't stay and sort out this problem with you. We'll talk about it tonight and see what can be done.'

They hugged each other in mutual support and sympathy. With the cattle gone, there was no work for Nicholas on the farm. Loveday could manage the few cows and chickens left, and then they too would be sold with the farm cottage. It was a regret for Nicholas that he could not give up his mining job, but after the farm was sold he would have difficulty finding other work in an employment market that was already overcrowded with desperate men. Loveday had to postpone moving into a cottage, and abandon her dream of working in White's shop in St Ives. She had to stay and manage the animals that were left, but without the help and companionship of Nicholas.

It was a drizzly, misty morning as Nicholas set off for work on his bike, on the long road to St Just. The weather compounded the already desperate situation facing the couple. The one bright hope would be if uncle Josh offered him a chance to take up fishing, once Annie sold the farm. He would write to him and explain. They would find a cottage in Newlyn. He would work hard, but he knew hard work was no substitute for experience. His education hadn't prepared him for manual labour, and this sort of life, whether mining, fishing, or even his chosen job of farming.

By the time Nicholas reached the mine, the drizzle had turned into a downpour, and the sea beyond the mine was a heaving mass of grey, whipped up by the wind. The spring tides had already decimated some of the boats in St Ives harbour, and two fishermen had been drowned. He could hear the fearful moan of the foghorn from the Longships lighthouse, warning fishing boats away from the treacherous rocks at Land's End. He was almost glad to be out of the weather and down in the warmth of the mine, which dried off his clothes in no time, only to be replaced by sweat in the damp and dusty air, polluted by fumes, which made it difficult to breathe.

Nicholas still did not have much of a rapport with his companions, but at least they had invited him to sit with them during a meal break. This was where he heard the stories and superstitions, which in this dark cavernous place, added to the truth of their tales. This team of men, their clothes damp and dusty, their dirty faces streaked with rivulets of sweat, drove Nicholas to both admire, and despise them. They, likewise, mimicked his 'toffs' voice and took delight in using his nickname, Pinkie. They scorned his habit of wiping his hands on his pasty cloth before eating. Their unwashed hands rarely threw away the crust by which they held their pasties, their diet was too thin to allow such a luxury.

Nicholas gradually learnt to understand the Cornish accent and relayed the tales he heard to Loveday. 'A miner's son had a number of warts on his hands and was cured by a woman digging a piece of turf for each wart. She turned the turfs upside down and when the grass died, the warts disappeared. Now can this really be true?'

'There are many tales of witches, of magic stones, and holy wells, little people, fairies and knockers, who you must know Nicholas are the little people of the mine. I'm surprised you haven't heard mention of the knockers. They can bring good or bad luck to a mine,' Loveday said.

'It's all superstitious nonsense,' Nicholas said.

'I suppose your education has taught you to disregard

such things, but don't voice your opinions, or someone will do you an injury, or put the evil eye on you. Even if you don't believe it, abide by what I tell you, please. Best be safe than sorry,' Loveday advised.

'And what about dowsing for minerals. Some of the miners say they are going out with a rod to discover more tin lodes. If the rod twitches they know there's tin in the ground, but the mine captains take no notice, and the miners have to go overseas to work when the lode runs out.'

'I've heard there's more money to be earned by families following the husband's trade. There's many a miner left St Just, Redruth and Camborne for jobs in other parts of the world. They don't come home.'

Nicholas soon learnt to listen to these men's tales, but make no comment. Loveday advised him to be silent. Today, at croust, there were no stories of magic, or witchcraft. The men stopped work and seemed to be waiting. Nicholas could feel the tension and suspense when the noise of hammering, and movement of trucks ceased. They could clearly hear the angry sea in the cavern of the abandoned mine throwing up stones and boulders at the wall, against which they rested their backs. The wall that protected them. In his nervousness, he wanted to make a joke about the knockers having fun in the abandoned mine behind them, but feared the gang's derision.

It was noisier than usual in that place. Nicholas felt panic, and had to exercise a tight control over his instinct to run and free himself from the noise and confines of that deep cell under ground. Even the men he sat with were nervous, though no one spoke. These men were stoic. It wasn't in their natures to voice their fears. Miners knew the hazards and dangers of their work, and accepted them. For the first time he experienced an unspoken closeness of these men to one another in their dangerous occupation. It was what he expected, yet he was still an outsider. He was a man alone.

Nicholas felt the fear like a knot in his stomach. His head ached with the thunderous sounds from the deserted mine behind the now shuddering wall. He trembled with the tension that coursed through him, and the anticipation of something terrible about to happen. He decided this would be his last day in the mine. Loveday was right. This was no place to eke out a living, with the constant fear of a disaster. He would work the farm with Loveday until they were forced to give it up. He would leave his future in the hands of fate. Anything would be better than this black hell under ground and his knawing fear.

Nicholas faced his fears and succumbed to them, and having determined his future course from tomorrow, he rose to his feet and made for the road to take him to an upper level, away from the threatening pounding of the sea against the wall. He would ride the man-engine and once free of the mine, he would peddle home on his bike. He could feel the fresh air on his face. Loveday would be pleased. He grinned at the puzzled faces of the men as he rushed past them, and then their expressions of ridicule at Nicholas's dash for freedom changed to ones of terror.

The wall began to shudder violently. The men showed

the alarm and fear they had tried to hide from each other. A trickle of water beneath the wall startled them. They rose with one accord. The trickle became a stream, the stream a torrent, but before they could run after Nicholas and take a step to safety, the wall burst open, breaking the barrier that separated them from the old mine workings. The screams of the men were lost as the wall collapsed. The sea roared and flooded into the chamber, knocking them off their feet, carrying men and machines in its backlash many fathoms under the sea.

Nicholas was caught by the flooding torrent of sea water as he neared the upper level. A few more yards and he would be free. But the relentless sea coursed up the incline, where a group of miners had gathered and watched helplessly as he was snatched by the last surge of the sea. The working mine was plunged into total chaos and darkness.

The women of St Just heard the wail of a siren, and with their children clustered about them, they ran to the mine, eager for news. There were many men who had come out of the mine from compartments above sea level, and others that were slower to flood. The women claimed them desperately. Others stood around waiting, hoping, and asking what sort of accident had happened. There were so many different types, including explosions, rock falls, failure of man engines, but fire and flooding were among the worst.

'We think the sea broke through from the old mine,' said one of the men to reach safety and able to give an account of what he thought had happened. 'I was on the man engine when the sea flooded past me, carrying men with it. Those working in Flowers Shaft would drown. It's narrow and would fill up immediately. The others further along would have heard and maybe escaped. Look, there's more coming up.'

Those who came first out of the mine were dry. They were bewildered, but safe, hardly knowing what had happened, except that general shouts and confusion, had led them to down tools, and make for the man engines and escape to the surface. Those who emerged from the lower levels were soaking wet and shivering with cold and shock. Each had an experience to relate, before handing in their identity disks, and being taken home by their families.

'That's your first, and last, day,' said a mother, clutching her fourteen year old son to her bosom. 'But Mum,' he protested, pulling away. 'I wasn't even down the mine. We were having some lessons in the sheds. Look, I've just got my helmet ...' The mother took the helmet, flung it away, gave the youngster a clout around the head, and dragged him away from the site. 'It took your father, it's not having you as well.' To the women the mine was a source of bread for their families. It was also a living, breathing monster, who devoured their men, husbands, sons, brothers, grandfathers and uncles.

Someone was trying to count the men who came up and assess the damage down below, but it was too soon to tell. By evening, most people living along the coast road out towards Land's End, and the other way into St Ives, had heard of the accident.

Loveday, alone in the cottage, waited for evening and

the return of Nicholas. He did not come, neither did his body arrive on a cart the next day, nor was he reported to be in the local hospital. Nicholas had been drowned with ten other men. Loveday heard his voice in her head repeating over and over, 'The mine is my destiny.' And so it proved.

When access was gained to the flooded area of the mine, it was evident that the bodies of the men had been sucked through to the old mine workings and into the sea. Their bodies were never recovered.

Loveday turned to her diary to confide her misery.

Loveday's diary. Age 19. 1902.
I am so unhappy. My life has turned to misery since mother has left and my Nicholas has been drowned in the mine. I have no comfort from anyone, or anything. I can only sit here and bemoan my losses. Last week I had a husband. I had Nicholas to help me through the trials that will come. Now I am a widow and he counts for nothing. He is not here. He is not with me. I don't know what I shall do without him.

Loveday did not go to the mine. It was the enemy. She regarded it as an unhappy place that Nicholas had no real association with. It had defeated them both. Loveday had decided that Nicholas should be buried with her father. Her father's grave had no headstone, the earth had yet to settle. There was no great attendance at the funeral service, Nicholas was an outsider and a miner. Loveday preferred it that way. She had written to his father, who had approved of his son's burial in Cornwall and explained that he was too ill to attend. Now, with her mother's departure, there would be no stone, or commemorative plaque. There was no money for such things. She had a wooden cross made, with Henry Care and Nicholas Godolphin carved on it and placed the simple cross on the grave in Zennor churchyard.

Several days later, and in a state of extreme exhaustion through working night and day to keep the small farm going, Loveday sat gloomily at the kitchen table. Her head drooped with fatigue, her eyes closed, and then her mother walked through the door. Annie Care had not heard of the tragedy at the mine, and launched into an explanation of her departure and return.

'John Fanshaw did not wait for me at Plymouth,' she said matter of factly, without sorrow, or feeling. 'He sailed the previous day.' She paused. Loveday said nothing, only stared at her mother in a sleepy uncomprehending way. Why were dreams of Nicholas and her mother haunting her both night and day?

Last night Nicholas had appeared at the end of her bed in the same clothes he wore when she first met him. He was untouched by the hand of work and toil. His eyes were bright, his face unclouded by ill fortune. He was as fresh as when she had first laid eyes on him at Lamorna Cove and he had walked over to offer his help. He held a sketch book and pencil, and was smiling at her as he worked on his drawing. 'I'm drawing you from memory, Loveday,' he said. Then he was gone. Loveday tried to will Nicholas to appear again, but when he didn't come, she knew it had been the final

194

goodbye, showing her that he was now following his artistic pursuits. She found it comforting. This apparition was of the same nature surely, but her mother was talking.

'I would have sold the farm.' Annie said. She paused. 'He should have waited, but what's the point. He didn't want me.' She offered no apology, but stood at the door waiting to be asked to enter, or for some reaction from her daughter. There was none.

As far as Loveday was concerned, her mother was just a phantom, come to provide her with reasons for deserting her. Everything was unreal. She got up from the table and without a word, went to bed and slept soundly for the first time since Nicholas and her father's untimely deaths. She was numb to any drama that required thought or feeling.

She wanted to blot out everything.

9

Zillah, having read the account of the accident in the mine could almost feel the sadness return to the room she was now occupying. It was where Loveday would have wept and slept. How unhappy she must have been. She looked at the framed sketches of Loveday, a young, lively girl, on the cliffs at Lamorna, done by her great grandfather, Nicholas Godolphin, and the photo taken by the Victorian lady photographer, posing a little shyly, but smiling. She breathed her sympathy towards the images. 'I'm so sorry, Loveday' she said and turned over another page of Loveday's diary.

Diary. Loveday. Age 20. 1902
My baby was born today, nine months after I was married, and nine months after I was widowed. It was a sad and happy moment when I saw my little girl. She has my flame red hair and her daddy's blue eyes. I loved her straight away and apologised to her for not taking greater care of her daddy, so that he would be alive to see her. Mother too was both sad and happy. We have had a terrible time between us since the deaths of our husbands. It is hard for two widows to manage, especially after John Fanshaw deserted her. Mother is so ashamed. But we don't talk about it. I don't want to hear how sorry she is, or how much of a fool she feels.

I don't allow her to mention it. I don't tell her I blame her for Nicholas's death, but if he had come back to work on the farm, he wouldn't have died in that horrible mine accident. My anger lies like a burden between us. But enough of miseries. I have my darling daughter, and I shall call her Karenza.

Gorsemoor Farm was no longer part of the farming community, Annie had sold most of the cattle, keeping only a few for their domestic needs. The fields too were sold to neighbouring farmers, except for those which led directly down to the cliffs or fed their cows, their pig, and their one horse, and on which they grew vegetables and daffodils, now too few to be sent by train to London's Covent Garden. Chickens still roamed the yard and their remaining stock was manageable. It was now a small holding, not the farmland built up by Henry Care.

No friends or neighbours visited these days, whether with horse and cart, or on foot. Gorsemoor Farm, and especially Annie Care, had become objects of disapproval, since Annie's brief and shocking interlude with John Fanshaw. St Ives and Zennor people were particularly unforgiving when one of their folk, especially their women folk, deserted their home, or sullied the name of their tight-knit community.

There was some talk of effigies being burnt on one of the neighbouring hills, and Annie had lost some clothes from her washing line. They had searched the near fields and cliffs and assumed that the garments had been blown away by the wind. Neither Annie nor

Loveday could believe that the torching of effigies, showing violent displeasure at a villager's misdoings, could still be practiced today. There was not a whisper in any of the surrounding parishes, though an unexplained fire on the top of Trink Hill, had clearly been seen from Gorsemoor Farm.

Later that year Loveday was in the yard collecting eggs in a basket when she heard a horse and trap moving smartly along the lane towards the farm. She watched it approach with some excitement. A visitor would be a welcome interruption to their days of sameness and hard work. Her mother had walked into Zennor to shop at the village Post Office, and Loveday was alone with the sleeping baby. She was surprised and astonished when Laura Knight stepped down from her trap and tethered the reins to the gatepost by the drinking trough. Loveday hurried forward to greet her.

'Loveday,' she said, as though they had parted only last week. 'I'm delighted to see you. I've been painting in St Ives and thought I'd drop by. May I release this poor mare into your field for a bit of a graze? She's had a hard journey all the way from Lamorna.'

'Of course, Laura. Of course,' Loveday agreed, stepping forward and releasing the horse from the trap and leading her into the small field, where she could be easily caught. Laura Knight stood by watching, taking in the scenery around her and then moving towards the cottage.

'Come in, come in,' Loveday said in a fluster, catching up with her and going ahead to open the door. She was on the point of ushering her into the unused parlour, when Laura helped herself to a chair and sat down at the kitchen table.

'Oh, this is nice. Now how about a cup of tea, if it's not interrupting your work too much. What lovely eggs. I'll buy a dozen,' Laura said, handling and admiring the basket of eggs on the table.

Loveday put the kettle on and was gradually accustoming herself to this most unexpected visit and was wondering how to phrase a question and ask why she was here without appearing rude, when Laura said.

'I've come to find accommodation for several horses, and a cow. I know it's a strange request, but then I thought of you, and remembered you lived on a farm, and found your address. Now, you remember Alfred Munnings?'

Loveday didn't blush. So much had happened to her in the last few months that she was beyond such shy reactions. She set out cups and saucers, indeed remembering the handsome man who had lifted her up and twirled her dangerously round on a rock over the sea. What an enchanting summer that had been when she posed for Laura Knight at Lamorna Cove, and had such fun. She had met Nicholas and everything seemed possible, even to a change in her lifestyle. She smiled at her recollections.

'Oh yes, yes, yes,' she stammered, 'I remember Mr Alfred Munnings.'

'Well, he is going to Zennor for a few weeks to work

on a series of paintings, horse and hounds, the hunt, that sort of thing and he wants somewhere for the horses, and his pretty cow, of which he is extremely fond. What a man! I thought of you. He'll pay, of course.'

Laura laughed, as Loveday opened her mouth in surprise and said, 'Is Mr Munnings coming to Gorsemoor Cottage?'

'Yes, with his animals, if you will allow it Loveday.'

'But of course. We've plenty of room in our field for a couple of horses and a cow, and Mr Munnings too.'

'I don't think Alfred wishes to stay in your field, Loveday. He has accommodation in Zennor with Mrs Briggs, next to the Tinner's Arms.'

Laura continued to laugh at Loveday, who was so overcome with the unexpected arrival of Laura Knight, that she was making no sense of what was said to her. She forgot to put tea in the pot and poured milk in the sugar bowl. But during tea the two women chatted and regained some of the ease of manner they had enjoyed while Laura was sketching her in Lamorna. Loveday became more relaxed when Laura peeped into the cot to admire Karenza, and to express her shock and sorrow at the death of Nicholas.

'Your daughter is so like him. He would have made a good artist. I hope you still have his sketches of you,' Laura said. 'I'm sure they're a great comfort. Remember the picture I painted of you standing on the cliffs, looking out over the sea at Lamorna?'

Loveday nodded eagerly, smiling at the image of herself, posing on her pinnacle of rock like a free spirit. Feeling loved and admired by Nicholas. Thinking that there were possibilities in life that she could aim for. She felt so much younger then, and carefree, but fate had snatched away her future.

'That painting of you was much admired. It was exhibited at the Royal Academy, and bought by a London Gallery. And you and I, Loveday, will remain forever young and hopeful for as long as the painting exists.'

Loveday expressed her pleasure. She did not know if the sale to a London Gallery was good, or whether a private collector would have been preferable, but Laura looked pleased, and Loveday took the hint from her obvious expression of delight.

'Of course,' she added, 'It will probably be sold on for a bigger price, and then who knows what will happen to it. It may even leave the country and turn up in America or Australia. Now wouldn't that be nice, to know that we have both travelled, without leaving our firesides.'

The remark made them both laugh.

'Will you mind your painting leaving the country?' Loveday asked.

Laura shrugged. 'I have absolutely no control over a painting once it leaves my studio and is exhibited and sold. In any case, I have to sell my work in order to continue painting, and build a reputation. I shall be happy if my pictures are as popular as those of Alfred Munnings. My dear, he's an absolute master, especially of the horse, and such a lively spirit. Harold says I am too enthralled with him, but then my lovely husband is a very quiet man, and Alfred is such fun.'

Loveday listened entranced to a tirade of events in

the social calendar of the artists, which consisted of parties and concerts and dances; a life so different from Loveday's work on the farm and looking after Karenza. She would be lucky to be invited to one party in five years, now that she was a mother, and a widow.

'Well,' said Laura, rifling in her capacious bag and bringing out paper and pencils. 'I shall do a lightning sketch of Karenza before I leave this afternoon. Such a dear little face. Better get started before she stirs and wakes up. It'll pay for my eggs.'

Laura worked fast. She completed two sketches, giving one to Loveday and leaving the other in her sketch pad to work on in her studio. 'Now, put it in a frame under glass and that'll protect it. It's my legacy to your daughter.' She signed it, waving away the words of thanks Loveday began to express.

Annie Care appeared along the field path as Laura's horse and trap swept away down the unmade farm road, waving her arm wildly in farewell. Loveday sat down at the table, exhausted by Laura's energy, and told her mother that she had arranged for the stabling of a number of horses, and a cow.

'A very strange request,' Annie said. 'The extra income will be valuable. We'll be able to buy some cattle and restock the farm; but how did you get to know two rich and important artists?'

Loveday went upstairs and retrieved a newspaper cutting of Laura Knight with her painting on varnishing day at the Royal Academy, showing her picture of Loveday, large and compelling, standing on a rock looking out to sea. Annie smiled, and somehow, the rift that had grown between them, quietly diminished.

During the week several horse boxes arrived and the occupants galloped to freedom in the fields. Their feed came, with great mounds of hay, and saddles, and harness and all the paraphernalia required to maintain them. The very pretty cow also came. She was a cross between a Friesan and a Jersey and found herself the object of attention from the last of the Gorsemoor herd. Loveday was glad Mr Alfred Munnings himself did not appear. She would have found the encounter embarrassing. He sent, Ned, his groom, who was to take care of the animals, and be the subject of the paintings.

Ned would transport the horses to and from the farm. 'It'll be convenient for me if I can sleep in the barn. I'll be on hand to manage the horses, and groom them, and generally make sure they're not an extra burden on you. Would that be possible? I shall be off early in the morning to have breakfast in the kitchen at Mrs Briggs's house, and when I've gathered up the hounds from the Hunt Master, I shall receive my instructions for the day from Mr Munnings. I'll be back with the horses to settle them for the evening.'

Annie and Loveday agreed this would be the best solution to housing the animals without any responsibility for them. It would be good to have a man around the farm too for any odd jobs that they couldn't do themselves.

Ned paraded before Loveday and Annie in his gentleman's outfit, his costume for the leader of the hunt. He was dressed in a scarlet coat, black velvet hat, white cord breeches and top boots. Alfred Munnings was to begin work on a painting on the hill leading down to Zennor, with Ned on horseback, surrounded by the hounds, and looking every inch a gentleman. Loveday took the red coat, hat, cravat and trousers and hung them from the picture rail in her bedroom. Annie kept the boots polished and they stood in the porch.

Over the next few weeks Ned made a welcome and cheerful addition to their company at the farm. He had supper with them, bringing in news from the village and the progress of the paintings.

'One of the large paintings is finished and it'll be sent to London or Paris I should think. The next one will be started tomorrow. If you look out over the hill to Eagle's Nest, you'll see me in all my finery leading a pack of hounds. I'll sound the horn for you so you'll know it's me,' Ned said. He put the horn to his lips and delivered his own particular musical call. 'Mr Munnings likes to make it look real and I certainly beat the gentry in my outfit, so he tells me.'

'Well, and aren't you proud of yourself,' Loveday laughed.

'Mrs Briggs is taking Mr Munnings in hand, and no mistake. He heeds what she says and comes home as soon as time is called at the Tinners Arms. I've never known him go to bed so early, but I expect he'll exert himself when he needs to be free.'

Ned helped out at the farm whenever Alfred Munnings returned to Newlyn, to break away from the confines of Zennor village and Mrs Briggs, and organise one of his famous parties. Then he didn't need his groom for a couple of days and Ned was freed from the restraints of posing on horseback, while struggling to contain the energetic animal and at the same time keeping him lively for the artist to capture movement.

It was during this time, with the return of that rabble rousing Alfred Munnings to their vicinity that the fishermen thought to have their revenge on an artist who had brought unfavourable comments about the drunken behaviour in the village of Newlyn. It also included Lamorna, previously a quiet backwater, with a couple of inns and local inhabitants who drank moderately with the landlord, Mr Jory at The Wink, but now Mr Munnings had taken up residence in the valley it had become a place of riotous assembly.

A great crowd of artists, students, musicians and their followers, gathered at The Wink in Lamorna. Carousing began early, prior to them setting off in various means of transport to carry on the party at Trewarveneth studios in Newlyn, where every artist offered hospitality of a liquid kind. Later that evening, as the boats returned to harbour from the fishing grounds, and the artists traipsed drunkenly down the hill to continue their singing and dancing on the quay and, so they said, paint nocturnes in the light of the full moon, the two parties met, with near fatal consequences.

Now the fishermen, on their own ground, saw their opportunity to show their disapproval of the artists' outrageous behaviour. The leading man of the drunken group, smiling foolishly, draped his arms in friendly fashion across the broad shoulders of two fishermen, letting them bear his weight.

'Hey Ho, my brave hearties,' he cried.

'And Hey Ho, to you,' the fishermen chorused. They took hold of him, a hand and leg each, swung him to and fro, and on the count of three released him into the harbour. This act met with great hilarity and favour from the rest of the party, and they began leaping into the water after him.

The groups of fishermen walking along the quay, anxious to get home, nevertheless saw the danger to these irresponsible drunkards and launched a few small dinghies to drag them out of the water, which was quickly sapping their strength and their ability to remain afloat. The fishermen spent the next hour pumping water from the lungs of near-drowned artists, who lay about the quay sick and shivering. Next day the fishermen were declared heroes and loudly praised for their prompt actions in the rescue. No one remembered they had tossed an unfortunate man into the sea, while the others followed like lemmings. The recovering artists were nowhere to be seen. The fishermen went to their work, as usual, but with secret, self-congratulatory smiles as they greeted each other.

For the next few weeks, Alfred Munnings, returning to his painting at Zennor, was a familiar sight among the locals, and although he was a frequent visitor to the Tinners' Arms, his landlady Mrs Briggs, for whom he showed a great affection, kept him soberly in place. He wrote very favourable remarks in her visitors' book, and drew a picture of himself sitting comfortably in an armchair, smoking a pipe and declaring, 'Wonderful woman, Mrs Briggs!' The drawing of Mrs Briggs showed her with two pitchers going to fetch water at the village pump.

Ned Berryman, during his stay at Gorsemoor farm, had endeared himself to Annie, and especially Loveday, and more especially still, to baby Karenza. When she was particularly fractious, and nothing would stem her tears, he took her in his arms, mounted a horse, and did a steady walk round and round a field, talking to her and soothing her. The movement of the horse and voice of the rider was often the only cure. It relieved the women of their worry and allowed them to continue their work on the farm. On the day of her christening at Zennor church, Karenza achieved a daddy, and Loveday acquired a new husband, Ned Berryman.

Once more, Gorsemoor farm began re-establishing itself. Annie bought more cattle and the milking sheds were full. She rented fields from her neighbour, Mr Paynter, who had bought them from Annie on her shameful return home, her savings gone with the man who had deserted her on Plymouth station.

Annie set about teaching Ned the rudiments of farming and husbandry. He soon learnt many skills and life on the farm was happy and successful.

For a few years fishermen and artists lived quietly side by side in the town of St Ives, and the villages of Newlyn and Lamorna. Pictures of faces, seascapes, landscapes, and narrative events in the lives of the fishing community appeared regularly on the walls of the Royal Academy and Paris Salon, and were highly prized and praised. Indeed, the west country artists sent in more paintings from their artists' colony than from any other area of Briton. They were a noted success. The Newlyn School paintings sold throughout the world and were destined for posterity and added to the collections of various national art galleries. Their fame was worldwide.

However, all that changed when one face in particular appeared throughout the country; it was the face and pointing finger of Lord Kitchener on a large poster telling the population that their country needed them. Over the next few months both fishermen and artists disappeared from the village scene, and reappeared after training in army and navy uniforms ready to fight for their country.

The most popular man and the most despised, Alfred Munnings, according to which group you belonged, was rejected by the army because he had lost an eye in an accident and was lame. However, in the next couple of years he was sent to France as a war artist. Laura Knight missed him and his gregarious company, but she was busy with her painting.

Because of the war restrictions were placed on the artists. They were not allowed to sketch any of the coastline, or to be seen painting out of doors. They could be accused of sending valuable maps and documents to the enemy, and would be imprisoned, and their work destroyed. It was a great limitation to those artists who chose landscape and seascape pictures for their subject matter. Julius Olssen the renowned St Ives artist of sea and sky, was vociferous in his objection to these limitations on a painter of seascapes, and questions were asked in Parliament, but to no avail.

Laura Knight's husband, Harold, warned his wayward wife to beware her careless behaviour. 'Laura, you are likely to get into trouble. Come inland and paint with me, where you won't be regarded as a spy, working for the enemy and sending sketches of the coastline.'

'Don't be silly, Harold. I'm not likely to get caught. I'll be very careful.' She was still painting down at Lamorna and Newlyn, but while in St Ives, a coastguard official came upon her in a quiet place on a rock, sketching and filling in areas with paint.

'What's this?' he said, pointing over her shoulder at a dab of blue.

'That will remind me of the particular blue of the sky.'

The man humphed. 'What's this?' he said, accusingly.

'The black bit is a rock.'

'And I suppose this green is seaweed,' he said.

'Oh no. That's a mermaid,' Laura replied, facetiously.

The coastguard warned that if he should see her in that spot again, he would bring a constable with him next time, and he would be witness to her breaking the law by sketching and painting in a forbidden area. She was lucky to be let off so lightly. She would not like the conditions in a prison cell.

Shortly after, Mr and Mrs Knight left for London. The First World War would come to an end with a great depletion of men from almost every village in Cornwall. In 1918, partly as a reward for the jobs performed by women during the war, Parliament granted the first batch of votes to women over thirty. Loveday noted in her diary this progress in the women's movement and wondered whether Emmeline Pankhurst, whom she had first seen at Chy-an-Porth house in St Ives, would take the opportunity to stand for Parliament in the new legislation that allowed women in Government, where she could tackle the unfinished cause of women's suffrage.

Zillah returned the diary, thinking of the sad events of Loveday's first husband's death, and the estrangement from her mother, Annie. Memories of her own mother came flooding back, but they were not happy thoughts. She had missed the opportunity of putting things right between them, by her mother's unexpected death, but now she questioned whether anything could have been mended. There had never been love and affection between them. There had been tolerance of a dutiful, but impatient kind. She had never been neglected, but was not precious to her mother as Amy and Ruth were. Given that fact, would her efforts have changed her mother's attitude towards her? These thoughts made the tears stream down her face, as the truth of it became obvious.

Although there was no rivalry between the sisters, their mother made a play of inventing competitions where Ruth and Amy came out winners and Zillah was accused of not trying, or being too lazy to exert herself in races where, because she was the eldest was given a handicap. 'Zillah, you have to start on my second whistle because you're bigger.' Their mother had made these rules, and the girls stuck to them for fear of a bad tempered reaction from her. They played in the park near home and Zilllah had made the mistake of winning one of the races, even though she had started yards behind her sisters. This had enraged her mother.

'Typical Zillah. Always the one to fight her way to the front. Always thinking only of herself. Always me, me, me, me, me.' Her mother had advanced towards her, then Ruth and Amy, laughing desperately, caught up with their mother and said, 'Let's all beat her to the café.' Miraculously, this had worked and Zillah never ever won another race.

Her father had always loved her. He tried to protect her when he was home, and she had seen warning looks that passed between her parents, but father wasn't at home during the day. She had learnt too, not to complain to her father because it distressed him and caused trouble between them, so she suffered most cruelties in silence.

Zillah felt unhappy enough to write to Carl. Her husband had always been aware of the sadness in Zillah's life because of the hurts inflicted by her mother. He had sympathised with her through some of the worst times. Now he was not there to sooth the pain as she remembered her unsuccessful attempts to please.

The three girls had been on an outing to the woods with school friends. While Amy and Ruth played, Zillah had picked the largest, bluest, bunch of bluebells, which she nursed carefully all the way home. She stood quietly in the doorway waiting for her mother to notice, and present them to her, but she was busy fussing over Amy and Ruth, drying their wet feet. Zillah put the bluebells on the table and went to her room to dry her own feet.

The flowers had gone from the table when she returned, but they were not in a vase, and no mention was made of them. The next time she saw the bluebells was when she was told to empty the bin. There they were, thrust deep into the dustbin, heads down; all those glorious blooms wasted; her present discarded. She did not question this act of violence to the flowers, but felt the rejection as a deep hurt.

Zillah wanted Carl's arms around her and his ability to make her feel loved. But she threw aside the pen and paper. She couldn't write to Carl. How could he sympathise when it was she who had caused them to part by coming to Cornwall? Perhaps she was like her mother, and wanted to make her husband suffer. The thought appalled her, but with difficulty, she thrust the idea from her. 'I have not inherited my mother's disaffection with this lovely place. I am like grandma Karenza. I am the natural inheritor of Gorsemoor Cottage.'

Having created a state of agitation in her soul, she got out of bed, went downstairs, and turned on her computer. She would start editing the novel that had arrived by email from her office, and work on it until the unhappy memories were erased. She knew she had succeeded, when some hours later, she caught the first light of dawn, creep over the window sill. Zillah had involved herself so completely in the storyline of the novel and its structure that she hardly remembered she was in Cornwall.

It was wonderful to look about her and feel completely at home, and somehow to be close to those people who had occupied Gorsemoor Cottage, Annie and Henry; Loveday, Nicholas and Ned; Karenza and Jack, and lastly, her mother Mary, who seemed to be the only discontented inhabitant. Now there was just herself. She would love to say Zillah and Carl, but it was not to be. However, in spite of the strange fact of Mary's discontent, and Carl's continued absence, her unhappy mood had gone.

Zillah determined she would write to Carl. Not a letter requiring anything of him; a friendly letter to tell him of her progress. Not to say she missed him, but about the freshness of the morning, the smell of the honey-suckle, the brilliance of the yellow gorse, the colourful heather, and now, opening the door to the perfumed air, she could see boats on the sea, coming out of St Ives to fish for mackerel.

'I love it here Carl,' she said aloud, as she walked through the courtyard and across the field to the gate of Dove Farm, where cows were gathered for the morning milking. They regarded her with serious eyes. 'I wish he was here,' she told the cows. 'I hope my darling husband misses me and comes home.' The cows continued to stare. Then a bird flew up out of the hedgerow and winged its way over the field towards the sea. 'Tell Carl I love him,' she shouted, and thought the bird would take her message.

'Are you weaving magic?' said a familiar voice. 'Are you sending words of love by the flight of a bird?' It was Beatrice emerging from behind the hedge, driving the cows to the milking sheds.

'It's your fault, you little witch,' laughed Zillah, 'You said anything could happen if I wanted it badly enough, and if it doesn't work, I shall blame you.'

'All right. I accept. But I think it will work. I'll give it my blessing if you come and help get the cows in. They are being awkward this morning. I'll show you how to milk them by hand too, shall I, before I hoist them up to those greedy milking machines?'

'These cows are probably the descendants of my great grandmother's animals, don't you think?'

'More than likely. Now get a move on. I've got my painting, my real work, to do when I've tweaked my way through this lot.'

The women felt exhilarated by the fine morning, and the promise of the day to come.

'How would you like to sit for your portrait?' Beatrice asked enthusiastically. Without waiting for an answer she invited Zillah to breakfast, in order that she wouldn't disappear and begin working on her computer, and forget about the portrait.

Beatrice was surprised by Zillah's natural ability to milk the cows.

'I believe you've done this before,' she said.

'I expect I'm a reincarnation of Annie, Loveday and Karenza, all in one,' Zillah quipped, and then half believed her joke. To her surprise, Beatrice took the remark seriously.

'I've often thought that I've lived before. You know, sometimes things happen, and you think you have a memory of it, as though it's not new. It's a sort of residual memory. A past event. It's why I believe in the ghost sitting in our window.'

'But I saw her too,' Zillah said. 'I also saw Lawrence and Frieda swimming in the nude in the cove. I think time was playing its tricks.'

'We are definitely two of a kind. The same kind of magical events happen to us. Come on, before our thoughts turn the cows' milk sour.'

Zillah enjoyed the quietness of the studio, and the stillness in sitting. The skylights allowed great squares of sunlight to light up the floor. She focussed her eyes on a nail sticking out of the wall. She realised that Beatrice didn't actually see her as a person, only as an object to be understood and recreated. She hadn't realised the intensity of the artist at work and that she, the sitter, could be almost anonymous. She could pose for a nude picture, without embarrassment. Zillah was surprised by how she too, could disappear within her own thoughts; it was a very meditative and withdrawing experience.

Zillah had not made a sequential reading of the diaries. If a page fell open, she read it. When she searched under the bed for one of the diaries, she picked up the one that came to hand. It could be Loveday's or Karenza's. She wanted to be surprised each time.

However, having read previously about Karenza meeting Jack Pender, the fisherman, on the harbour, and their walking out together, she wondered when and where they got married. She leafed through the pages, trying not to stop at interesting snippets until she came upon what she was looking for. Tucked into the diary was a wedding photograph, taken outside Aunty Millie's, the middle cottage on the harbour beach. Karenza and Jack smiled to camera surrounded by the wedding party.

Diary. Karenza. Age 16. 1918
Jack and I were married at the Parish church, in St Ives. He is to join the merchant Navy. Mother agreed to our marriage because she had such a short time with my real father, Nicholas Godolphin. She didn't want the war to part us and Jack said he would divide his time between work on the farm, and fishing, when he comes home. It will be such a help since my step dad, Ned Berryman, was kicked by a horse and is very lame and hardly capable of the hard work on the farm. I felt so sorry for him, sitting on the end of the pier in his wheel chair. He tried to be happy for my sake, but he hated his disability.
All the fishermen's lodges were decorated with flags, and everyone seemed to be on the harbour waiting for us. It was a lovely day, thank goodness, because we walked from church along the Wharf, round the harbour and along the quay. Jack had decorated the boat and it rested on the sand gleaming with new paint and fresh from scrubbing. I made sure of it being clean

*because my white bride's dress is needed for a cousin in
Newlyn. She is getting married in a few weeks time. We
bought the dress between us from a lovely bride's shop
in Truro.*

*We posed at the end of the pier for the photographers.
There were so many relatives and friends that we had
difficulty fitting everybody in. The only person missing
was grandma Annie, who had died of influenza the
previous year. Afterwards everybody watched and
laughed as Jack lifted me over his shoulder and walked
down the steep steps to the beach. I couldn't manage in
my soft shoes and with my skirt bunching around me.
He carried me over to the boat, and we had more pictures
taken, then he and I boarded and everybody was
involved in pushing the boat out as the tide crept in.*

Zillah was so engrossed in reading the account of
Karenza and Jack's wedding that she jumped at the
sound of someone hammering on the kitchen door. She
leapt off the bed and flew down the stairs, carrying the
photograph and diary with her.

'Oh, you're into your other world. I'd better leave
you in peace to uncover all those secret lives. Who is it
this time, grandma Karenza or great grandmother
Loveday?' Beatrice said, already backing away from the
door, to leave Zillah to her reading.

'It's grandma Karenza and Jack's marriage. I can't
leave it. You'll have to come in and read it with me. It's
so fascinating, and amazing.'

Zillah left Beatrice sitting at the kitchen table looking
at the sepia photograph of her grandparents while she

put coffee in the coffee pot. Her cheeks were flushed with the excitement of reading about two people who had loved her.

'I never knew grandpa Jack, but he sounds so lovely. And I've just read about the fate of great grandma Loveday's second husband, Ned Berryman. Poor man. Here, read this first page while I pour the coffee, and we'll finish reading the next page together.'

Zillah and Beatrice poured over the pages in companionable silence.

As Zillah read the words she could imagine the whole lovely wedding. It must have been such a charming and simple affair. It endeared her even more to Loveday and Karenza and their lives in Cornwall. She couldn't understand her own mother's rejection of this wonderful history and the furious desire to rid herself of the farm and cottage, and the area where she was born and grew up. Mary wanted her life to begin from when she left home. She never looked backwards; never talked to her children of her childhood, her parents, her school, or the farm.

Beatrice had been harangued with Zillah's constant worrying about her mother's attitude towards her. And why had Mary been so distant with her own parents, Karenza and Jack, and her home in Zennor?

'You see what lovely people my grandparents were,' Zillah said. 'I don't understand.'

'Well, perhaps there's no explanation,' Beatrice said, patiently. 'Some people don't have an association with their past. And perhaps we can't love everybody equally. Doesn't mean there's anything wrong exactly. That's just how we are.'

'But it's so alienating; though come to think of it,' Zillah said, thoughtfully. 'I think of this place as home, not my parents' house. I loved grandma Karenza more than my mother. I can say it quite openly now, without feeling guilty.'

'There you are then,' Beatrice said, 'You are imagining a mystery when there is none. Forget it. Get on with the present, and leave the past to look after itself.'

'You're right. I worry too much.'

'Come on. I need to do another sketch of you. Leave everything and come over to the studio. You need a good blow of fresh air.'

10

It was Loveday who put an end to the festivities of Karenza and Jack's wedding, and sent them off to Gorsemoor farm, 'As long as you can be trusted to milk the cows in the morning,' she said. She and Ned had decreased the herd again after Ned's accident. They were staying at Millie's cottage on the harbour beach, so the newly weds, who weren't having a honeymoon, because of Jack's call-up, could have time on their own.

Jack had learnt to drive because his father and uncle wanted to get their catch off to the Newlyn fish market as soon as possible for auction. The van was scrubbed and cleaned and decorated. It was parked on the pier and the couple drove off to the clutter of old boots and anything that would make a row on the large granite slabs. Amid much cat calling and shouting, they waved goodbye and drove off into the sunset.

'I thought we'd never get away,' he said, his arm around his new wife, and the other on the steering wheel. When they got to Trevalagan Hill and were about to drop down the road to Gorsemoor Farm, Karenza made Jack use both hands to drive, to negotiate the twists and turns of the road.

'I don't want us both killed on our wedding day, or me to be a widow, or you a widower Jack Pender, so watch the road.' Jack did as he was told and spent the next fifteen minutes telling Karenza how he was looking forward to undressing her.

'It's a skilled job,' she told him with a laugh, 'and I don't think you've had enough practice. Well, I hope you haven't, Jack Pender.'

When the moment arrived, and they were up in their bedroom, they were too impatient to wait for Jack's clumsy hands to undo delicate buttons, and untie satin ribbons, and lace trimmings and hooks and eyes.

'We've got enough to learn tonight Jack. Maybe you can dress me in the morning.'

'All right,' Jack agreed, 'but I want to watch you undress. I've been looking forward to seeing you take off your clothes, and be naked.'

They had explored each other's bodies but had obeyed the rules, which forbid them to make love until they were married. It had sometimes caused much unhappiness and frustration. Now they were free of restraints, but still they took their time, caressing and holding each other.

The soft light of the lamp threw a romantic aura around their naked bodies. They stood, close and touching, in front of the cheval mirror, admiring themselves, taking no heed of various religions which declared the naked body sinful and its display an effrontery to God and mankind. Then Jack could wait no longer and picking Karenza up he carried her to the bed.

They woke at dawn and turned to one another with delight. They made love in a frenzy of excitement, and fell into an exhausted sleep. They were woken by the cows in the adjoining field complaining, waiting to be relieved of their milk-laden udders. They scrambled out of bed and ushered the cows into the milking shed. Times had changed for the farmer in terms of his work-load. There was no butter or cheese making. Milk was put into great milk churns and collected by lorry. It was sold to large commercial dairies, which distributed milk in bottles and made butter and cheese in factory dairies and sold to shops.

Loveday and Ned returned to the farm and found the lovers still enthralled with one another. Loveday was glad of their happiness, remembering how little of life she had enjoyed with her first husband Nicholas. She hoped they would not be caught up in the war that was raging in Europe. Jack's job in fishing was essential work, and for a couple of years he had been safe, but that had changed and he was required to report for duty.

Jack was assigned to the Merchant Navy, to escort convoys of supply ships of food and necessary items, around the shores of Britain. He confessed to Karenza in letters that he enjoyed the job, the comradeship of the company on board, and the feeling that he was doing essential work in making sure that Britain was supplied with food.

Karenza had to be cautious in what she wrote. She would like to have told Jack that submarines were offshore, but she didn't dare risk a letter being destroyed for containing information that might be useful to the enemy. People living by the coast had seen the black floating monsters come to the surface, the conning tower had opened and German sailors had appeared briefly, breathing in the fresh air, and surveying the skies for aircraft. They quickly returned to their confined quarters. The submarine then dived and disappeared into the dark sea.

Some farmers took to patrolling the coast path with their shot guns, hoping to take pot shots at any German sailors daring to surface in their waters and pose on the sub's conning tower. And though there were various exaggerated reports of shots being fired, there was no evidence to back this bravado. 'I was just too far away, but they saw me alright, and quickly dived. They got a fright, I can tell you.'

She sent Jack the local paper which told of a musician living up by Bosigran who was fined twenty shillings for showing a light in his window. 'We thought he might be signalling to the enemy. We keep guard on each other. We're like spies. People don't even trust their neighbours. Things have changed,' Karenza told him.

In a farming and fishing community the basic essentials of food were not in short supply. Only luxuries were hard to come by, but then, it had always been that way, so people were not deprived of anything. There were always supply ships with their convoys steaming away on the far horizon, and every now-and-again, one of the boats fell victim to the dark, marauding shadows under the sea. In the distance black plumed smoke could be seen, and sometimes a vessel would be on fire.

Karenza knew that Jack was somewhere up around the waters of Scotland and its many islands, so he was not likely to be a victim of the stricken convoy or supply ships off Cornwall.

Karenza didn't mention the unfortunate fate of some of the merchant ships in her letters to Jack. It would be inappropriate to boast of the treasures that came their way on the tide, while he risked his life trying to prevent such things happening. In any case, it wouldn't do to warn the authorities of such activities.

Leave didn't come around often, but Jack told Karenza he would be having shore leave in Plymouth. Would she meet him there? They could stay somewhere cheap, but they would be together, even for a short time. Some of the men weren't so lucky if their wives were a long distance away.

Plymouth was a town, bigger than Penzance or Truro. It would be exciting to be with Jack in a big town.But what would she wear? She must be smartly dressed for town. Karenza traded eggs, butter and cheese, which Loveday made for their own use, to people with cars, who often called at farmhouses for such goods and were hapy to pay the price. With the money Karenza bought herself a new costume and a hat. However, before the trip could be made, tragedy struck.

Loveday wished Karenza a happy weekend with her husband and sent her off to catch the train from Penzance. She decided to go for a walk in the fields to cheer herself up. She had been feeling unwell over the last few months, but farm people didn't bother with doctors for themselves, or vets for their animals, unless the situation was dire. In this instance it proved to be so. Loveday collapsed in a field while picking mushrooms. She was found by a stranger walking across country who, not knowing where she lived, flagged down a passing motorist, who phoned for an ambulance from a call box in Zennor village.

Loveday recovered consciousness in hospital and gave her name. She demanded to be sent home, but wasn't allowed, since there was no one there to look after her. She was worried about how Ned would cope, left on his own in a wheelchair. In her desperation she explained that her daughter would be waiting on the platform at Penzance station to catch the train to Plymouth. When Karenza heard the announcement over the tannoy to go to the station master's office, she feared the worst.

'Is my husband all right?' she asked anxiously.

'I'm sorry, I don't know madam. It's your mother. She's at Penzance hospital.'

Karenza was relieved, frightened and disappointed. Jack was alive and wanted her; mother was ill and needed her. She was in a dilemma. If she didn't meet Jack, it might be the last time she would see him alive, or dead. If a ship was torpedoed, seamen more often drowned than were saved. On the other hand, her mother was ill. If she ignored this call from her mother, and she died, she would never forgive herself, and it would ruin any enjoyment she had with Jack. Sadly, she knew she wouldn't be going to Plymouth. From the

225

station master's office window, she could see her train pulling out of the station, going all that way without her. Her heart ached for Jack, who would be waiting at Plymouth station, and hear the announcement over the tannoy, as she had done, to go to the station master's office and learn that his wife wouldn't be coming.

By the time Karenza arrived at the hospital, her mother had slipped into unconsciousness and because of this wouldn't be allowed home. They would keep her in overnight and do some tests. Karenza sat at the bedside and wept. Because of the war, there was much relaxation in the hospitals, people visited at any hour. Karenza sat in the chair all night. Her mother woke briefly and they held hands and smiled.

'Send a message to your uncle to look after your father, and the animals,' Loveday instructed.

'I've done that. The station master let me use his phone to ring Mr Paynter. He said since he's bought most of our herd anyway, our last few might as well join them. He took dad to St Ives to stay with aunt Millie. He'll be able to chat with the fishermen.'

Loveday relaxed. 'Thank you Karenza. That's made me feel better.'

'I'll tell you something funny Mum. Mr Paynter said it was the first telephone call he's had since it was installed two weeks ago. He said he couldn't think where the sound of the bell was coming from. It took him ages to realise it was the phone.'

Loveday smiled. 'Well, I think it's proved its worth. I'm sorry I've upset your plans, but what would I have done without you?'

Mother and daughter looked fondly at one another. They had shared so much together, had battled through difficult times, had increased and decreased their herd as circumstances dictated, had sold off most of their farmland, but still they held on to their family home and were happy.

'There's still a day and a night left of Jack's leave. I shall be all right. Go to Plymouth to meet Jack. I'll still be here when you get back. Such a fuss over nothing.' Loveday said.

Reassured by her mother's words, Karenza caught the first train out of Penzance, and slept throughout the journey to Plymouth. Jack met her at the station. They flew into each other's arms and cried. They spent a few precious hours in lodgings in the Barbican. The landlady thought the sailor had brought home a prostitute, because she found them creeping up the stairs in the afternoon, when they were only allowed into the house after six o'clock. She stood at the foot of the stairs and shouted after them.

'I will not have women of the streets soiling my sheets. Out you go!'

'This is my wife,' Jack said in anger. Karenza burst into tears.

'Where was she last night? You were on your own then,' she accused.

'I'm on leave for two days and two nights, but my wife couldn't come last night because her mother was taken into hospital.'

Karenza sank down on the stairs in a pitiful state, and it was her evident distress that made the landlady change her mind and believe that the young couple were telling the truth.

'Don't cry. Off you go upstairs, and I'll bring you a cup of tea.'

The room was surprisingly bright and clean, with white rugs either side of a brass bedstead which was covered in a gold coloured satin eiderdown, and matching gold curtains. The bedside light had a gold shade. The walls were painted a honey yellow. In the late afternoon sun the room took on a magic element of its own and cast a golden glow around them. They stayed in their room making love, until hunger drove them out in the evening to find something to eat.

Returning to the hospital a day later Karenza discovered that after she left Loveday had fallen into a deep coma. She had not come round and her mother had died in her sleep. It was simply heart failure. She was desperately unhappy and feeling ill herself. She walked into Zennor to telegraph Jack, but his ship had already left for a secret, unknown, destination.

Ned Berryman was distraught with grief. His disability, which prevented him from working on the farm, made him useless. He shunned going back to the farm and remained living on the harbour beach with Millie, but he hated having to rely on her. He was a very independent and proud man and since his accident felt himself a burden to everyone. He could see no future now that Loveday had died, and he was worthless to Karenza. 'Please dad, do come home,' she pleaded. 'I need you here.'

A few days after burying Loveday, Ned asked Jack's father to take him out in the boat. 'I'll be no trouble boy. You won't have to look after me. Just get me aboard and leave me to watch the sea. That's what I want above everything. I'm closer to my Loveday out there. She'll see me from where she is in heaven, and I know she's waiting for me.'

'Forecast's not good,' the crew told Ned. 'Likely to be a storm brewing. Why not leave it till a better day, and good weather?'

The fishermen mending their nets on the quay warned Ned in their kindly way of the black clouds moving up slowly from the west. 'Don't look too good,' they said. 'We wouldn't go out in such a threatening sky unless we had to.' Ned assured them he was not bothered by sun, sea, wind, rain or weather. 'Nothing can touch me now,' he said.

They trundled his wheelchair awkwardly over the great granite blocks on the pier. Ned was carried down the steep steps to the boat. The wheelchair was tightly roped on board and Ned safely secured. The crew of three worked cheerfully round him. He was no problem. They dropped their nets in their usual fashion. They drank the whisky Ned had brought on board with him and toasted Karenza and Jack and just about everybody whose names came to mind.

The little crew worked and sang in great good humour, encouraging Ned's excess drinking, but remaining sober themselves. They ignored the stiffening breeze. Ned was drunk and happy and oblivious of any threatening danger. When they were about to return to port, the wind howled, the sky blackened with cloud and daylight was all but extinguished. The sea rocked the boat and threw it among the mountainous waves. The rain poured in a deluge.

There was no shelter for the man in the wheelchair. The crew huddled in their oilskins, taking turns in the tiny cabin to steer the boat and escape the lashing of the storm. Above the howling of the wind, the crew turned to hear the howling of Ned Berryman, his face stricken and ghastly. He had loosened the ropes and hurled himself from his wheelchair as the boat listed seawards. The sea took him without a struggle. His body was never found.

In St Ives they discussed the accident. The men acknowledged it was foolish to take an invalid out in a boat. They accepted the criticism, but argued it was Ned's wish to take the trip, carefully not revealing it was also his wish to take his own life. This they kept to themselves and suffered the harsh condemnation of the fisherfolk for Ned's sake. It was considered a wilful and sinful act to take one's life and they wished to preserve his character.

In the next month, Karenza discovered she was pregnant. With no help on the farm, Karenza, pregnant, was in a difficult situation. She was coping with the unexpected deaths of both parents, and the absence of Jack, but providence brought her relief in the shape of a man from the Ministry of Food, Mr Hawk. He was a very efficient and officious young man. He walked over the fields with her, mapping out the terrain, and told her she should be making more use of the land, 'With a war on,' he said, 'we need to provide food for the towns. If we're self-sufficient, we won't need to import, and put our boys in the Merchant Navy at risk.' Karenza could only heartily agree with him.

'More potatoes mean we eat less bread. I will provide you with a couple of girls from the Women's Land Army. They've all had their month's training at a farming institute. You can grow potatoes, carrots, sprouts and other vegetables. They will plant and work the land, and help you look after the cows. We'll need to restrict the cows grazing area, but grass is good here, and I see no problems arising.'

'What about accommodation?' queried Karenza.

'We've taken over premises in the Wesley chapel in St Ives, which will be converted to provide sleeping and eating for a large number of women. They can cycle in, or will be dropped off by lorry, which will be taking the women to other farms in the area. We will provide them with a packed lunch to eat in the fields, or in a barn under cover if it's raining. No need to cosset these young women. They are here to work.'

Karenza couldn't help disliking this puffed up young man who found himself in a situation of authority and intended making the most of it. She doubted he'd ever had such power and his final salute and rallying cry, 'We must dig and plant,' made her look at him and suspect he'd never dug a spade in the earth in his lifetime.

Within weeks several fields had been tilled and the land army girls arrived to plant potatoes. Karenza was allotted three women, who never ceased to startle her by arriving each day whistling cheerfully along the lane, having been dropped off by lorry. She admired their working overalls, which consisted of brown dungarees, with matching jacket and wished she had specially designed garments for work, instead of wearing old clothes. She determined to modernise and buy some trousers, which were so serviceable for work on a farm.

For walking out, and parading, the land girls were issued with fawn shirts, with a tie, a green v-necked pullover, brown corduroy breeches, thick khaki knee-length woollen socks and heavy brown shoes. The cowboy style hat was worn with panache and pride. They brought with them their boldness, their different way of life, their tales about their particular part of the country, and a liveliness and fun that seemed to be missing in Karenza's rather isolated life.

Karenza invited her new friends in each morning for a cup of tea before they started work in the fields, with milk drawn fresh from the cows. It was a good start to the day for all of them. They sat around the kitchen table, and laughed with the sheer enjoyment of being alive.

'Better not tell our supervisor about the tea, Karenza, or we'll be in trouble from the hawk for shirking our work,' Kitty, from a Midlands town warned her.

'And it'll be my fault,' Sasha interrupted. 'I'm supposed to be the ring-leader for any trouble the girls get into, because I'm prone to sleep-walking, and was led back to the hostel in my nightgown, having tried to sneak in the back door of the cinema. Honestly who, in their right mind, would go running round the town dressed only in a nightshirt?'

'It's your right mind that's in question,' laughed Alice.

Karenza enjoyed lunch times too when she invited the girls to sit at the table and often provided pasties and tea in exchange for one of their corned beef or fish paste and cucumber sandwiches. But all of them were alert for the sudden arrival of the hawk supervisor. It didn't do to let him think they were on friendly terms, and house guests, or he would suspect them of ganging up and deceiving him in some ingenious way.

Karenza's baby was born in Penzance maternity unit and, while she was away, Kitty, Sasha and Alice were detailed to take over her jobs with the cows and chickens and general farm duties. The girls were delighted to be living in the cottage. 'On no account,' the hawk warned them, 'does your job include nursery duties. Household chores and baby minding are not your responsibility.' Nevertheless on Karenza's return home with her baby they made a great welcome-home tea party.

The company of the women was one of the delights of Karenza's life at the moment. There were plenty of hands to help with the fractious new baby, in spite of the dire warnings of the hawk. Their light hearted manner, and the capable way they tackled their tasks, and relieved Karenza of the heavy field work, was a great help in the smooth running of the farm. Her letters to Jack were full of the lives of Kitty, who had suffered badly from dermatitis in a munitions factory, and been transferred to farming. Of Sasha, the daughter of a landowner and leader of the hunt, in Derbyshire, who had never got her hands dirty in the acres surrounding their country estate. And Alice, a girl from the east end of London, whose father was a Beefeater in the Tower of London, and whose family actually lived in a house within the walls of the tower.

'They seem to have led such exciting lives, and they're only the same age as me,' she told Jack, 'and you are sailing the ocean, and I am living in the place I was born. Perhaps after the war we will travel somewhere together – though I can't think of anywhere I'd like to go. Anyway, I've got Mary to look after. She's getting quite big. She's not a smiley, or very cuddly baby, and hates you to hold her tight. She'd rather be kicking away on her own on a blanket on the floor.'

In the early days, the supervisor would drive out to the farm in his lorry and observe the girls at work. Mr Hawk would question Karenza and tick off items on a clipboard, so she felt very conscious of how she answered his questions, and whether her responses were important in awarding good, or bad, marks against the girls.

'Are you quite satisfied with their work?'

'Certainly.'

'Do you feel they are pulling their weight?'

'Oh, yes!'

'Any one, or all of them can be replaced if you are not happy with them. And if you have any complaints, they can be dealt with.'

'None at all.' Karenza would invariably reply.

She got the feeling that he would like to have some complaints and show his authority in dealing with them, so she pretended to an employer type relationship with the girls on his visits. She objected to his keenness to establish his power over their lives and behaviour and resented his interference, but knew she was also under scrutiny and dare not question his right to inspect the land and the work.

'Why are you growing daffodils?' he asked.

'I'm not,' she said.

'Will you walk out to that field over there, and look at the yellow plants.'

'Certainly, Mr Hawk.'

Karenza could quite easily have explained the yellow plants, but she wanted him to walk out to where the girls were working and knew that they would somehow put him at a disadvantage. It was an opportunity not to be missed. At that time, Karenza was heavily pregnant, and stumbled over the rough earth. The women, who were hoeing between the rows of potatoes, stopped and looked up.

'Careful! Mrs Pender,' called out Sasha, remembering to use her surname. 'What are you doing? Shall I hold your arm?'

'You'll fall over. You shouldn't be stumbling around these fields in your condition,' Kitty added. 'If you fell and your waters broke, it might be good for the potatoes, since we haven't had much rain, but quite dangerous for you. How would we get you back to the house, Mrs Pender?'

'You don't want to give birth among the potatoes, do you?' Alice said, as they came to a stop beside her. She leaned on her hoe, and smiled sweetly at Mr Hawk. Karenza hoped they wouldn't overdo the sarcasm and criticism, or it would upset the apple cart.

The girls achieved what they had been aiming for. Their rather stuffy, critical supervisor, began to feel very uncomfortable and embarrassed. His face was bright red, and he looked ashamed and subdued. His conscience was telling him he should have considered the woman's condition. He hadn't even taken her arm and helped her. He did not like being at such a disadvantage.

'I've been asked to come and look at some yellow plants,' Karenza explained.

'Oh, the daffodils,' said Alice innocently.

'There's even more in that patch further over. You can't see them from the farm,' Sasha told him, anxious to assure him of their co-operation.

Mr Hawk perked up. The land girls had informed him quite accurately that there were daffodils growing among the potato plants. He had definitely spotted an illegality. The evidence was irrefutable.

'Yes. They are daffodils, just as I thought. Did you realise you were growing daffodils, Mrs Pender?' he questioned triumphantly.

'I know this is where I planted daffs. We used to send them to Covent Garden.'

The man made a great pompous play of marking something on his clipboard. He drew in a breath and with a great shaking of his head he explained.

'It is not permitted to plant flowers. They are a luxury item. It is certainly against the rules to send flowers on the train to Covent Garden. I'm afraid this will have to be reported.'

The girls looked suitably crestfallen and chastened.

'As you see. We've planted potatoes, but those old daffs will come up, whether we want them to, or not. They'll probably be around for years, even if we dig up the bulbs after the flowering. Looks rather pretty though, I must say.' Karenza laughed; much to the man's annoyance. 'Oh no, you couldn't send such a few blooms to a place like London, now could you, Mr Hawk?'

The three girls smiled their sweet, innocent smiles, looked with sympathy at Mr Hawk's discomfiture, and bent to their hoeing.

'Heed the warning,' Mr Hawk said, and made off in stumbling haste, across the field. Just as he thought he'd made it on his two feet over the rough terrain, he fell. It was a wonderful sight. 'Goodbye, Mr Hawk!' the four of them called, suppressing their giggles, but letting him know they had witnessed his humiliation.

The bumper harvest that year on all the Zennor farms was due to a warm, delightful spring, with just the right amount of rain early on and a blistering heat later, so the hay was cut early.

The land girls moved from farm to farm following the threshing machines but Gorsemoor and Dove farms were the first to be cut. Karenza busied herself baking pasties, heavy cake and scones. She boiled eggs, picked tomatoes, cut lettuce from the vegetable plot, made fresh bread and provided tea and cider for the workers. She put Mary in a blanket in the wheelbarrow, along with the provisions, and set off across the fields with their lunch.

She was a welcome sight. As she approached a whistle was blown, the threshing machine was silenced, people jumped down from the hay carts, bags of oats were thrown over the horses heads and from all corners of the field peopled gathered under the trees or in the shelter of the hedges and eagerly devoured their lunch.

Eagle's Nest was the traditional venue for celebrating harvest and Mr and Mrs Arnold Forster, the present owners, were aware of their social duties and threw the expected party, providing a lantern lit garden and gramophone and records for dancing on the lawn in the evening.

But the idyllic summers ended, and so did the war. The girls who made such a joyful sight in the countryside gradually drifted off home as their fields of hay, corn, potatoes and broccoli were gathered in and their labour was replaced on the farms by returning soldiers to their farming jobs in their villages.

Mary was nearly two by the time of her father's late return from sea. Jack had been assigned to minesweepers, which were clearing the oceans for peacetime shipping. Mary very much resented this man's big frame sitting at their table, and sharing her mother's bed. She also rejected her mother, who spent much time talking and laughing with this male person. It was some time before they built up the relationship of a threesome. But Mary was a very independent child and seemed not to need either of her parents. She had no fondness for any of the animals and was often to be found wandering the road into St Ives, for no apparent reason except that she wanted to be away from the farm.

School offered some escape, and she enjoyed being there and learning. The learning offered some reason for her to leave her parents, her class mates and her village and to become completely free of them. As she grew older this was clearly part of her ambitious plans, so she was very much the successful student.

The farm was an obstacle. She made it very clear to her parents that she had no intention of taking over, or helping out. She was busy studying, planning her escape route, wanting to be rid of Karenza and Jack, who were so close, who loved each other so much, she felt like an intruder. They felt rejected because she didn't want to be part of the love they wished to share with her. It was a strange situation.

'I've sent off applications to several colleges, so I shall be leaving home, and Cornwall. There's really nothing for me here.' Mary told her parents, when she left the senior school.

'You could continue at the school in Penzance,' Her mother said, hopefully. 'They have the same courses ...'

'No!' Mary shouted. 'I want to get away. I don't want to be buried in the country. I don't like animals. I don't like the sea. There's no job that would suit me anywhere in Cornwall.'

'If that's your wish Mary, your mother and I will support ...'

'Support? I don't need you to approve, or disapprove.

That's what I've decided.' Mary did her usual flounce out of the room to ensure she had the last word and to prevent any further discussion. Her parents knew better than to pursue the subject, or to point out that she still needed financial help, even if she regarded their support as pathetic and unnecessary. Mary paid no heed to the money necessary to launch her into the adult world; that was to be expected, and was not her concern.

Mary accepted a place at a college in Bath, to learn secretarial skills. There was no farewell party for the friends she left behind, and no promise to come home as soon as the term ended. There were no letters that said she missed home, or her parents. She was smugly satisfied with her student accommodation, and quite unaware of the hardships at Gorsemoor farm that allowed her this delightful freedom.

Jack became more involved in fishing, which left Karenza largely managing the farm. It was decided, once more, to cut down the herd and sell most of the animals and the remaining fields to their farming neighbour, at Dove Farm, who wished to expand. This would give them a nest egg, which would ensure that Mary could continue her studies, and live away from home.

Her one letter home was to send the name and address of the letting agent for her flat and to give a box number account into which her parents would pay the agent the monthly rent and living allowance.

'She's forgotten to put her own address on the letter,' Jack said. 'And wouldn't it have been better to send the money direct to her? Oh well, perhaps she'll remember the address next time she writes.'

'We can only hope,' Karenza replied doubtfully. 'I can't think what arrangements she's made for getting her money, but it's no good suggesting we send money to her, she thinks if she doesn't receive it personally, then she hasn't actually been given any money. Though how she justifies that, I can't understand.'

'And she doesn't have to say thank you. The two most difficult words in the English language for Mary to say,' Jack said bitterly. 'And she's free, which is what she always wanted.

Mary flourished surrounded by strangers. She liked the anonymity of being a student in a large town, and being known by very few people. She had no wish to make friends. When she finished her studies she launched into a successful career in Bath, becoming a secretary at Bath University. There was no wish to return home, even for a visit. The parents often discussed the 'where did we go wrong?' question, and there was no satisfactory answer. They habitually covered up their hurt. The conclusion was 'Mary is Mary, and that is that.'

11

'You've dropped your head slightly,' Beatrice said, peering round the edge of her easel and pointing her paintbrush accusingly at her subject.

The voice disturbed Zillah in her reverie, thinking of the lives lived at Gorsemoor Farm through the diaries of Loveday and Karenza. And now, here she was on the scene. It was strange that there was a repeat pattern in the way Loveday and Karenza had both become pregnant so soon after their marriages. This certainly hadn't happened to her. They had been married for some years and hadn't bothered about a family, but if Carl visited and she became pregnant, would be stay? She dismissed this thought. She couldn't trap her husband. No. Carl would have to be a willing occupant of Gorsemoor Cottage.

Zillah also compared the relationship of Karenza and her daughter Mary, and Mary and herself; except that she was not aware she had distanced herself from her mother, rather her mother had proved the one holding off her daughter.

'There must be a faulty gene somewhere,' she said aloud.

Beatrice peered once more round the edge of her easel, and again pointed the paint brush at Zillah.

'You've gone into a daydream. I've seen it happen

before with models sitting for portraits. It's a fault of that profession. I get to hear some of their innermost secrets.'

'Oh. I wasn't aware I was talking out loud.'

'I'm intrigued about this faulty gene. Is it the red hair, do you think? It's such an extraordinary colour. It must have come over with the Vikings. Anyway, I've had enough for one day. I'm whacked. I think you'd better explain yourself over lunch. Come on, Caffe Pasta, in St Ives. I'll treat you. I know I've been a bit hard on you today. You should have told me.'

It was the third sitting and Zillah had got tired of the view of the nail on the wall. Her neck was stiff, her shoulders seemed to be locked into position. Beatrice had been so engrossed in her work; she hadn't given her model enough rests, but she had informed Zillah, 'After twenty minutes you should give yourself a shake and move your bones, otherwise you'll turn into a statue.'

They sat in the window overlooking the harbour and watched with amusement as unaware holidaymakers were deprived of their ice-creams and pasties by the swooping, skilful gulls, who dived over their shoulders and snatched a free lunch. It was fun if it wasn't happening to you. Sometimes a squadron of gulls attacked, swirling and beating theirs wings around people's heads until the victim was forced to throw his paper of chips to the ground in order to escape injury. The gulls hurled themselves on their plunder and demolished the chips in seconds, being quite untroubled by feet advancing towards them. People had to skirt round the gulls.

The gulls rose into the air, searching for their next

victim. It was interesting to watch the reactions of men and women. The latter took protective action, cowering into themselves, screaming. Men took offensive action, and swung their fists, and kicked out, but the gulls were seldom victims.

Over coffee Beatrice said, 'I've got to pick up some paintings from a gallery near Falmouth. I need a lot of work for my exhibition at Space Gallery in Penzance. The wall area is huge, and they are already double hung, as you know. Anyway, I haven't heard from Rosie for ages, so she can't have sold anything.'

They drove and chatted, liking one another's company. Zillah confided her worry to Beatrice 'For some reason grandma Karenza has stopped writing her diary. She seems sad. It just says, Mary has gone, and then there's loads of blank pages.'

'Nothing sinister in that. She just got fed up,' Beatrice assured her.'

They reached the town of Falmouth, enjoying the countryside and the luscious greenery of trees that flourished in the slightly milder climate of the south coast. They walked through the cobbled streets of the town, which showed glimpses of the sea through various alleyways, where a great variety of ocean craft were moored. It was the second largest natural deep harbour in the world and the Falmouth repair yard could handle large ships. Nearby, the newly opened maritime museum housed a display of boats for every purpose and occupation. The windows looked over a forest of moored boats down to Penryn and over to the small village of Flushing.

They eventually reached the gallery tucked away, and

off the main tourist route. Rosie, to whom Zillah was introduced, was a very personable woman, charming and likeable. As well as running the gallery, she wrote romantic novels, and was often to be heard reading out the juicy bits to any passing stranger or friend, who happened to drop by. She was just concluding a piece from her latest book when she spied Beatrice. The friend quietly made her escape, under cover of Rosie's rather boisterous welcome.

'Beatrice!' she yelled, dashing forward and giving her an affectionate hug and kiss. 'Lovely to see you. It's been ages. What can I do for you?'

'Well,' said Beatrice, recovering from her over zealous greeting, 'I've got this rather big exhibition looming, and if you haven't got a cheque for me I'll take my paintings, if you don't mind.' Beatrice looked around the walls of the gallery hoping to alight on one of her works.

'Ah!' Rosie exclaimed, 'There's the dilemma.'

'What does the doubtful sounding ah! mean?, and what's the dilemma?' Beatrice asked, becoming alarmed and suspicious by Rosie's hesitant approach and her attempts to remain jovial.

Zillah busied herself looking round the gallery at a variety of pots, pieces of sculpture and paintings. There were none of Beatrice's paintings on view. She tried not to listen to the conversation or concern herself with what appeared to be developing into an interesting situation.

'Well, the truth is, I got into a spot of bother and needed some money. I sold several paintings at a reduced price – yours were snapped up,' Rosie said, beaming. 'You wouldn't believe the number of people who admired your work.'

'Well, you should have asked me, Rosie,' Beatrice admonished, 'but I suppose a sale, is a sale, is a sale, even at a reduced rate. I could do with some cash myself.'

'I haven't got any cash.'

'A cheque will do, as long as it doesn't bounce.'

Zillah could hear Beatrice and Rosie laughing uproariously.

'I haven't even got a cheque. Well, I could write one out, but I'm afraid the bank wouldn't honour it. I'm skint.'

'You're what!' Beatrice said, coming dangerously close to losing her temper.

'Broke,' Rosie repeated, with a shrug of her shoulders.

'But what about the money you got for my paintings? That's my money.'

'Yes, of course it is,' Rosie said earnestly. 'But I had to pay my rent for the gallery, or get chucked out, and that wouldn't do any of us any good. Then there were other debts, and some bloke threatened to punch my face in if I didn't pay him immediately. And just look at my face, it certainly wouldn't improve it.' She burst into laughter at her own joke. 'It's been one thing after another.'

'Well, I agree it's very sad for you, but even sadder for me Rosie. I have no money and no paintings. What the bloody hell do I do now?'

'I promise I've got you on my list. You'll have the money as soon as I sell something from the gallery. There's a few other people as well, and they've been very kind and agreed to wait. They know I won't let them down.'

'How jolly for you to have such good friends,' Beatrice said sarcastically. 'But I shall be in again in a couple of weeks, and I expect to have cash for my paintings.'

'Of course, of course; hopefully, yes,' Rosie agreed.

Zillah kept a good distance away, carefully avoiding any involvement in the argument, and hoping she wouldn't have to step between Beatrice and Rosie to prevent any further threat to Rosie's face. But Rosie was still smiling and quite unembarrassed by the predicament, while Beatrice was controlling her anger.

'Right, Zillah, let's go.' Beatrice called, marching swiftly to the door.

'Oh, and by the way, congratulations on the exhibition at Space. I've received an invitation, so see you at the Private View. Nice to meet you er, er,' Rosie called as they left the gallery.

Beatrice was quietly seething as they walked hurriedly back to the car. 'I bet I never get that bloody money, and there's nothing I can do about it. Her actions don't live up to her intentions. Trouble is, you can't help feeling sorry for her. I heard she was in a financial mess, but somehow people rally round her. She's what's known as a charming rogue. Completely amoral. Somehow, you can't be angry with her for long. People absolutely love her. It's so unfair. I'm sure if I was in trouble and couldn't pay my bills, I'd be run out of town.'

They arrived back in Zennor quite late, with Beatrice despondent that she had achieved neither paintings, nor money. Zillah took her bath and she began to think about the events of the day and realise what it was like to live in Cornwall and rely on the sale of paintings and arts and crafts to make a living. The people that bought your work came in droves for a summer, and left in droves, so that the county was empty of people with buying power for half a year. Was she capable of living with that uncertainty of being able to make a living? To comfort herself, she reached under the bed for one of the diaries. It was Karenza's. She opened it at random and to her great surprise found a letter addressed to her.

My dear Zillah,
I owe you an explanation for what happened years ago. You were very curious about a man coming to the door. He gave me some money. I said one day it would be yours. My grandmother Annie, employed John Fanshaw to help on the farm. He planned to buy a sheep farm in New Zealand and asked Annie to come with him. Unfortunately, he left the country, taking Annie's money but leaving her behind. The grandson of John came to return the money. It had remained in a bank account gathering interest, until mentioned in John Fanshaw's Will. I never intended to touch it, but when my arthritis got the beter of me I used some of it to pay for my care home. Thank you for visiting me so many times darling. I didn't sell Gorsemoor Cottage, because it's your home. Use the money to repair it. Enjoy life there as we used to. We had such good fun, you and I.
Love grandma Karenza.

Zillah burst into tears. This was the woman who had loved and mothered her. Where would her self-worth be without that constant support and affirmation of herself as a valued child? A child who was unfailingly welcome in the cottage she felt was home.

The revelation of the source of the returned money, the likelihood that Karenza's father, Nicholas, would have lived, had the money not been stolen, and he forced to work as a miner. These things must have haunted Karenza. All those years later, she could obtain no comfort from farmhand John's stricken conscience.

Zillah was disturbed by this piece of news about the money. She had the diaries, and this was the other part of the 'pirate treasure' grandma had promised her. She had wondered how grandma had managed to keep herself for the last couple of years of her life. Zillah had spent the rest of the money on the farm buildings and out-houses, just as grandma had wanted. She had also left instructions with the stonemason to carve grandma Karenza's name on the granite headstone, with grandad Jack Pender. This should have been her mother's respon-sibility, but Mary had neglected to perform this duty.

'How extraordinary life can be,' Zillah exclaimed aloud. 'I must ring Amy.'

'I can't bear late telephone calls. I always think something bad has happened,' Amy said.

'Something has happened. But nothing nasty. I'll read you the letter grandma Karenza wrote to me. She wrote it on a page in her diary.'

'It's the treasure you kept going on about when you

came home from Cornwall,' Amy said, when she had listened to the reading. 'Ruth and I were quite jealous of this unknown pirate treasure.' The sisters laughed.

'You don't often get pirate's returning their stolen treasure,' Zillah said.

'Oh well. Think yourself lucky. You'd never have managed to modernise Gorsemoor Cottage without it.'

'And that reminds me. I've had all this work done and nobody's visited yet. When is dad coming?'

'Dad's still building up his courage to come on the train. Shouldn't be long now. Ruth, baby Lisa, and I will come together. It'll be lovely, us three sisters again. Can't wait. Ruth and I always wanted to go to Cornwall with you, but mum wouldn't let us. I suppose we were quite envious at times.'

'Grandma Karenza always hoped you'd come, when you were old enough to decide for yourselves, but somehow it didn't happen. Mum's influence was too strong. The only time you met grandma was at my wedding. She was so thrilled that you came and hoped it would be the first of many visits, but of course it was the first and last.'

'I know. And that was difficult too. Mum made herself ill trying to persuade us not to go to the wedding,' Amy said. 'She got it into her head that we would be persuaded to go swimming and would drown off one of the beaches in St Ives. She was terrified of water, especially the sea. That's why we never learnt to swim. Any further visits to Cornwall would have been impossible. You didn't know any of this, of course, but Dad was really firm about the wedding and insisted we go, and he would stay behind with her. It really upset dad that he couldn't be there for you, but I'm afraid mum always came first. Apparently, mum had nightmares every night when she knew we were going to the wedding.'

Zillah was sad to learn this latest piece of news, but it was consistent with her mother's obsessions and odd behaviour towards her, and the sisters' connivance in order to remain on good terms with their mother. It must have created difficulties at home. But, having learned of the promise of the family visit, Zillah couldn't let this latest news upset her.

At least Dad had offered his support and protection, when it was needed. Zillah wondered how someone as good natured, patient and kind, as her father, David, had married someone as calculating and cold as her mother. But he had truly loved Mary, of that she was sure. She leafed through Karenza's diary and found another entry hidden among blank pages.

Diary. Karenza. Age 41. 1943
Thank goodness Jack is too old for this war, but fishing is a dangerous occupation. I've got the Land Army girls again. Mary could have come home but she preferred clarical duties in the Wrens. She doesn't visit, or write, just to express her horror at the idea of coming home and to tell us she's returning to her job in Bath after the war.

With the arrival of the Land Army Girls came a group of Commandos, who were being trained in cliff climbing by local instructors and other army experts. This caused the land girls working on the farms to spend more time on the local beaches, or walking the coast path, in order to meet up with these illusive and fascinating young men. Jane and Ann were no exception. They made Gorsemoor Cottage their headquarters, from where they would survey the area and plan their campaign to entrap the commandos, who were only too willing to be lured into whatever snare was awaiting them. So, with the two sides determined to meet, they met; even though the first sight of one of these illusive male creatures was dangling from a rope, half way up, or down, a cliff face.

Karenza encouraged the girls' endeavours by letting them stay weekends at the cottage. They spent all day Saturday repairing their faces from the ravages of wind and fresh air. They painted their lips red, filed away their broken nails, luxuriated for hours in the bath and washed their tangled air in soft rainwate. In the evening they danced the Waltz, the Foxtrot and Quickstep at the Palais de Dance on Barnoon Hill in St Ives. Living at the farm on weekends the girls were free to stay out late and ride home on their bicycles. Women who stayed at the hostel had to be in at 10.30pm.

The transformation from muddy farm labourer to ladies of glamour and sophistication made Karenza laugh. They forgot their hard, skilful work on the farm, and became rather helpless, and utterly feminine. To see them in their best frocks and shoes and stockings, nobody would have thought they could milk cows, plough, hoe and weed fields, repair dry stone walls, dig potatoes, clear ditches, spread muck, build stooks in haymaking, and plant and harvest any number of crops. Added to this were stray commandos who turned up whenever they were free and worked alongside the girls to secure a date for the weekend. If some of the other girls struck lucky on Saturday night, Karenza allowed them to invite young men home to Gorsemoor farm for Sunday tea, and put on their most delicate airs and graces. Yet still, they managed the required number of working hours on the farm.

The postman arrived at Gorsemoor farm one morning with a message from Jack to report that the fishermen were picking up tins floating in the bay, and along the coastline from Land's End to St Ives, from one of the sunken merchant ships. They were also, sadly, picking up bodies, but no survivors. Karenza and the Land Army girls downed tools and did what was common among people living by the sea; they went down to the nearest cove and scavenged among the rocks and caves for bounty thrown up by the tide. They met people along the coastpath, and in the fields, laden with bright metal tins. All the labels identifying the contents had been washed away.

'I reckon it must be tinned fruit, and tinned meat. We won't know till we open one and find out,' said a neighbour, passing with his load. 'I hope it isn't fish, else I'll throw it back in the sea.'

They laboured all morning collecting tins from the beaches, pushing their wheelbarrow over the bumpy fields and storing them secretively for fear of them being discovered and taken away by customs men.

Back at the farm Karenza opened a tin with some

excitement. Inside were tinned peaches in a sweet syrup liquid, a luxury unknown in St Ives, even in peacetime. They sat at table, each with their own jug of cream and smacked their lips over such delicious fruit. They set off again in the afternoon for another consignment, discarding any tins with a dent, where sea water would have destroyed the contents. By the next day, the authorities had caught up with events and were to be seen combing the beaches to recover some of the lost cargo. The locals were absent, as though completely unaware of the treasure on their shores.

The barn at Gorsemoor farm had been shortened by at least a foot at one end, where tins were stored hidden behind bales of hay. People soon learnt to judge the contents of a tin by shaking it. If it was fairly solid, it was meat. If the inside sloshed around, it was fruit; peaches, apricots, pears or pineapple, and more rarely, fruit salad. Parties held in the town were enriched by these unlawful luxuries, and for some years best red tinned salmon and mixed fruit salad were fashionable fare at wedding receptions. Guests coming from up country questioned the provision of such delicacies, but their questions were never answered; a raised eyebrow, a wink, or a finger tapping the side of the nose were the only replies.

Mary Pender was an efficient and competent secretary. She lived for her work, and rarely had time for a social life. She lived alone, and liked it that way. She had worked for a confirmed bachelor, David Ward, for five years, and was more than a little surprised when he told her he was leaving his position as bursar of the college. He had always shown his appreciation of her commitment to her duties, although she had declined to be anything more than formally friendly. He had given up inviting her for an evening drink after work, or talking to her about her personal life. However, on being told he was leaving, Mary was intrigued to know what he would be doing in the future and he was agreeably surprised when she agreed to join him for a drink.

That morning Mary dressed in an outfit which would be suitable for the office, and for socialising afterwards. She didn't dress to please. The thought wouldn't have occurred to her. She wasn't in the least excited about meeting David, only curious to know his plans and who, if anyone, had been appointed in his place and, out of self-interest, what would be her exact position in the college?

They left the office together, much to the surprise of people they passed in the corridors. David smiled as their prolonged walk excited curiosity from offices along the way. Mary looked straight ahead, feeling irritated, acknowledging no one and wishing they'd arranged to meet outside the workplace.

'Where's Miss Frosty drawers going with Mr Heart-on-his-sleeve,' said their knowing colleagues.

'Must be something dramatic.'

'Must be something deadly serious.'

'Perhaps she's noticed him at last.'

'Never. Not that cold fish.'

'Don't know why he bothers. He should have given

up by now.'

'Wish he'd look at me like that. I'd soon notice.'

'I hope you don't mind,' David said, 'but I booked dinner in a little restaurant, where we can have a quiet chat, and not be interrupted by colleagues.'

'Oh,' said Mary, stopped in her tracks. 'I hadn't planned to eat out. You should have asked me. I don't like surprises.'

David was immediately apologetic. 'Well, as it's my last week, I thought ...'

'I like to plan ahead.' Mary gave in, not too graciously, and made it plain that it wasn't exactly a pleasant surprise, more of a nuisance really. She rarely ate out.

They sat opposite each other at a small table by the window. They ordered red wine and Mary proposed a toast to his new job, or career, or whatever plans he had made when he left the college.

'Are you moving away from Bath?' she asked.

'I'm not exactly sure of my plans. I seem to be incapable of any decisions about job prospects; whether I should sell my flat and move to Newcastle, London, Scotland or Timbuctoo,' David said wryly. 'Sadly, it's a matter of indifference to me at the moment.'

Mary was clearly shocked. She had worked for this man and known him to be decisive and able. She had admired him, she now realised. What was the matter with him? He had distorted her judgement.

'I don't believe you haven't made plans. You're not ill?' Mary said, showing the first signs of concern for him.

'In a way, yes, I am. Have been for the last couple of

years at least. I need a change.'

'Are you getting married? Have you got a girlfriend? We have always been so busy, I'm afraid I don't know anything about you.'

'No. No girlfriend. And much to my regret, Mary, I know nothing about you, but that's because you are a very private person.'

'Well, yes, I suppose so. But let's not talk about me. I want to know what this big secret is. What is this change you need, and why do you need it? And what's to become of me. Who will be my new boss?'

'I didn't want to go into all that. I don't think anyone else has been appointed in my place yet. I just wanted us to get together for a farewell dinner, and to say goodbye to you away from the impersonal nature of the office.'

'I think, now you've got me here, that you should explain yourself.' She gave a little snigger of amusement. 'Come on. Confess. I won't tell anyone.'

'Believe me Mary. It will be embarrassing for me, and for you.'

'Me! How could it be? I insist,' she said, looking at him intently, and with some impatience. What was the point of asking her out if she wasn't going to be privy to his secrets.

'Ah!' he said with relief, as the waiter placed their meal before them. 'Let's enjoy dinner first.'

Mary gave in with a sigh. 'But afterwards David, please.'

'All right. Afterwards,' he agreed.

They talked quite easily to each other on trivial

matters. It surprised them both when they began to enjoy each other's company, and to learn a little about activities and interests that they were involved in. Over coffee Mary returned to her insisting tone.

'Tell me.'

'You are not going to like it.'

'Tell me."

'You may regret having asked.'

'Regret nothing, is my motto. Tell me.'

She was quite unprepared for what was to follow.

'I love you,' he said simply.

She sat back in her chair abruptly, and stared at him, open mouthed, in disbelief. What was he talking about? Had she misheard?

'I can't ask you to say that again, even though ...'

'I love you,' David said, more deliberately.

Without waiting for any response he told her how he had loved her for about two years. In fact he hadn't wanted to fall in love; especially not with someone who never noticed him. At first he had hoped she would realise his interest in her. Now, he had given up hoping, and could only absent himself from her company.

'I can no longer sit there looking at you, and wanting you.'

'Wanting me!' she cried, with some distaste.

'It's what people feel when they are in love,' he instructed her.

There was silence between them. She was thinking he couldn't possibly be in love with her, she hadn't given him any encouragement. Why hadn't she known instinctively about this. Why hadn't she even guessed?

Why hadn't someone told her? But nobody would. She wasn't popular. She didn't invite friendship or confidences. She examined her feelings and decided she wasn't offended, only shocked.

'You must appreciate my hopeless situation. I cannot subject myself any longer to your indifference. It is beginning to depress me,' David told her.

'I do understand,' she said, matter of factly. 'It must be difficult for you, I suppose,' she said, not really understanding.

'Not difficult. Impossible.'

For once, Mary was thinking rapidly. It was going to be difficult to walk back into the office. Probably everyone knew of his unrequited love. Now they would be wondering about the outcome of their walk together. They would be waiting, those people, smirking, whispering. She wouldn't satisfy their curiosity.

'You have served your notice and will be leaving shortly?' Mary enquired.

'Yes.'

'Oh. Pity.'

'Pity?'

'We have worked together so well. I shall miss you.' Mary said. 'I don't know quite what I shall do without you. Things will never be the same. I like things to remain constant.'

She could only look at the matter from her own point of view. Her voice trailed away as she panicked at the change about to happen. She looked at him, as though seeing him for the first time, but it wasn't a look of love, more a summing up of a character, and a situation, and how to resolve it for her own good.

'I can't possibly work with you again; not after this,' she told David. 'I shall not return to the office to say goodbye. You must make some excuse for me at your farewell party. I shall not be there.'

She then put forward her proposals. She wanted the following week off and another week would serve as her notice in lieu of her holiday period.

'I don't want to see you during that fortnight, but I want to meet you again here for dinner in two weeks, and you can tell me the whole story again, so I can see if there is any truth in what you have said.'

David was surprised at such a response, and agreed to her terms gladly, with the prospect of meeting Mary for a second time, even if it was for a final goodbye. In all the time they had worked together, she had never made any demands upon him, though he thought he had clearly signalled that he was there for whatever purpose she had in mind. They each had time to weigh and consider the situation.

The two weeks travelled slowly by. As soon as they met again, David said, 'I love you, Mary. I want to be with you. I would do anything for you, as long as we could be together.'

Mary looked at him and smiled with enormous satisfaction. 'What are your plans?'

David had secured a job with London University in their annex near Finchley Road, and taken a flat in Golders Green. Over dinner he talked about the job and looked at her hopefully, but he thought he knew what to expect. It was more than likely she would reject the idea of their being together.

'I'm coming with you, David,' she told him over coffee. 'I'll get a job in London. Is the flat big enough for two?'

He was visibly shocked. 'You don't love me. You've never even given me a thought.'

'So. Shall I come?' she demanded, saying nothing about love.

'Yes. I love you enough for both of us.'

Mary was immensely pleased. She wasn't expected to return any revelations of a secret love, held in her heart. She didn't love David. Perhaps she would never love him, but it was an interesting state of affairs, and one that contented her. If someone like David loved her then she was wise enough to take advantage of the situation.

'My God, Mary. I can't believe you are actually saying you will come and live with me, in London. It's what I want more than anything in the world. I would do anything for you,' he repeated. 'What a wonderful evening this has turned out to be. It exceeds my wildest hopes and dreams.'

In the mid 1950s David and Mary were married quietly and moved to Hampstead Garden Suburb, where they had a house and garden in very pleasant surroundings. Karenza knew nothing of her daughter's marriage until she wrote to say she would be bringing her husband to meet her parents, and could they stay a weekend in

261

Cornwall at Gorsemoor Cottage.

By this time Karenza had sold the animals and fields and used the money to turn her barns and outbuildings into holiday accommodation. Jack occasionally went fishing, but mostly he took visitors line fishing out of St Ives. He still owned a share in the boat.

Karenza and Jack greeted the newly weds with pleasure, asking for no explanation of why they hadn't been informed about the wedding. This was Mary, and she took her own course. David loved the area and surrounding countryside, the sea, Jack's boat, the harbour at St Ives. He couldn't understand why Mary should want to leave, but even now, she was impatient to be away and annoyed at David's enthusiasm for the place. The weekend was enough.

After many years of contented marriage Mary discovered she was pregnant. She was horrified by this invasion of her body, and being near the menopause had not thought she could be pregnant. The discovery gave her no joy. She attended the Royal Free Hospital in Hampstead and was with difficulty and drama, delivered of twins, a boy and a girl. Mary was ill and depressed. She stayed longer in hospital than the other mothers. She refused to feed the babies. The boy was put into an incubator. She went into hysterics when the nurses offered the girl to hold.

'Look, Mrs Ward. You've got a most beautiful girl.'

Mary caught sight of red hair and turned her face away. She refused to look at the twins. In the hospital's opinion the experience and trauma of the birth made her reject them. Her negative response to the children lay in her being an older mother. David tried one more time to persuade Mary to accept the twins, and wheeled them into her private room. 'I've been thinking Mary,' he said. 'We could give the babies family names; after your mother and father perhaps ...'

Mary turned on him with ferocity. 'I don't want to talk about names. They've got my mother's hair. They're hers. I don't want them. Take them away. Take them out of this room.' Mary's voice rose higher and she became hysterical. The nurses wheeled the cots out of the ward, while David calmed her down.

David was distraught. In desperation he telephoned Karenza. She and Jack drove to London and took the babies home to Cornwall. They devoted their time to caring for the infants. Every room in the cottage was turned into a safe haven for their grand children.

Mary seemed to recover once the babies were out of her sight. She felt no desire to contact her mother to ask about her firstborn children and left these problems to David. Then suddenly, after a month, she wanted the boy to be brought home, but by then it was too late. He was named David after his father. The girl, Zillah, who had been named by grandma Karenza, could stay until she was ready for her.

Mary wasn't ready for Zillah until five years later. By then Amy and Ruth were born, in quick succession, and living quite happily at home with their parents. Only her father visited Zillah in Cornwall every few weeks, driving by car all the way from London and staying the weekend.

'Dad,' Zillah said over the phone. 'You're coming at last. I'll meet you at St Erth station so we can ride the branch line train to St Ives. You'll love it. It travels right by the coast and beaches. You can see Virginia Woolf's lighthouse out in the bay. It's much better than coming by car.'

'Good. I look forward to seeing you my darling. We'll have a good chat, and I'll answer any of the questions that seem to be bothering you. It's about time you knew some of the circumstances of your birth.'

Before Zillah could utter her surprise at the statement, 'circumstances of your birth' her father had put the phone down. What was she likely to hear? Was she adopted, or something? Surely not. It was no use ringing back. She must wait until dad came. But maybe, there was something in Karenza's diary. She would carry on working at her computer, making up for lost time, and read the diary in bed tonight. There could be other secrets to uncover.

Zillah recalled the many times she had stayed with grandma, when they took the little train from St Ives to Penzance, just because Zillah loved it. She loved going to Zennor school too, walking through the fields to the village, and meeting up with other children from farms along the way. There were times when mother needed a rest, so Zillah was told, and she was sent off to Cornwall. Grandma Karenza always said, 'Ah it's my favourite grand daughter,' as she stepped off the London train, and Zillah was made to feel special.

Amy and Ruth always stayed in London. 'Because,' grandma said, 'Your mother needs some company.' Zillah's happiest memories of childhood were of Gorsemoor Farm

Zillah had married Carl in Cornwall, with special permission to marry in Zennor church because she had been a pupil at the local school and was the grandchild of a resident, whose family had lived in the parish for a couple of generations. Mary had been ill at the time of her daughter's wedding and was unable to come. Her father was nursing her through a particularly bad time, so he too was absent.

Zillah had thought to postpone the wedding until both her parents could attend, but grandma Karenza and her father insisted it should go ahead as planned. In fact it suited Zillah to have her grand-mother as her parent. She had always been a real mother to her. She even looked like her. She had hoped dad could be there, but his wife always came first with him, much as he loved his eldest daughter. It was a delight to Zillah that her two sisters could be with her at last.

Zennor church was decorated with floral bouquets at every bench end, and the mermaid chair, with its ancient and crude wood carving was brought forward for Zillah to perch on and Carl to stand behind as the minister conducted that part of the service. Amy and Ruth were resplendent in their light blue maids-of-honour dresses. It was the first time they had visited Cornwall and met the grandmother who was not welcome in their house in London. Their mother was always too busy to receive guests, or to pay a visit home, and had constantly invented reasons why Amy and Ruth should not visit grandma Karenza in Cornwall.

Many times plans were made and the three young girls would eagerly pack their suitcases. They lay awake late into the night, with Zillah telling her sisters about grandma, the farm, the chickens, the cows, the big farm down the lane, the sea and the miles of sandy beaches. 'I sleep in a big feather bed all on my own, but there's plenty of room for three of us, and grandma makes lovely scones and jam. I can show you my school. We can see wild goats that live in the hills ...' Gradually Zillah's voice faded and the girls slept.

One time the sisters very nearly made it to Cornwall, with Dad taking a day off work to take them by taxi to Paddington station. Their mother stood waving at the gate as the taxi drove off, then suddenly she was on the ground, lying still, with her head on the stone kerb. The taxi was stopped and the driver returned to the house. Their father leapt out, followed slowly by the girls, dragging their suitcases.

'Mary,' David cried, picking up her inert form and cradling her in his arms. He rocked her to and fro, while the sisters watched, their dumb faces resigned to the knowledge that they wouldn't be travelling to Cornwall.

'Amy, get your mother's tablets. Ruth, get some

water. Zillah, get back in the taxi. You've travelled enough times to get the train to Penzance on your own.'

Their father carried their mother's limp form back into the house, while Amy and Ruth were despatched to their duties, and Zillah was whisked away in the taxi with never a wave of farewell. She would have to tell grandma all over again that her sisters couldn't come. Something happened to prevent it every time.

Only Zillah spent time at Gorsemoor Cottage during all the seasons of the year, and during the long summer holidays. Why weren't they invited again? It couldn't be helped that circumstances always cancelled their plans. What had they done to be always excluded from the visits to Cornwall? 'Your grandmother has her favourite. She won't invite you again. She blames me for being ill. You wouldn't like it there and I like you to be at home, so there it is,' their mother informed Amy and Ruth. It was a sadness that did not heal.

In the summer of 1992 Zillah and Carl's wedding took place at Porthminster beach café. It was a glorious June day, with a light breeze ruffling the edge of the sand, and the water so shallow it was the palest turquoise and blue. The terrace tables were decked with helium filled balloons with trailing ribbons. Inside a four piece band played a long list of musical requests. There was room for dancing, and for the tables piled with food. Friends and work colleagues came from London to join guests from St Ives and were visibly enchanted with the place, especially when a school of twelve dolphins delighted them with their leaping passage through the bay and out towards the lighthouse.

Zillah and Carl had hired a horse and open carriage to take them from Zennor church to St Ives. It was grandma Karenza who was their coachman. She drove them from the village along the coast road, past Tremedda Farm, and Eagle's Nest sitting high on its hill, past Wicca Farm, and then up to Trevalgan, and all the way downhill to St Ives. On the road they were passed by everyone travelling in cars so that when they arrived at Porthminster beach, the whole wedding party was there to greet them.

It was a memorable day, of course, with photos taken on the beach. Carl had carried her into the sea, and laughing, she held her dress away from the lapping water. Zillah threw her bouquet from the balcony of Porthminster café, to the cheers and laughter of those struggling on the sand to catch it. Most of the guests stayed on the beach until the sun disappeared behind the houses in the harbour. Amy and Ruth caught the night train back to London because their mother needed them. Then Zillah and Carl said goodbye to their guests and followed the setting sun back to Zennor, with grandma Karenza.

They spent the weekend at Gorsemoor Cottage. It was the last time that Zillah would see her grandmother in her home, when it was warm and comfortable with her presence, reminding her of her childhood years. On returning to London they shopped to furnish their new home at Highgate, and enjoy their life together. A few years later, grandma Karenza died and Gorsemoor Cottage was hers. It was sad, neglected and rarely visited, while Zillah took some years deciding what to do with it. Her office friends advised her to sell the place and splash out on a holiday. Carl also wanted to sell and exchange their flat for a house in London. Her father wisely said she should wait. 'The time will come when you will know the answer.' She Clung to the last advice, and waited.

12

Zillah was pleased at the prospect of welcoming her father to Gorsemoor Cottage. What would he think of the alterations she had made? It was an exciting prospect, but also tinged with apprehension. She took herself to bed early in order to feel refreshed and ready the next day to welcome her father and enjoy his company, but there were niggling thoughts preventing her from sleeping. What did he mean about revealing some of the circumstances of her birth? What could he tell her that she already knew; that she was the least favoured of the three children? Perhaps it would just be to confirm this. It would be a relief if only he would be honest and admit it. Why must he continue to protect her mother and deny such a fundamental truth?

However, she would wait to see what tomorrow would bring and curb her anger. She would leaf through Karenza's diary. She had more than made up for the neglect of her work on the book, and had emailed a couple of chapters to the office. Now she was free of her workload and began to feel good about herself. She happily turned the pages, looking for something, which might jump out at her; something of significance in her life with grandma. What eventually caught her eye shocked her to the core.

Diary. Karenza. Age 64. 1966
Poor little souls. The twins couldn't be more different.
Little David is so tiny and frail, but Zillah is blooming
and quite big. It'll be hard work looking after them
both, but I've got young Susan, from Zennor
village, to come in every day to help with the house-
work while Jack and I feed, bathe and dress the babies.
Susan wants to be a children's nurse. She has left school
and this will be her first paid job. It'll be good
experience when she applies to train for her profession.
The question is – how will Jack and I cope?

Zillah couldn't carry on reading for the tears that
pricked her eyes. She leapt out of bed, holding the diary
against her chest and pacing the floor as though in pain
and breathing in great sobbing gasps.

'Oh my God. Why didn't someone tell me? I had a
twin brother and no one told me! I don't believe this. I
really can't believe it. Why didn't Grandma tell me?
Why didn't dad tell me?' She had been grossly betrayed.
Did Amy and Ruth know and hadn't told her? No, she
thought not.

The questioning of everybody's behaviour and their
obvious collusion in keeping it a secret from Zillah and
her sisters, made her at once both sad and angry. She
had trusted grandma; thought they had a very special
relationship. Mum had deceived her; well she was not
surprised, but dad too. The hot, angry tears, continued
to flow, but she wiped her eyes and carried on reading,
unable to believe the words that floated before her,
magnified by tears that filled her eyes.

271

Diary. Karenza. 1966

Jack is so upset by the arrival of the twins, and the boy's poor condition, that it has made him ill. He can't understand our daughter's attitude, and he is angry, but I tell him Mary is unwell and can't help herself. It's safer for the little ones to be with us. I think their father understands this too and can't be on hand to look after their welfare. Yet again, we ask ourselves, 'where did we go wrong' in bringing up such a child as Mary, who has no love for us and worse, seems to have none for her babies.

Little David is looked after by Jack, who sits in the rocking chair nursing him all day. He feeds him and changes him, but we have decided he can do without baths. What is the point of exposing such a little one to cold and shivering, despite the warmth from the kitchen range.

I look after Zillah, who is a lovely little girl. She takes her bottle well and is putting on weight. The District Nurse, who comes daily, is pleased with her progress, but is not happy with the boy. She says the placenta probably wasn't enough to feed both babies and Zillah, by chance, was the one to benefit most.

Zillah screamed. 'Oh God. All that weird treatment from my mother about me being a greedy little pig, who was made to finish up her sisters' left-overs. It stems from me being a twin and depriving my brother of food. Oh how cruel. How absolutely bloody awful! My mother blamed me, and hated me. Here's the proof.'

There was now an unstoppable flow of tears and heart-rending sobs. She wanted to know what happened to her brother, and leafed through the diary. But in her distress couldn't find anything. She turned back to that fateful page that was open before her in case there was something she had missed. It was now smudged with tears and almost unreadable. She threw the diary on the end of the bed and ran downstairs. She dialled Carl's number.

Carl, picking up the phone pleaded with Zillah to stop crying.

'I can't hear what you're saying darling. Please. What is it? Calm down. If you're not in any danger, put the phone down, dry your eyes, and in five minutes exactly, I will ring you. Now do as I say.'

Reluctantly, Zillah put the phone in the cradle, and did as she was told. She was almost sick as she swilled cold water over her face. Her throat was sore from deep sobbing, and her chest felt bruised. Within five minutes she was controlling her emotions and physical reaction to the news of having a twin brother, and not knowing what had happened to him. She sat by the phone willing it to ring. Carl seemed to be the only person she could trust, and she had betrayed him. The thought of it brought tears to her eyes again, but she knew she had to contain her anger and sadness in order to tell the whole story to Carl. He was shocked and desperately sorry for her.

'If only I could be with you, this instance. I'll get the car out and drive down immediately. I should be with you in a few hours.'

'Darling, thank you so much. It's enough to hear your voice for the moment. I don't want you driving at night, but I do want you, so please come when you can in the morning. I do need your arms around me. I do love you Carl.'

'Needless to say baby. I love you. Can't tell you how much I've missed you. We need to be together, Zillah. Let's talk about it, shall we, but only when I've made you better.'

'Yes,' she said.

'Ring me during the night if you're desperate to talk again.'

'I will Carl, but Dad's coming tomorrow, and I need an explanation from him. I can't tell you how angry and let down I feel. How utterly betrayed ...'

She couldn't finish the sentence; it was too hurtful to think of such a situation.

'Tomorrow my darling, I'll be with you. Goodnight for now. Try to sleep. My best love to you. Tomorrow darling. I'll see you tomorrow.' Carl found it difficult to put the phone down, yet he couldn't say anything more. He wished he could take her in his arms and comfort her.

'Tomorrow,' Zillah vowed, 'I will be so angry with my father.' Tomorrow she didn't know how she would greet him at the station. Tomorrow couldn't come quickly enough. Tomorrow she would be unhappy again. Was it her father's intention, to tell her about her childhood? She could recall his exact words when he said he was coming to see her, 'It's about time you knew something of the circumstances of your birth.'

'Yes, about bloody time,' she told the midnight air.

She opened the window of her bedroom, wishing she could see a light in Beatrice's window at Dove Farm and take comfort from it, but all was dark, the occupants sleeping. She stood looking out to the fields, feeling the damp perfumed air rising, with just that chill that made it sweet smelling.

She remembered her father's anger, when soon after her mother's death she had asked him why her mother didn't like her. Now she knew it was true, and Karenza's diary confirmed it. She slept fitfully, dreaming about her mother; dreaming about a wasted little body of a boy; dreaming about her flying over him, a great big girl, giggling and eating, and eating, and becoming fat, while the frail little boy faded into a shadow. When she woke with a fright, she remembered another appalling episode of her childhood and the angry, spiteful, accusing expression on her mother's face.

'Come along, eat up. Can't let all that good food go to waste. I'll sit here and watch you eat, make sure every little scrap leaves that plate. You'll get even bigger. You can lick the plate if you like. Go on lick it. Lick it!' She became angrier with each word. She pushed Zillah's head down, until her nose was touching the plate and the food stuck to her cheeks and hair. Her mother rubbed her face in the mess on the plate. Then her father walked in unexpectedly.

'Mary,' he screamed, and took hold of her mother's arm, almost wrenching it from her shoulder, so forceful was the quick-tempered action. Zillah was so humiliated, so abjectly unhappy, that she let her face remain buried in the plate. Her stomach felt engorged with eating; and then she was sick; and still she did not move.

There were angry shouts and accusations from her father, and whimpering from her mother, as he pushed her out of the room. He picked Zillah up and carried her limp body into the corridor, shouting, 'Clean that up!' to her mother. The child caught a glimpse of her sisters scampering out of the way as her father carried her to the bathroom. He washed and undressed her, and next day, without seeing her mother or saying goodbye to her sisters, he took her to Paddington station and put her on the early morning train to Cornwall, with a word to the guard to keep an eye on her. Grandma Karenza met her with open arms, hugging and kissing her, and the pleasure in being loved and treasured soothed away the hurt of the previous day.

'You're home again darling,' grandma said joyfully, and Zillah couldn't understand why there were tears in her eyes, but her smile was one of happiness. She told her nothing of the treatment by her mother, the shame would be too great, but Zillah felt grandma knew. There were always these unspoken secrets between them.

As the train pulled into St Erth station Zillah tried to compose herself for meeting her father. She saw him alight at the far end and began a slow walk towards him. He spied her, and waved. She did not wave back. Her face was frozen in a hostile glare; her eyes dull, red and swollen. They stood facing each other, his face questioning and puzzled. He put out his arms and pulled her to him. She did not respond.

'My darling girl; whatever is the matter?'

He held her and kissed the top of her head; and still her arms remained firmly at her side, stiff with anger and resentment. He held her from him, searching her stricken face.

'Something's happened. Tell me.'

'Grandma's diary. I'm a twin.'

She released herself, turned and began walking swiftly away. He could only follow in horrified silence. What could he say to her? He had intended breaking it gently this weekend, and now it was a shock to her. He followed her down the platform, not knowing what his next step should be, only knowing that she despised him for the deceit they had practised on her for so many years, he and Mary and Karenza.

The journey she had intended to be such a pleasure, taking the branch line to St Ives, was suffered in silence, with neither of them looking out of the window to enjoy the views along the coastline. Everything had been spoilt. They got into the car at the station, still without speaking. Both remained wrapped in their thoughts; the journey a mere interlude in the storm that was to follow.

Zillah had imagined she would rant and rave at her father as soon as they entered the cottage; instead, she remained frozen. Her mood was one of quiet, hurt, resignation. This thing had happened, and she must accept it. She put on the kettle and made coffee, indicating he should sit at the kitchen table. This same table, used by Annie and Henry Care, Loveday, Nicholas Godolphin and Ned Berryman, Karenza, Jack and Mary Pender, had seen many problems brought together and discussed. She sat opposite her father, waiting for him to begin.

'Your mother was very ill when you were born, and remained so for a long time. Grandma Karenza and grandpa Jack brought you...' he hesitated, 'and your brother, to Cornwall.'

Zillah winced, and clenched her fists against a rising tide of anger.

'My brother, who until last night I didn't know existed. What happened to my brother?'

'He was called David. He died, three weeks after he was born.'

'Died. Where did he die?'

'Here. In this cottage.'

'Where is he buried?'

'He's buried in Zennor churchyard.'

'But there's no grave, only grandma and grandpa Pender. I would have found a headstone for David Ward if it was there, so where is it? I would have questioned my name, and the fact of him being born at the same time. What happened?'

'There's no headstone because he hadn't been christened. But he's there.'

Zillah sobbed quietly at the sadness of having had a twin brother, and of his death. She cried too for grandma and grandpa's suffering. Oh the pity of it.

Her father, once started, was anxious to get the ordeal over, and for his daughter to know, and understand some of the details of the matter, and come to terms with this rather shocking news.

'After the baby died, the whole neighbourhood rallied round. They knew grandma Karenza had the care of you both. They also knew that your mother was ill. Even so, grandma was conscious of questions being asked, and what sort of mother could refuse to look after her babies. It was a source of shame to her. It was a fearful and worrying time for us.'

'It's my mother who should have been ashamed. She didn't want either of us?' Zillah said, with a terrible anger and bitterness, that she hadn't felt before, in all the trials of her childhood under her mother's roof.

'She wanted little David to come home; just one of you at a time, you see. And I had to tell her he was dead and buried. It was truly awful.'

'Poor little David.' Zillah realised the truth. 'I was alive, but she didn't want me.'

'She went into a decline after hearing of the death of David. She wasn't capable of looking after herself, let alone a baby. I decided to leave you here with grandma.'

'But she had Amy and Ruth soon after. She looked after them.'

'I know. It was strange. That seemed to cure her, but she was over possessive with the girls and couldn't bear them to be away from home.'

'Grandma was always more of a mother to me. How long was I here?'

'Nearly five years.'

'I can remember you used to come and visit me at grandma's, and then one day you took me on a long

279

train journey to a house I didn't know, and into a room. You said, 'This is your mother, and these are your two sisters.' I think I just stared at them, and they stared back. I wanted to go home to Cornwall, but I didn't want to hurt your feelings because you told me it was a very special treat.'

'Yes. That must have been an ordeal for you.'

'We three sisters loved each other straight away. My mother looked at me in a fierce way, but I got used to her because you said she was my mother. She didn't cuddle me and love me like grandma did.'

'It was my fault for bringing you home. I couldn't bear that you should grow up without knowing your mother and sisters, and she wouldn't come here to visit because it's where the baby died. She didn't go to her father's funeral either.'

'Or her mother's. I was the only one of the family there. But the whole of Zennor and people from miles around came. She was truly loved; unlike my mother.'

Zillah was struggling with her emotions, her anger, her hatred, her hurt and feeling of being betrayed and deceived. She felt she would explode with all this anguish. It was torture. There was the distress too of dealing with the sorrow for the death of her little brother.

'God. No wonder she didn't really want me, when she thought I killed her other baby. That's why she called me a greedy little pig, and pushed my nose in the trough. That's why she hated me.'

'No, Zillah, she didn't hate you,' he said gently.

'Yes! Yes! Yes!' she shouted at the top of her voice, clenching her fists and rising to her feet. 'She hated me.

280

You had to protect me from her. There were lots of things she said that you never heard. Ask Amy and Ruth if you want to know. You should have left me with grandma, my real mother.'

Her father remembered only too well the number of times he had to step in to prevent his wife abusing his daughter, and he was desperately sorry that it was necessary. He reached across the table and took Zillah's hands, unwrapping her fists and telling her to sit down. The anger, which had flared so violently, had suddenly subsided. She was exhausted.

'I always loved you best, Zillah. Amy and Ruth seemed to understand this, and didn't mind. They encouraged our togetherness because they couldn't bear mum's indifference to you.'

'Now you're admitting it. It's what I wanted you to do; admit that mum didn't like me. Of course I now know why, but why did she blame me for my brother's death, just because I was the biggest twin. How could I possibly be responsible? It was probably her fault. Did she ever think of that? If she had chosen to feed him, he may have lived. She killed him. She killed him by neglect.'

'No. No. I can't think like that Zillah. In her way, she was sorry.'

'No wonder she never, ever, came back here. I wouldn't have wanted her to either, if I had known this. I'm glad she died. I'm glad she didn't come here. She would have spoilt my cottage with her hatred.'

They were both now in a more sober mood but Zillah's tears continued to flow. There were no more passionate outbursts, or recriminations. They sat holding hands across the table, trying to mend things between them.

'I couldn't tell you while your mother was alive. It would have meant an even greater rift between you and her. There would have been a big family upset, and I couldn't bear that. You do see, Zillah. Please try and understand it from my point of view.'

'I'm sorry for you dad. It must have been difficult.'

The silence and tension stretched between them. There was no immediate forgiveness from Zillah, or more conciliatory pleas from her father. The situation was saved by the sound of a car drawing up outside, and within minutes, Carl had opened the door, lifted Zillah to her feet, and hugged and kissed her.

'My darling, darling girl,' he said, and he waltzed around the kitchen with her before seating her once more at the table. He greeted his father-in-law in a peremptory manner, not yet knowing the situation that might exist between father and daughter after the revealing of so many family secrets. They then engaged in the trivial pursuit of talking of Carl's journey, their well-being, and the weather, which helped calm the situation and brought some light relief.

Carl realised he would have to take charge of making lunch since Zillah and David seemed traumatised and frozen into inaction. He set sandwiches before them and made tea and persuaded them to eat. The afternoon passed slowly, with each of them engaged in their own thoughts. David went to his room to rest and Carl took Zillah on his knee and rocked her in grandma's big old rocking chair.

The afternoon sun blossomed into a red and gold evening sunset and settled over the sea in a huge disk of fire, setting the sea ablaze. The kitchen, facing west, was bathed in a fearsome light. The wooden surface of the old kitchen table showed all its scars in the fierce dying glow, and then suddenly the sun had gone, leaving Zillah, Carl and David sitting at the dinner table in shadow. As though released they rose and took their coffee through to the living room. David broached the subject of his wife again.

'I want you to understand something about your mother. Something I learnt only recently. Something of which, I think, she was unaware, so was her mother, and most other people but,' David hesitated, 'she had a mild form of autism.'

Autism!' Zillah and Carl said together.

'Well that, or something similar. She couldn't relate easily to people. I knew that when I first met her, but I loved her anyway. That's why grandma Karenza was so upset. She and Jack brought up a child in a beautiful place, in a loving environment, and that child couldn't love them; and they didn't know why. Also, at some point, Mary decided she couldn't live here. In her head, that was irrefutable. She made judgements, often with no good reason, and no amount of commonsense would change her mind, so you see, once a decision was made, it became a habit, a sort of obsession. She was a victim of her fixations.'

'Oh dear!' Zillah exclaimed again. 'All that stuff she

collected and hoarded. Those familiar sayings she used over and over again. There's not even a wedding photograph, or photographs of us as children. She wouldn't allow us to wash our hair on a Friday. We could only ever have Christmas cards displayed on Christmas Day. You indulged all her stupid phobias. She was obstinate, pig-headed and inflexible. All those entrenched attitudes; those tunes she never tired of hearing you play.'

'I know. I used to sing all those old songs to her *The Very Thought of You*. Always trying to convince her that she was the only girl for me. Her favourite was *I Can't Get Started*. She clung to it like a trophy. It was our tune. The one I wooed her with, time after time.'

'Dad, I'm sorry. I don't want to hear all your sentimental anecdotes at the moment.'

Her father winced at her rebuke, but carried on talking. 'When we married I loved her, in spite of her having no feelings for me. Although she agreed to marry me, it was merely to help her life move on. Those tunes marked the progress, or lack of it, in my pursuit of her. I made up my own words except the line *Still I'm broken hearted 'cos I can't get started with you*. When Mary realised the effort I put in to win her affection, she was proud of my persistence, and gradually, I believe she did learn to love me.'

'Learn. Why did she have to learn everything? Why couldn't she love like ordinary people. Why was she so obstinate? Why couldn't she understand simple things and accept them as the truth, rather than stick to her stupid ideas?'

Her father paused in his explanations, upset by Zillah's lack of understanding, and the memories which flooded back of Mary and their early years together, and the sorrow he now felt with having to live the rest of his life without her.

'That's why I want you to understand, Zillah,' he continued, recovering his composure. 'I want you to realise that it wasn't her fault, and especially, to try and forgive her. It might take time, but if you could appreciate the circumstances, you'll know she wasn't consciously to blame for her behaviour.'

'Don't ask me to think about forgiving her for the moment Dad. I'm still trying to come to terms with being a twin, and knowing that I had a brother, who died.'

'I only found out by accident about your mother's disability when I asked for the notes from the hospital after her death. One of the doctors who examined her behaviour after the birth of you and David, wrote, "I suspect this mother to be autistic to some degree. Further studies need to be done with this patient." Of course they never were because Mary discharged herself.'

'This is all too much to take in at one time. I suggest we go for a walk to clear our heads a little. Zillah could do with some fresh air,' Carl said.

The three of them walked through the fields and down to the cove in the full glare of the evening sunshine. Zillah felt weak, as if she were recovering from some serious illness. They only spoke to point out a ship on the horizon, the colour of the sea, or a flight of birds. It was soothing on their nerves to walk by the sea and hear its shush on the sand, the rippling and tinkling through patches of pebbles. There was the louder splash further out as the sea hit the big rocks and ran in foam over the gleaming surface. To their joy, seven seals leapt and played not far off shore, and treated them to a fine display of water activities.

The light was fading fast as they stumbled home through the fields, now lit by the full moon. Zillah had left a lamp in the cottage window, and it beamed a reassuring guide to home, and warmth, and comfort. Bed was a welcome thought. There were still unanswered questions but they were too emotionally distraught to think about them.

'We'll talk again in the morning Zillah. I think you've suffered enough for the moment. I promise to explain everything else that is worrying you,' her father said. 'Goodnight my darling. Please forgive me.'

Zillah avoided her father's goodnight kiss. She wasn't going to forgive him that easily. Years of suffering at the hands of her mother couldn't simply be forgiven and forgotten whatever valid explanation was given.

'I must know where David is buried. We must go to Zennor tomorrow,' Zillah demanded, in a sudden blaze of energy and hysteria. 'I have to find his grave. I have to take flowers, say a prayer, even if you can't be sure exactly where his grave is,' she said. And then, in anger, she rounded on her father. 'No. Of course you can't be sure. You don't know. You weren't there. You were looking after your stupid wife.'

'I'm going to bed now Zillah. I can't talk to you when you're so angry. Goodnight.'

Her father did not attempt another goodnight kiss.

He looked beaten and tired.

Zillah didn't say goodnight. She ignored her father but turned to Carl. 'Grandma should have told me before she died, so that I would know I had a twin brother.'

'She left you the diaries, Zillah. Calm down, darling. I'm here now, and tomorrow when you've had a good sleep, we'll do exactly as you wish. Please don't get so anxious and upset,' Carl pleaded, 'It was all such a long time ago.'

'Not for me it isn't,' Zillah replied defensively, 'For me it happened yesterday when I read about it in grandma's diary. It happened yesterday, Carl. Do you understand?'

Carl gently took Zillah's hand and guided her upstairs to the bedroom. She seemed incapable of undressing herself. She stood in a trance by the open window, looking out over the fields. The clouds had moved away, and the moon lit up a silver pathway on the sea.

'Two people very like me, Loveday and Karenza, stood here looking out of this window, and felt the sorrow I feel tonight,' Zillah whispered to the night air.

Carl sat in bed watching and listening to Zillah's quiet words, knowing she was trying to deal with her distress and perhaps evoking the spirits of her grandma and great grandmother. He hoped it would help. Eventually, he went to her, leading her to the bed, where he undressed her and tucked the blankets cosily around. She was too tense and nervous to lie still, so he turned on the two bedside lights. 'Talk to me, darling.

287

Tell me what you're thinking; if it'll help,' he said.

'I was thinking how grandma must have been shamed in front of her whole community. She had to see one grandchild die, and the other left in her care, and neither of the parents was there to help her. How could she explain their absence to people for whom family was the most important element in village life? How could she excuse the behaviour of her own daughter to her neighbours?'

'She was just a very remarkable woman,' Carl said soothingly. 'I'm sure the people around here knew of her qualities.'

Carl gradually dispelled the ennui that had settled on Zillah's spirit after her anger. They shared the delight of being together again. They sat up in bed and Zillah showed Carl the diaries of Loveday and Karenza, from which she had learnt so much of their lives. They turned pages and talked about the legacy of these books that had brought such painful revelations, but also a gift of dreams, and the lives and loves of the people who had lived in her cottage.

Zillah, although emotionally exhausted, could not sleep. Over and over in her head was the injustice of her mother's treatment of her and the unfair belief that Zillah was responsible for her brother's death. A brother would have been the same age as her, if he had lived. Perhaps together, they could have withstood their mother's onslaught, but would Zillah always have been the black sheep? There probably would have been a preference for the boy. She would never know but it was more than likely she would still have been the one to suffer her mother's outrageous behaviour.

Carl stayed awake too; ready to deal with Zillah's troubles, ready to absorb some of the anger and sorrow that engulfed her from time to time.

'I want to see if there's anything else about my brother David in grandma's diary,' Zillah said.

'Why not leave it until morning?' Carl advised. 'I don't want you suffering any more upsets. You'll be rested and able to deal with things better in the morning.'

But Zillah was adamant. They sat with the diary between them and opened a page towards the end of the book. They had one more shock from Karenza's diary, before Zillah lay weeping quietly in Carl's arms.

Diary. Karenza 1966
What I would have done without my darling Zillah, I do not know, so great was my sorrow. Her sweet face and bright eyes held me entranced, and her loving little body was warmth and comfort, and soothed me. What it is to have a child to love, and who loves you. She is my little miracle, my one hope in my sadness.

Jack had been restless during the night, so had the little one, who cried weakly on and off. He took David from the cot and went downstairs. Zillah woke, and I brought her into bed with me. We found great comfort together, and slept well. In the morning I saw that Jack hadn't come back to bed, and David's cot was empty.

I went downstairs. Jack was in the rocking chair, and the baby was lying on his chest. It alarmed me that Jack's arms were hanging at his side, and not nursing the baby. I didn't want to look any further, but I did,

289

and I knew Jack was dead; with a dead baby lying on him. It was a dreadful discovery.

Zillah sobbed and her breathing was laboured with the blow of this new discovery. 'Oh Carl. This is awful. Grandpa died too. What a terrible shock. Poor grandma; and she still had me to look after, and no daughter to turn to for comfort. A daughter who wouldn't come to her baby, or her father's funeral. How despicable.'

'I think your mother must have suffered, Zillah. She must have questioned her attitude to her babies, and then when she came round to wanting them, it was too late. I imagine she couldn't face the neighbours here for her neglect of you both. Perhaps she was too full of remorse to even face her mother …'

'She didn't have any remorse, or pity, or any feelings at all. She was incapable of compassion. She could only think with her brain. She had no heart, so don't find excuses for her Carl. I can't bear it. I can find no justification for her. I must finish reading the diary.'

'Darling,' he pleaded, 'Enough. Don't put yourself through this ordeal.'

'I must know, Carl. It has been hidden for so long that I'm now desperate to know everything, however distressing I might find it.'

Diary. Karenza. 1966
I don't know how I phoned the doctor, but I remember opening the door to him, and hoping he'd say they were both all right. When he told me that Jack and David were dead, I still couldn't believe it. It was expected the

baby would die, but not my Jack.

I came upstairs to tell Zillah, who lay on the bed looking at me with those lovely blue eyes. She seemed to understand me, even at that little age. Jack was taken away by the funeral people. It didn't seem right for him to leave home, and I made them bring the coffin back, so I could say goodbye properly, and talk to him. I think I sat up all night holding the little dead baby and then I tucked him in the coffin beside his granddad, who had looked after him and tried to keep him alive. I was happy about that, and so was Zillah. I didn't tell anyone, or know if it was permitted, but people seemed to know what happened to the baby and everyone turned a kind blind eye.

On the day of the funeral, people came for miles around to walk behind the coffin all the way to Zennor. I carried Zillah in my arms, wrapped in the shawl my mother, Loveday, crocheted for me when I was a baby. I felt her presence very strongly.

'What a good thing grandma Karenza had her own darling mother, Loveday, to think about and find comfort in good thoughts,' Carl said, pulling Zillah to him and holding her firmly.

'I'm so glad that at least that mother and daughter loved one another.' Zillah said. With shaking hands she leafed through the diary to find the page she had inadvertently closed.

Diary. Karenza. 1966
Some of the wonderful people who came to the funeral,

291

thought to carry candles, other groups sang hymns. Some carried the banners of their chapels. It didn't matter that folk were either church or chapel. They were united in their sorrow for Jack, and their support for me.

The Vicar looked at me, and I knew the question that was in his eyes, but he said nothing, and I stared back at him, admitting nothing. People sat and stood in the church, and outside. There were enough chapel people to fill the church over again. I think there would have been a riot if the vicar had guessed the baby was in the coffin, and refused to bury little David with grandpa.

'Oh Carl. That's why there's no headstone for David. What a wonderful thing grandma did, to put my little brother in the coffin beside his granddad. What would have happened if the Vicar had questioned it, and demanded he be removed from consecrated ground because he wasn't christened. How could she bear the whole ordeal? Poor grandma.' Zillah felt her heart would break and she would never stop crying.

'Well, she had you to help her through that nightmare. Isn't it good that she compensated for your vengeful mother, and you compensated for her unloving child?'

'Yes. We were a great comfort to one another.' Zillah agreed. 'I know what I shall do, Carl. I shall write to the Bishop and ask for David's name to be put on the headstone. I don't think these days they dare make a distinction between babies who've been christened and those who have not, do they? If they do, I'll want to know the reason why.'

'I'm going to make you a cup of tea, and then, my darling, perhaps we can get some sleep. Take a few deep breaths while I'm gone, and try to relax.'

'All right,' Zillah agreed, resigned to the good advice.

After the tea, Carl took the diary from Zillah, turned out the lights, and made her lie down. He gently rubbed her back, until she was relaxed and sleepy, and finally slept himself. In the morning Zillah confronted her father with the truth, that the baby was buried with his granddad. Her father confirmed this.

'Don't be angry, Zillah. I hadn't intended keeping it from you. I was going to tell you this morning. I thought you'd had enough to deal with in one day. But then I heard you crying last night and realised you must have discovered more from grandma's diary. I'm sorry.'

They had all risen early and Zillah demanded that they go to the churchyard. She picked a few wild flowers from the hedgerows as they walked through the early morning fields, passing cows enveloped in mist, their hides gleaming wetly, their eyes curious at the intrusion. They arrived at the church as the bell was tolling for morning service. They did not enter with the Sunday congregation, but made their way to the right of the church door and came upon the grave of Jack and Karenza Pender, and little David, and stood there.

The singing of hymns in the church reached out to Zillah and acted as a balm to her ragged nerves. All her tears had been used up. She even smiled at her father and husband, feeling better, now that she had discovered her twin brother, and feeling too, that he was safe with the only parents he had known, in a quiet and beautiful corner of Cornwall.

'I hope grandma was able to forgive her daughter for causing her such grief,' Zillah remarked philosophically.

'She had always tried to understand Mary,' her father replied, 'But it was difficult for her, in spite of her good commonsense, which does not come naturally to everyone. Normal well-meaning parents brought Mary up but acceptance of their daughter's behaviour was all that Karenza and Jack could achieve, because there was no reason why they should understand. Only we know about her autism directing her actions, and shaping her nature.'

'But remember,' added Carl, 'grandma Karenza had you Zillah. And so my darling, you healed each other, and one day perhaps you will forgive and understand your mother?'

'Maybe.' Zillah replied, with another flash of anger. 'I'm too hurt by the memories at the moment, but because I've been given a reason for my mother's conduct, I can accept it more. I'm glad to know it wasn't really my fault.'

'And it wasn't really her fault,' her father said in defence of his wife.

'If you say so,' Zillah said, dismissively.

They turned away from the graveyard and went to the Tinners Arms. While David ordered the drinks, Carl took Zillah's hand.

'Tomorrow we'll make plans for both of us. I hardly care what they are as long as we're together. What do you think?'

'Together is the big thing, whatever, wherever. We

don't have to decide anything quickly. Stay awhile and we'll get to know Cornwall; have a holiday, then we'll talk about what we'll do.'

Zillah was surprised to hear herself say this. She loved her cottage, her real childhood home, but realised she would be prepared to give it up to live with Carl. He was essential to her emotional well-being. He was her rock. She hoped she meant as much to him, but for the moment, she couldn't tell. These were new circumstances in which they found themselves.

Back at Gorsemoor Cottage, Carl and David were inspecting the newly decorated units for holiday-makers. All that was needed was the furniture. Zillah set about making lunch. She wanted to leave them alone together, in case there was anything they wanted to discuss and put right. She was relieved to see them chatting in the courtyard and note there was no tension, or argument, or disagreement between them. Then there was a burst of laughter, and Beatrice had come upon the scene. She walked into the cottage linking the arms of the two men.

'They've invited me for lunch, ' she said in the doorway. Then she stopped and looked with concern at Zillah's troubled face. She lifted a questioning eyebrow, which clearly said, 'What's wrong?'

At that moment, Zillah would have loved to sit down with Beatrice and tell her the whole sorry story, just to get her sympathetic response and good down-to-earth opinion on the matter, instead she indicated that they would discuss it later. Beatrice gave her an understanding hug. She was the welcome spirit needed to dispel any gloom remaining from the previous day.

'I've come as the spectre at the feast, to make sure you don't have any excuses for not making an appearance at my private view at the Space Gallery on Wednesday,' Beatrice told them.

'You're as welcome as the spirit of light,' Zillah said, and kissed her on the cheek. 'And we'll come to your exhibition.'

'So that's three of you I can expect,' Beatrice said. She sighed with satisfaction, as though congratulating herself on a job well done. She was completely confident that they would come, and no one thought to deny her. She had that effect upon people. As usual, Beatrice made herself entirely at home, taking a seat at the table, and inviting the men to sit either side of her.

Beatrice had brought some freshly made bread from the batch her mother had baked and Carl and her father wolfed it down with relish, liberally spreading farm butter on chunky slices and dipping them into thick tomato soup.

13

After they had feasted Beatrice got up from the table and said, 'Zillah and I are going for a walk, while you two do the washing up.' She grabbed Zillah by the elbow and hoisted her off the chair. She fetched her coat, thrust her arms through the sleeves, buttoned her up and marched her to the door. 'See you in a while,' she said.

Zillah gave a helpless smile to her men folk and let her friend propel her through the yard to the gate in the wall and the field beyond. They walked in silence, slowing their pace, gathering their thoughts, each unwilling to unfold and reveal their feelings. A tight string of tension grew between them until Beatrice broke the impasse, 'Are you going to tell me what's creasing your poor little face and bothering your poor little soul, or do I have to hire a detective agency?'

This made Zillah smile. 'I don't know where to begin,' she said, 'whether to tell you about my horrible mother, my deceptive father, my grandma's diaries or,' and here she hesitated and drew a deep breath, 'or to tell you I had a twin brother.'

This stopped Beatrice in her tracks. 'A twin brother? I think we can start with this one. What happened to him? He's obviously not around, or you would have mentioned him.'

'No. He died a couple of weeks after we were born. It was a case of survival of the fittest. Poor little thing. I've only just learnt of his existence; through the diaries, and then confirmed by my father.'

'Wow!' Beatrice said. 'No wonder you look devastated. How come it was such a secret?'

'It's a bit painful,' Zillah said. And bit by bit, the story was told.

By this time they had walked to Zennor and called in for coffee at the Backpacker's hostel. There they met the artist Anthony Frost, sitting on the bench outside talking to a small group of students from Falmouth School of Art. They waved and he got up to greet them. The students looked balefully at them, not welcoming the interruption.

'So what are you doing here?' Beatrice said.

'Ah well, it's choose your artist day. Some of us were at Falmouth art college this morning, talking about our work and this four have chosen to spend a few hours with me. We're on the way to my studio.'

'Sounds like a great idea. I wouldn't mind getting in on that circuit.'

'Send some slides in. Say you're willing to come and talk. See what happens.' Anthony advised. 'You've got a great studio to offer too.'

The students' hostile looks softened, as they realised Anthony was talking to an artist. They even smiled a group smile.

'Well, we'd better get going. We've got two cars, can we drop you anywhere?' Anthony offered.

'Yes, great. You can drop us at Bosigran,' Beatrice said.

By the time they reached the mine engine house at the side of the road to Bosigran Farm, the students were prepared to wave a fond farewell. The women turned their backs to the coast and took the inland footpath over the National Trust moorland, struggling over the rough terrain, and feeling at one with the birds, which would suddenly rise from the undergrowth at their feet. There were wild flowers amongst the purple heather, lichen covered rocks, moss and rare plants. Overhead, the Kestrel hovered.

They walked into the silence of the moorland, each engaged with her own thoughts, until they came upon the Men-an-Tol, a set of three ancient stones, the centre one with a hole pierced through the middle. 'Magic stones,' Beatrice said. 'I don't suppose you'd want to crawl through that, but children with whooping cough or some other childhood illness, were said to be cured by being passed through several times.'

'I know. I've read about the Men-an-Tol. In fact grandma brought me here when I had measles, or some childhood illness. She carried me on her back after we left the horse and cart. I remember her helping me through the hole in the stone. She told me that many children were brought here when there was plague in the villages. And then it was supposed to be a cure for infertility and something else, which I've forgotten, but it was to do with a full moon.'

'I suppose the ancients thought anything was worth a try when they had to rely on herbs and folklore and witches.'

'I'm so glad we've come. Grandma would approve. I

remember she told me I was born for magic, because of our red gold hair. I think I'll struggle through and release my feelings of anger and sorrow and even hatred. Here, take my coat Beatrice. Hold my bag,' Zillah demanded, dropping to her knees and beginning to crawl through, feet first.

'And don't tell them back home. This is our secret.'

'I'm all for it,' Beatrice said. 'It's just as well it hasn't been raining or you'd be kneeling in a puddle right now.'

'Say a few prayers, or something magical; some incantation or mantra. Release me. Release me. Set me free!'

Zillah tumbled through the hole and sat on the ground rubbing her hands inside the interior walls of the round rock. 'I'm healed. I believe I've done it,' she cried, jumping up and kissing the top of the rough stone.

'I'm sure you have. Yes. You've done it!,' echoed Beatrice. 'I can feel it.'

'Well,' Zillah said. 'People still believe in its healing properties today, so why not me.'

'And me too,' Beatrice added with conviction.

'Now what?' Zillah said. 'We need a back up. I remember something else grandma told me. We find a bush. We dip a piece of cloth in a magic well and hang it on the branches of a tree. When the piece of cloth is dried in the wind and blown away, your prayers are answered, or you are healed.'

'Let's go,' Beatrice said. 'I know we've already walked miles but we could make our way back to Foage Farm; a strange place, remote, medieval. There's a stream running through the valley. The area is so ancient that it'll be as good a place as any to wreak our magic.'

The two women set off across the moorland fired with the expectation of their next adventure. They tramped doggedly along the narrow footpath, of mud, water, gorse and heather, not talking, but measuring their footsteps to their desire to reach their destination. They had not planned this expedition and yet Beatrice had led Zillah to this course of action as though it were pre-destined.

They walked down into the valley, leaving the high song of the skylark upon the moors, and came upon Foage Farmhouse. There was not a soul around and a mist was beginning to descend upon this quiet deserted place. They hit upon the road which led to Zennor village. Beside it a stream, banked by small trees and bushes, ran alongside.

'A good spot,' Beatrice said, stopping beside a sheltered overhang of branches. 'What material have you got?'

'None. Where would I get some? We haven't come prepared. Will a tissue do?'

'I don't see why not.'

Zillah pulled out of her bag an unopened pack of tissues. 'There. Uncontaminated. This should send a pure signal.' She bent down, cleansed her hands in the running stream and pulled out a clean tissue. 'I desire forgiveness. I desire to be cleansed of all hateful thoughts. I want to live with hope and relinquish all unkind, spiteful, vengeful, bitter thoughts. I want to find joy and happiness.'

Zillah took her fragment of tissue and secured it to a

branch overhanging the stream. She offered Beatrice a tissue to invoke her own thoughts, which she did quietly, not revealing her secret wishes. She released her tissue into the stream.

'That's for the river god. If one doesn't work, the other will,' Beatrice said. 'I endorsed everything you said.'

'Good. Evil and misfortune are washed away in Holy wells and springs. And you helped me do it, Beatrice. Thank you.'

'Well, desperate situations call for desperate measures. The thing is, you just believe in what you are doing to free your head of your worries, and it works. Good psychology.'

They continued their walk into Zennor and came upon the open-top bus on its way from Land's End back to St Ives. It was just pulling away from the bus stop. They ran across the road and the driver stopped. They were dropped off at the top of the lane leading to Gorsemoor Cottage.

'Don't ask where we've been,' Zillah entreated of the questioning faces of Carl and her father. 'We are just exhausted.' The two friends collapsed into chairs and allowed tea and sandwiches to be served.

'I've never walked so far in my life,' Beatrice said. 'We are full of scratches and bruises. I shall easily cure myself of moorland walking.'

'We thought you might have got lost on the moors, or fallen down a mineshaft. We'll call off the air sea rescue,' Carl said.

'Oh stop that,' Zillah protested. 'Just pour us another cup of tea.'

Zillah, Carl and David put on a brave face to go to Beatrice's event at the Space gallery. All three were rather washed out and weary, but they needed something to relieve their thoughts of the past few days. There was a live rock band, noisy and raucous, that Martin Val Baker had booked for the occasion. People and voices were obliterated by the blast. Martin raised his eyebrows at Beatrice in a questioning look, which asked 'OK?' Beatrice replied with a shrug of her shoulders. Anthony Frost came and gave her his big bear hug, and grinned.

The paintings were not seriously studied. Private views were gatherings of friends and clients, but mostly friends. Buying was for the enthusiast, the gallery's clientele, or follower of the artist's work, on the opening night. Beatrice hoped there would be enough of these present to make it a success. Sales often took place over the phone the next day, or people came back to buy days later. The internet also accounted for many sales from a source not previously available, and then there was the casual art lover, who dropped by chance into the gallery and liked what he saw.

Beatrice insisted on hauling Zillah and Carl around the room with her, to introduce them to other artists, neighbours and friends, until their heads were awash with names and faces.

Ethan was there, clinging tightly to the arm of a great strapping girl, who seemed to be dragging him around the place. 'This is Dora,' he said to Beatrice and stepped back. The girl came forward with outstretched hand.

'Ethan's doing some wonderful work,' she said.

'I'm glad to hear it. What colour is he using now?'

'Yellow,' the girl replied. 'I'm going to ask about an exhibition here. They're just right for this gallery.'

'Well, you've obviously had a tremendous effect upon Ethan, and all for the good I'd say. I wish you luck,' Beatrice said, moving away.

From behind Dora, Ethan looked directly at Beatrice and grinned triumphantly. Dora pulled him away.

'I wish her well of him,' Beatrice muttered. 'Come on, I want to introduce you to some saner characters. You won't remember any of them, but it's a way of making you feel you belong here. Gradually, things and people start to gel. You'll see.'

Carl wasn't at all sure that's what he wanted to happen, and he eyed Zillah in such a way as to indicate he wouldn't allow himself to be dragooned into staying in Cornwall. Zillah merely shrugged. Her unspoken reply said, 'Don't blame me for this.'

Rosie, from the gallery in Falmouth, was loud in her praise of Beatrice's show.

'If you can get together enough paintings for next year, I'd like to give you a spring exhibition, or maybe summer, or autumn, if that doesn't suit.'

'I'd be pleased to consider it, if you pay me what you owe,' Beatrice said, and rather cruelly added, 'and you still have a gallery by that time.'

'That was a bit unkind,' Zillah remarked.

'Not so unkind as owing me money,' Beatrice said, defensively. 'And it might make her realise she has to be a bit more business-like. She can't always rely on the good grace of friends; not me anyway.'

Somehow, it seemed like a chaotic event to the ordered minds of Zillah and Carl Brook; and an assault on the senses of David Ward. It was a complete mystery to Beatrice's parents, Sylvia and Arthur Paynter, who had ensconced themselves at a table and bravely endured the experience. The evening concluded in a satisfactory number of sales. ' Phew!' Beatrice breathed a sigh of delight and joy. 'You don't know how rotten I'd feel if nothing sold, especially with a new gallery too, who've yet to build their mailing list and claw back the cash they've put into the project.'

David, always a moderate drinker, drove them home by the light of the moon. The morning found them at Dove Farm with Mr and Mrs Paynter discussing the previous evening over coffee. They were beaming with pride at their daughter's successful exhibition. In retrospect, they decided it had been a good show. There was plenty of wine and food. The place was heaving with people, and apart from having to shout at close range into someone's ear, they had met some really nice folk.

'We've decided,' joked Mr Paynter, 'that as we now have a famous daughter, she can be excused milking. In fact I might even sell the cows, convert the cowshed, and take up painting myself. It's easy money, compared to farming.'

'You'd better develop some talent fast,' Beatrice teased. 'Pay up, and you can be my first student.'

In the afternoon Zillah drove Beatrice, and replacement paintings to the gallery, taking the route over the moors into Penzance. Then she and Carl accompanied dad to Penzance station. He promised a longer stay on his next visit, feeling that the young couple had much to discuss about their future life, and needed to lick their wounds. They could best do this alone.

Feeling somewhat at a loss after David's departure, they strolled along the beach at Marazion and watched the colourful sails of the Penzance sailing club out on the water near St Michael's Mount. They held hands and walked, each dealing with their own thoughts and feelings, not reaching any conclusions about where they would live, only that they must be together.

Zillah hoped that Cornwall would provide a clue. She wanted to fulfil grandma Karenza's hope that she would find happiness in the cottage where she had found sanctuary and love. She did not confide this to Carl, nor attempt to argue or persuade him to her way of thinking. She just waited. In fact, they did not discuss their future. They drifted through the days, enjoying the good weather, exploring the countryside; its standing stones and quoits, and its prehistory strangeness. It was a time of quiet contemplation.

'It's a strange and fascinating place, Cornwall,' Carl admitted to Zillah. 'It's got a heart beating somewhere. It takes hold of you and I think it's wise to get out quick, before it captures you.'

'Yes. I've known about it since childhood,' Zillah said cautiously, 'and so many artists and writers have been captured. Cornwall appeals to creative people.'

306

During a mild evening walk along the beach, near Zennor, which Zillah had named Lawrence and Frieda cove. She related her strange dream of seeing the couple swimming naked out to the rock, their being in danger, and their difficulties in returning to shore. The episode had remained vividly in Zillah's memory.

'I think it was probably a warning to you not to swim there,' Carl said laconically. 'On the other hand, there could be something more profound, but I don't know what.'

Zillah stared at him. He was being serious. Not only was his pragmatic and practical side showing, but Cornwall was beginning to ensnare him. Magic was beginning to creep insidiously into his thinking. She must tell Beatrice about this.

'There's some lovely driftwood here,' Carl said, picking up a fairly large lump of odd shaped timber. 'Looks a bit like a boat. And its sea washed and smooth. Only needs a bit of sanding here and there. Let's collect a few pieces.'

While Zillah worked on her computer, Carl had converted one of the units Zillah was planning for holiday accommodation into a workshop. With his redundancy money he bought a workbench from a car boot sale, and was quietly squirreling away tools and equipment. Zillah watched him from her office window, wondering where this project was going, and why he hadn't talked about it.

She dared not raise the subject of his working day, where he sawed and planned, and hammered, and painted. She did not dare to enter his private world. She felt excluded, but understood the need for his secretive behaviour, which made him lock his workshop door every night. She only hoped that what he was engaged in, pleased him, and the outcome wouldn't disappoint, or prove a failure. So much depended on her desire to have Carl stay in Cornwall.

One evening Carl appeared in the kitchen doorway, with a grin on his face. 'I've been making things,' he said, 'Come and see,' Zillah followed him, intrigued and excited. He opened the door to his workshop and there, displayed on the bench were several boats, dolphins, and a beautiful mermaid, 'All from the drift-wood,' he explained. 'You look at the shape and it tells you what it wants to be.'

Zillah was amazed at the ingenuity of the designs and the charm of the objects.

'They are wonderful. Beautiful. I love them,' she said, with genuine admiration.

At that moment, Beatrice came along and beamed her approval.

'Oh, you've changed the unit into a workshop. What a good idea. Looks as if my painting students will have to stay at our farmhouse. You could have a craft centre here,' she blurted out, 'I know several people making lovely objects who are looking for premises like these.'

'It's a great idea,' Carl said. 'What do you think Zillah? To tell you the truth, a plan of workshops in the countryside had occurred to me. And we won't need to go to the extra expense of buying furniture.' Carl's face was a picture of enthusiasm.

'It's perfect. Absolutely perfect,' Zillah agreed, noting

the 'we' in his sentence, meaning that they were a partnership. She hoped it wasn't a slip of the tongue.

But it wasn't that easy. How and where, did one sell such objects in order to enable one to live by such a venture? Where did one find a ready supply of driftwood, seasoned and smoothed by the sea? It couldn't be left to chance finds. There were plenty of beaches, but one had to be there at the right time, or the objects would be washed away with the next tide.

Carl took to going into St Ives and tracking down anyone working in wood. He found a woodcarver living by the harbour and studied his work exhibited in the St Ives Society of Artists. These pieces of birds and animals were smooth-honed, beautifully crafted, expertly carved. 'I could never achieve the like,' he told Zillah. 'He works with all kinds of wood, oak, yew, holly, laburnum, cherry and walnut. He showed me pieces of wood where he had mapped out the shape of a dolphin, or gull, and they were just perfect.'

Over a pot of tea at nearby Bumbles Tea Room in the Digey, Carl expressed his disappointment with his own crude workings on driftwood. 'It's depressing to compare my efforts with an expert wood sculptor. They are not nearly good enough to exhibit.'

Zillah tried to tell him that his were unique objects and found through exploration of the material he worked on. There was a market for such natural, crafted pieces. 'You got such joy working on them,' she said. But he wasn't satisfied.

'I'm going back to Bristol,' he told Zillah. 'I might get a job there and see you at weekends. I can't quite see what I'm doing here, and where I'm going. The city will restore me, I think. There seems to be purpose in bustle and excitement, whereas I'm just drifting and dreaming down here, with nothing to show for it.'

Zillah knew better than try to persuade him that what he had discovered and made in his driftwood sculptures was meaningful. She knew how he felt and it was important to uphold his view of his progress, rather than persuade him to accept a life that offered him only illimitable freedom. He needed a rudder.

Zillah took a deep breath and found some courage from deep within her. She made a reluctant, if sincere, promise to Carl. 'If you find what you're looking for in Bristol, and are happy to stay there, then I'm prepared to sell this cottage, so we can buy a house. Bristol's a good city and I can work from home anywhere in the country.'

'Thanks, Zillah,' he said. 'You do understand what I mean, don't you? But I'll miss coming to this place. It has a strange hold on you.' Zillah resisted the temptation to say, 'Well stay.'

The days after Carl's departure were lonely and hopeless. She took to travelling around and saying goodbye to some of her favourite places. She drove to St Ives and parked at the Island car park and lunched at Porthgwidden beach café. She sat outside on the terrace, drinking coffee, staring out to sea and looking at Godrevy lighthouse and over to the Towans in the distance. She watched families of children playing in the sand and envied their simple happiness.

At Godolphin Manor, she visited the dining room

housing the painting of the famous Godolphin Arab stallion. The first of its line. The bluebells were just emerging in the woods under the shelter of the leaves of the early spring trees, where sunlight pierced through the lacy branches. There was a promise of milder days to come.

She visited St Michael's Mount and its surrounding gardens, and Lanhydrock, touring through the variety of kitchens for preparation of different foods, enjoying the nursery, the bedrooms and bathrooms of this modern Victorian House. At Zennor she walked once more through the museum with its huge water wheel, and tools and artefacts showing the interesting history of the district and its fascinating Cornish kitchen.

The St Ives Museum which housed the history of the town, its fishing, mining, shipping and domestic memories, had always held her affection. She wished it a final goodbye.

At Gorsemoor Cottage she looked out over the fields to the sea and knew she would miss, not only the cottage, but everything about the area, the stone stiles and hedges over which she climbed, heather, the spring flowers, primroses, violets, daffodils, sea pinks, foxgloves and brilliant yellow gorse smelling of coconut. The cry of a gull on its way to the cliffs brought thoughts of deserted coves and scavenging for detritus thrown up on the sands. The treacherous coast path crossed streams, detoured down to secluded stretches of sand, took high stepped pathways to elevated platforms of rocks, and imperilled the traveller at every stage. It was a dream filled journey.

Many a novice walker started from St Ives, drank his triumph at the Backpackers café in Zennor and, suitably refreshed and energised, continued the expedition to Land's End. She would miss too, the special magic road, which meandered narrowly between wild moors, and isolated farmland and sea, all the way between St Ives and Land's End. It was a road unfit for the nervous driver, with its sudden turns and tilts and its high stone Cornish hedges, and though covered in wild greenery, were unyielding. Late evening, moonlight and starlight cast an intimidating sensation around the lonely traveller on the road at night. It could be scary.

In considering a move to Bristol Zillah realised she would miss Beatrice too. A really good friend. After Carl's departure to Bristol, she had come to supper and listened with warmth and sympathy to Zillah's troubles about the future with Carl.

'You've already dealt with my past by taking me over the moorland to the Men-an-Tol stones and the silent stream and somehow, magically, the agony of it has left me. I really do feel cleansed. I hope you don't think we were just playing childish games.'

'I should think not, indeed,' Beatrice said vehemently. 'It was I who led the way. Remember?'

'OK. Now try working on the next problem,' Zillah said with a laugh.

Carl's telephone calls and letters, were a continuing story of applying for jobs, looking at houses to rent or buy, and missing Zillah. Her letters did not tell of her dread of leaving her cottage, only of missing Carl and confirming her desire to be with him, wherever he happened to find contentment in living. She encouraged his endeavours, while at the same time complaining to Beatrice that he hadn't given Cornwall a chance to convince him he could live here.

'Leave them alone, and they'll come home,' was Beatrice's favourite quote.

'Well, he's been away a month, and spent a couple of weekends here. I need to know quite soon whether I'm to put the cottage complex in the hands of an agent.'

'Don't put pressure on,' was Beatrice's advice.

Zillah dreaded the weekend to come. 'Carl has had a reasonably good interview with a local newspaper.' She told Beatrice. 'He'll know by telephone on Saturday, whether the job is his or not.'

When he arrived on Friday, Carl was hopeful of a good result. 'I think my luck's changing,' he said. 'I felt pretty positive about this one. I've seen some very nice houses too, which I think you'll like. Good gardens and within reasonable walking distance of the city centre.'

'I'll come back to Bristol with you. Take a look. It's lovely to be with you again, Carl. I don't know how much more I can take of us being apart all the week. So if the news is good, I'll put the cottage up for sale. Beatrice can have the keys and show people around. I couldn't bear to do it.' She smiled bravely.

Carl's anxiety lifted with Zillah's decision to return to Bristol with him. 'I think you'll like it there,' he assured her. But her attempt to cover up her real feelings about leaving the cottage weren't lost on him. At this juncture, when each was engaged with their thoughts, Beatrice burst in upon the scene.

'I'm having a dinner party tonight, several painters, also Martin Val Baker and Anthony Frost, who you both know, a couple of potters, a wood carver, a sculptor, a writer, and you two. Sorry about the short notice, but it took time to persuade mum to give up the kitchen and the big table to my little orgy. The oldies are banished to the much polished, but unused, dining room. Must dash, got shopping to do before the big cook. See you.'

Beatrice had run off before they'd been given a chance to consider whether the invite was acceptable. Well, that was Beatrice, and they would go.

'I don't know how she does it, but she makes things happen,' Zillah said, with affectionate envy.

Late afternoon, Carl and Zillah walked to Zennor across the fields. The young calves on Dove Farm followed them, getting closer, but when they turned to face the herd, they stopped, their bravado halted. The geese at Wicca Farm gave their usual chase, heads lowered, prepared to see off the trespassers. The geese were not to be intimidated and Carl and Zillah gave the victory to them. The dogs at Tremedda stood upon the wall and barked a warning.

Zillah knelt to put flowers on the grave of Karenza, Jack and her little brother, David.

Under a thorn tree she placed flowers and read the inscription on another gravestone, 'Sacred to the memory of Nicholas Godolphin, lost in a mine disaster. To Loveday, his wife. Also Ned Berryman, lost at sea.'

In an older part of the cemetery was the grave of Henry Care and his wife Annie.

'I'll come again, before we leave,' Zillah whispered, as Carl turned to watch a tractor toiling across a far field.

Back at the cottage they were both reluctant to further any discussion of their future so Carl busied himself tidying up his workshop and Zillah took a long bath. The window of the bathroom was plain glass and framed a view across the fields to a glimpse of the sea. She lay there, letting the silent tears obscure the picture. Everything seemed to be winding down, coming to an end. And yet there was the strange, comforting, feeling of being freed of the childhood oppression that had obsessed her.

'This party will probably be the last event to happen in Cornwall,' Zillah said quietly to Beatrice, as she entered the big farmhouse kitchen, lit by candlelight.

'Not if I can help it,' Beatrice replied.

Beatrice had organised her seating arrangements so that Zillah and Carl were separated by the long length of the table. The conversations were fairly animated, each person engaged in telling of the latest developments, exhibitions, or drama, in the lives of their chosen occupations. Beatrice hardly sat, but danced around the table, bottle in hand, filling up glasses and throwing in a remark here and there.

Beatrice was particularly attentive to the end of the table where Carl and a rather quiet man, were making tentative forays into the general discussion. Beatrice wedged herself between the two men. 'Now Luke, have you got Carl's address? He'd love to see your exhibition in Bristol. He's been admiring your work at the Waterside Gallery in St Ives and, would you believe, dabbles in wood carving himself.' The two men turned to each other with interest.

'As you probably noticed from the pieces in the Waterside Gallery,' Luke said, 'my specialist studies are of birds. I work mostly in driftwood, or from fallen trees, where the sea or elements have treated the wood and transformed it into a malleable state. It becomes supple and reveals its hidden depths.'

'That's exactly what I thought, when I began my first carvings. The wood is so pliable and alive,' Carl enthused.

'And often suggests a subject,' Luke said. Beatrice abruptly left the scene.

The woman writer was talking of publishing and the difficulties of getting an agent, and of promoting a book. Zillah countered with the problems of editing and the careful consideration of not losing the author's voice. 'You should try writing yourself,' the novelist suggested. 'I've often thought about it,' Zillah remarked, mentally noting that it would be a good idea to put into practice. 'I believe she'll write the stories to my illustrations, one of these days,' Beatrice remarked, in passing.

The potters were discussing clays and glazes, the problems of getting pots to the shops, of breakages and being in an ideal situation where they could sell direct to the public. 'What we need is a community of crafts people.' Beatrice dropped the suggestion in while pouring drinks for the artists, who were already talking of a cooperative run gallery, manned by the artists whose work was exhibited.

The sculptor was complaining about the cost of the foundry casting his works in bronze and steel. He was going to try a special resin bronze process. 'I have a friend who has already tried it, and it's really successful. I'll put you in touch with her,' his companion offered. 'Much cheaper for the artist and the buyer,' Beatrice chirped in.

Inevitably, the party succumbed to the temptation to drown the creative processes in good food and wine. By the end of the evening they were much too far-gone to drive to St Ives or Penzance, or villages along the route, but the painter, Anthony Frost and his wife, decided on a romantic walk home and set off calling loud goodbyes to their companions. Beatrice gave up her double bed to the two potters and she and Martin crept away to the sofa in her studio, listened to music, and talked the night away. The sculptor, heavily sunk into his beard at the kitchen table, had been persuaded to lie under it. He was wrapped in a duvet, being too heavy and helpless to walk up the stairs. The novelist then gratefully slept in the now available spare room.

Zillah and Carl took the wood carver home to Gorsemoor Cottage, staggering through the fields, and helping him upstairs to the spare bed, and flinging a blanket over him, before collapsing onto their own bed, half undressed.

Next morning, on looking out of her bedroom window, Zillah saw a bedraggled bunch of comatose artists being led towards the cottage by Beatrice and Martin, who seemed to be the only two to have escaped the excesses of the previous night. 'We've come for coffee,' they yelled, as Zillah looked down at the sorry looking bunch below. 'You invited us, remember?'

Fortunately, Carl had remembered and coffee was prepared and waiting for their new found friends. It was drunk in a morose silence at the kitchen table, until the reviving liquid began to pump their hearts into greater activity, and adrenalin forced them to wake up.

'What did you dose us with last night?' Zillah questioned Beatrice.

'Well, Martin and I had this recipe. Nothing special. Just home-made wine, well a sort of mead, a sort of cider. We thought we'd try it.'

'Beatrice thought we'd better warn people, but nobody listened. If you're not used to pure organic stuff, it's a bit of a knock-out. I suppose it's more fermented, more alcoholic than everyone's used to,' Martin said.

'I notice you and Beatrice were the only two not to succumb to the dreaded potion,' Zillah complained

'Ah, well it's a question of understanding its potency.'

'And I had to be fit enough to clear up. Mum wanted her kitchen back by five this morning.'

Recovery for everyone was eventually achieved. They dragged themselves off home when they felt capable. Carl and the wood carver took their third reviving coffee to the workshop, where sounds of chopping, sawing and sanding, drifted into the kitchen. At last they emerged. Carl declared he was well able to function and would be driving Luke home.

'Luke is taking me to his workshop,' Carl said. 'I won't be back for some time Zillah. We're going to the woods to collect some fallen trees. Luke'll need help. OK? I'll probably bring some back here.'

'Perfectly. Enjoy yourself. But what about your important phone call?' she added as an afterthought.

Carl shrugged. 'You can take it. Tell them I'll ring back.'

'But if it's important, shouldn't you be here when they call?' Zillah protested. 'What shall I say if they offer you the job?' Carl was already through the door and Zillah would have followed for the answer to her question, but was held back by Beatrice clinging to her arm, and silenced by a desperate look from her, which clearly said, 'please don't rock the boat.'

After the two men had gone, Beatrice said, 'You wouldn't believe the trouble I had trying to get Luke, who is practically a silent man, to the party and getting those two talking. Anyone would think you wanted to live in Bristol.'

'It's the only hope of us being together, and if this job comes up, then that's what we'll do, live in Bristol.'

Beatrice sighed heavily. 'That's all the thanks I get. Everyone loves the idea of the craft centre,' she said, 'they couldn't be more enthusiastic or willing to discuss it. Didn't you hear them last night? Martin and I talked about it. He said he'd print some advertising for you. You'd have the place up and running in no time. It'll be like the William Morris craft workshops all over again.'

'We haven't got a craft centre, or workshops. We haven't got anything here, only a few decorated but empty buildings. So there's no point in being enthusiastic over nothing. You have to face reality,' Zillah said bitterly.

'You should go to bed and sleep off your irritation,' Beatrice advised, and walked off.

It was the first mild tiff the friends had had, but Zillah was feeling sorry for herself. She showered to wake herself up and succumbed to lying on the bed nursing her belief that she would soon be house hunting in Bristol. She was already grieving for those lost plans for staying in Cornwall. She was awakened two hours later by the telephone. She picked up the receiver and still dazed, received the news that Carl had got a job with the newspaper. The message was being passed on to her because of the urgency of the situation. He was expected to start work on Monday.

By the time Carl returned, she had packed two travel bags, so determined was she to show her willingness to depart Cornwall forever. Tomorrow was Sunday and they would have to travel on that day if Carl had to start work on Monday.

'Good news!' she called cheerfully, as Carl came through the door.

'How did you know?' Carl answered with surprise.

'The phone call, of course.'

'Oh that!' Carl dismissed it with a careless wave of his hand. 'No, I mean I've signed up as a mature apprentice to woodcarving. Luke thought I had some good ideas, but needed a little more experience in using tools, learning about wood, knowing the anatomy of animals.'

'Signed up?' Zillah said under her breath. That sounded permanent. 'You'll need some professional woodcarving tools,' she said. 'And I think Beatrice has a library of books on animals, their behaviour, their habits – could be useful. Beautiful studies of them in their natural habitat. There's also the bird sanctuary ...' Then Zillah paused mid sentence, conscious that she was being over enthusiastic. She could just tip things over the edge so that Carl felt pressured. Let the passion come from Carl.

'Of course,' he said, enthusiastically. 'I can take the camera. I tell you Zillah, there's more to carving animals than you would ever imagine. As well as working with old wood, which I can do on my own, I shall also be tackling other varieties of new wood, cherry wood, apple, oak, beech, and learning about their characteristics. I'm starting on Monday. Going to tidy up my workshop.'

Carl paused on his way out of the kitchen. 'Where are you going?' he said, noting the two bags.

'Nowhere,' Zillah said, mentally unpacking.

'Bristol has lost its appeal. I hope you don't intend going without me,' he said, and gave her startled face a smiling kiss on both cheeks.

'It worked, didn't it?' Beatrice pronounced, poking her head round the door. All it needed was a little manipulation of a few people of like minds.

'You witch,' Zillah said, as the two friends embraced each other, and laughed.

321

And so, as if by osmosis, without discussion, or decision, or argument, Carl was absorbed into Cornwall; but for how long, Zillah couldn't guess.

'Beatrice, I'm scared,' Zillah said. 'I have to finish reading grandma Karenza's diary, and I'm worried that I might find more tragic events like the ones I've told you about.'

'That's a possibility,' Beatrice agreed, 'but what we could do is make a cup of tea, and read it together. I believe you're strong enough to take anything now.'

The friends sat at the table and Zillah and Beatrice read the final page. The first words made them catch their breath and jump in fright.

My darling Zillah.
I hope you are sitting at the table reading this. It's what I've dreamt of for many years – you occupying the cottage. Be brave. I know much of what I have written in the last few pages has been a great shock to you. We all carry burdens in this life and I'm afraid I have passed my burden on to you. Please forgive me for that, but it is part of the life grandpa and I shared and lived through together. You were also a great part of my life and I loved you, and knew that love was returned.
Bless you darling Zillah. Love grandma Karenza.

Zillah and Beatrice looked at one another and smiled.